" And what do photograph as she reach began unbuttoning her jeans. And amazing herself, she did not stop her.

"Passion," she answered, her voice husky and excited, betraying her calm exterior; her head now leaning ever so slightly back, eyes closing, dark curls falling back away from her face.

Carrie left Nina's jeans loose and moved her leather-clad hands up along Nina's belly over the cotton of the white poet's shirt, unbuttoning the tiny buttons one by one, feeling the silk of Nina's bra beneath the cotton, then slipping the blouse slowly over the woman's creamy shoulders. With a quick glance towards the archways, Nina allowed her. Swiftly Carrie unhooked the white lace push-up bra that held Nina's beautiful, full breasts captive. Instinctively Nina reached up to cover her suddenly exposed chest. Carrie gently pried Nina's hands away, lowering them to her sides.

The Rosebud Reader

ROSEBUD

THE ROSEBUD READER

Lindsay Welsh

PRIVATE LESSONS

The most recent group of students was doing well, Devon decided, as she perused the reports on her desk. She had asked all of the teachers to submit at least one report on each of the students, so that she, as headmistress, could send letters to the parents of the girls reporting on their progress, as she did periodically. She divided the reports into two piles.

One pile—the larger of the two—contained a page on each student which listed the students grades and comments on her education. Devon put these aside.

The second pile—not quite as large but still a very impressive size—contained reports that the parents would never see. Also penned by the teachers, they were much more interesting and would eventually go into the huge files that Devon kept for herself under lock and key.

She picked up the first one, noting the neat script of riding instructor Rebecca Briggs, herself a favorite with the headmistress of this most impressive finishing school.

"Regarding Amy Gates," the report began. "Miss Gates has been at the Academy for nine months now and has proven to be a very interesting student."

Devon smiled. Rebecca was as difficult to please as Devon was; her standards were almost impossibly high. Any student described by Rebecca as "interesting" was bound to be delightful.

She is a young blond student, well fleshed; and this led me to believe that her asscheeks would be very creamy and nice to spank. The first time I had reason to bring her in for discipline, and to haul up her skirts and pull down her drawers, I immediately saw that I was correct. Her sweet buttocks are like the finest ivory, and even sweeter in that they go a brilliant shade of red once the hairbrush is applied. She is somewhat tolerant of pain, which is very good also, for a spanking may be carried on and on before she starts to cry and scream. Her little cunny is very blond also, and gets wet when she is spanked. I believe that if I were to allow it, I could bring her to a peak simply by smacking her sweet ass long enough.

Of course, spanking is not the only thing I have discovered with this young wench. Her breasts are very firm and pert, and her nipples respond well to being squeezed hard; in fact, they seem to erect themselves at my lightest touch. One evening I placed clips upon them and left them there for almost three-quarters of an hour; but even though Miss Gates was obviously in distress, she did not cry for them to be removed.

I have inflicted almost every punishment at my disposal upon her. She responds well to the riding crop, to the buggy whip, and to that delicious whip that you keep in the discipline chamber. As for paddles, she is divine. Although, the wooden and rubber ones worked well, the metal-studded one was the finest, as that beautiful white skin came up in dots of red. Eventually, after repeated paddling, her sweet fanny was covered with a lovely red rash from the marks of the studs overlapping with each blow.

While I do not wish to influence your judgement in any way, I would heartily suggest that this student not be moved forth at the end of the semester, but kept from her home and retained here at the Academy. If you require a cause, I will state that while her hands are good, her seat in the saddle is not yet perfect. I implore you, for your own pleasure, not to send this student forth *until you have personally enjoyed her young breasts and fleshy buttocks. I assure you that you will not be disappointed.*

> *Your obedient servant, Rebecca Briggs.*

Devon smiled. She enjoyed Rebecca's reports most of all. Among all the teachers, Rebecca put the most thought and care into her prose and insisted on relating every intoxicating detail. Devon made a note to herself to find Amy Gates guilty of some infraction and have the pleasure of calling her into the office and experiencing for herself the satisfaction that the riding teacher had so obviously enjoyed herself on more than one occasion.

She was just about to pick up another report when there was a gentle knock at the door. Annoyed, she called out, "Who is it?"

The heavy oak door opened slowly, just a little, and a young female face appeared behind it. Devon recognized her immediately: Lilian Smith, a student whom Devon had had the pleasure of disciplining herself on a number of occasions.

"What do you want?" Devon demanded.

Lilian stepped into the room, dropping her eyes to the floor and performing the required curtsy before speaking. "Please, Mistress Whitfield," she said. "Mistress Briggs requests the pleasure of your company."

"Where?"

"In the chamber, Mistress," the young woman replied.

Devon's eyebrows rose. "In her private chamber?"

"No, Mistress," Lilian replied, and she caught her breath. "In the discipline chamber."

So the morning would be an interesting one, Devon decided. She looked at the young messenger, whose cheeks had flushed scarlet at the mention of the special room on the very top floor. She had spent time in there herself, at the hands of her teachers and also Mistress Whitfield's. Half of her envied whichever student was up there now; half of her pitied the captive, who assured had done something very wrong to warrant such a measure. She could almost see the racks and feel her wrists pulled tightly together and shackled in place. How she wished she were there!

"Dismissed," Devon said. The young woman thanked her Mistress, then slipped out the door.

Devon put her papers away and stepped into the hallway. She still had time before her interview, and the treat waiting upstairs would fill it quite nicely.

The discipline chamber was only one of several rooms that comprised the top floor of the east wing. Access to all of them was through a single door which was always kept locked and could be opened only by the teachers and by Devon herself. Not all of the Academy's students received these special private lessons, and the locked door was intended to keep them out. It was also a valuable tool for punishing the students who did receive lessons; many reported that the sound of the door locking behind them and the walk to the discipline chamber down the long hall could be as terrible a treatment as the actual punishment itself. The teachers' living quarters were directly below the private wing, and that section was also protected by a lock and key. However, there were sufficient secret passageways from the top floor to the one below, to best accommodate the teachers and their pleasure.

Devon opened the door with her key, then firmly closed and locked it behind her. The long hallway, with its huge window at one end, was all gleaming mahogany, smelling faintly of the lemon oil rubbed in by submissive students who begged to do the job on their hands and knees—mostly naked, as ordered by their dominatrices. The magnificent oil paintings that graced the other halls of the Academy were noticeably missing here. Instead, the walls were sparsely but effectively decorated with the tools the teachers loved to use behind closed doors. Here was a riding crop, a rug beater; farther down the hallway hung a pair of leather wrist-cuffs shackled together, and a bridle specially made to fit a young woman's face. Beside the door to the discipline chamber was Devon's favorite; a beautifully executed drawing of a young woman across her Mistress's knee, with her bare buttocks exposed and her tormentor's hand raised to deliver a stinging slap.

But today this was just an appetizer for the feast that waited inside. Devon opened the door to this most delightful chamber and stepped inside.

The chamber itself was a huge room, with windows on two sides that could be covered with heavy velvet drapes. Today they were open, and the sunlight revealed the room's secrets. In the center were several wooden horses, a table with iron hooks screwed into it, and a horrible wooden rack which could accommodate two slaves, one on either side of it. Along the walls were more racks, huge iron rings, shelves filled with all manner of toys and devices, and a row of comfortable stuffed chairs for an audience. Unknown to any of the students who had been enslaved in here, there were also holes in the west wall, hidden amid the ornate carvings of the wainscotting, and a small hidden chamber in behind them where teachers and guests could watch the proceedings in the room without their presence being known.

The tall ceiling was crossed with huge oak beams, into which were screwed several large iron rings. From two of these hung young ladies, their wrists shackled together and then tethered to the rings. They were pulled up just far enough that they were barely able to keep their toes on the highly polished floor. Both of them wore their long skirts and petticoats, with no shoes or stockings, but they were naked from the waist up, their breasts pulled up and their nipples sweet and rosy.

"Mistress Whitfield! How good of you to come!" Rebecca Briggs was seated in one of the chairs, admiring the two nubile creatures that dangled so enticingly from their cruel bonds. She stood up and walked over to the door where Devon waited. She was a beautiful woman who moved with an easy grace and a long-legged stride. For this occasion she was wearing hunting attire, and her tight-fitting jodhpurs and tailored shirt complemented the stern leather boots she wore. Like Devon, she wore men's riding clothes whenever she could, for she also knew the secret pleasures of mounting astride.

"How good of you to ask me," Devon said. She admired Rebecca, admired her cold, firm eyes and the set of her jaw that intimidated all of the students below her. Rebecca's beautiful body and dominant ways made her a favorite with Devon among all the teachers, both as a disciplinarian and also, in the privacy of their chambers, as a lover.

"You have set them up very nicely," Devon continued. She walked over to them. Both of the girls were trembling now; for, as harsh as Rebecca was, she was no match for Devon and her punishments, and the captives knew this.

Devon reached forward and touched the nipple

of one of the girls. The young woman drew in her breath, and her face went red. Devon moved her hand so that she cupped the firm young globe and massaged it. The girl's breathing increased. It sounded improbably loud in the empty room.

It feels so good, doesn't it?" Devon asked.

The girl nodded her head slightly and whispered, "Yes, Mistress," so softly that it was almost inaudible.

Devon continued to play with the girl's breast, with both hands now, one hand tweaking the nipple and the other massaging the flesh. She could feel the flesh hot in her palm and hear the maiden's breathing. The other captive watched, longing for her Mistress's hands to be on her body.

Straining on her toes, the young girl was panting in the way that indicated she was close to her peak. Devon looked at her and smiled coldly. Then she gave the tit a final squeeze and stepped away. Crestfallen, frustrated, the young woman panted and for a moment considered begging for more, but suddenly remembered her place and held her tongue.

"What were their transgressions?" Devon asked.

"Improper care of their charges," Rebecca replied. "The one on the left was in a hurry when she came back from her ride, so she hurried her horse's brushing and missed several strokes. As for the one on the right, I found some dirt on her saddle when it was supposed to have been cleaned."

"Serious charges," Devon said.

"Serious indeed," Rebecca agreed. "And deserving of punishment. That is why I thought you would like to be here, to witness their humiliation."

Rebecca went to the shelves that held the implements. Two pairs of eyes, wide with fear, followed her movements as she selected a heavy whip and brought it back with her.

The young woman who had been frustrated by Devon's touch was first. The whip snapped across her back, and she clenched her teeth together so that only a grunt escaped. Devon beamed. The cruel lash left a delicious red welt across the girl's pale back.

A similar stripe was raised along the spine of the other girl. Then Rebecca began a regular routine; one lash on the first back, one lash on the second. Soon both backs were striped with lashes, and the girls were screaming for mercy, tears streaming down their cheeks. Of course it was pointless. No one could hear them here, save the two Mistresses who savored every desperate cry for help.

Finally Rebecca decided that the punishment was complete, and she took the whip back to the shelves. The girls still hung by their wrists, sobbing, battered and tear-stained. Without a word, Rebecca loosed their bonds, and they dropped to the floor, their legs too numb to hold them up. Devon thought they looked magnificent; their skirts disarrayed, their backs worked over, their bare nipples hard and pink.

"Now get out of here," Rebecca hissed. "Go to your classes, but once tea is over, you are to report back to me here."

"Yes, Mistress," the two replied. Stiffly, their backs burning with the red welts, they gathered up their blouses and left. Of course they would be blocked in their progress by the locked door at the end of the hall and forced to wait however long it would take for either Devon or Rebecca to open it for them. They only hoped that which ever Mistress it was, she would not be carrying a riding crop when she came out to open it. Their poor backs were sore enough, without their skirts being lifted and a harsh leather whip applied to their backsides!

"Another session with them after tea?" Devon asked.

"This whipping was for punishment, to correct their errors," Rebecca explained. "Later on there will be spanking, both to reinforce their lessons and to amuse me."

"A good idea," Devon agreed. "But remember that tomorrow is the day for our trip into town."

Rebecca smiled; her eyes were bright with anticipation. "Of course I have not forgotten," she assured the headmistress. "I have been looking forward to it all this month."

Devon reached forward and kissed her passionately, then turned to leave. "I, too, will enjoy tomorrow," she said. "But when you are finished with their spanking, Rebecca, you might come visit me in my own chamber. There's nothing like a little fun of our own to get us in the mood for a day's trip into town."

"The first thing you will discover here at the Whitfield Finishing Academy," Devon told the young woman who sat before her, "is that the school utilizes a set of very strict rules from which no deviation will be permitted."

The pupil before her was Elizabeth Dunn, her newest student. Earlier that morning the young woman had arrived at the Academy, along with her mother, in the family's coach. Watching from an upstairs window, Devon noticed the terrible task the girl's mother had in forcing her daughter to alight from the coach. In mortal dread of the well-matched team that stood perfectly still at their harness, Elizabeth grasped the doorframe and would not come out. Exasperated, Elizabeth's mother cracked her open palm sharply across her daughter's cheek, but even this would not convince the young woman to leave the coach. Only the combined efforts of the driver and footman, using plain brute strength, got her out of the coach, and as they dragged her, her hysterical eyes never left the horses, who had not so much as stamped a foot or swished a tail at flies. When she was far enough away from the dreaded animals, she broke free of the servants and raced up the stairs to the safety of the Academy's huge carved front door.

Devon shook her head and left the window. There was no doubt about it: this young lady would require private lessons. It was obvious that no amount of reasoning or timid approach would change the young woman's mind. She was going to need the healthy fear of a domineering Mistress if she was ever going to get over her incapacitating problem.

The footman brought in the trunks and was instructed to place them in Elizabeth's room. She would share quarters with Emily, the winner of the previous day's exciting wrestling match and also the recipient of the coveted prize of a good hard spanking, which had been carried out so well by Anna Crowell. Emily had been warned against letting Elizabeth know anything specific about the private lessons until Devon gave her permission to, but the headmistress felt that the subtle influence of a young woman who naturally grovelled before her teachers might help break in the new student gently, but firmly.

Now, with her mother on her way back to their home in London and her new living quarters set up, the Academy's most recent student was receiving her subtle initiation into the world of submission and slavery that she would eventually reside in totally, even if she was still completely innocent of its existence.

"Sometimes the rules may seem harsh or unnecessary," Devon continued. "It may seem that way to you at first, but you will quickly discover that there is a reason for all of them. Without them, the school could not operate efficiently, as it now does. With them, everything runs as it should."

"Yes, ma'am," Elizabeth replied. Devon was pleased to note that her manners were already very good and that she seemed to have respect for authority, except when it came to the matter of horses.

"That will be our first lesson," Devon said. "Every teacher at the Academy is to be addressed as 'Mistress,' each time you speak to her."

"Yes...Mistress," Elizabeth said. The title came as an afterthought, but Devon knew that very shortly it would slip off her tongue as naturally as breathing.

Devon continued, "Another rule is that when you are with a teacher, you do not speak to her unless you are spoken to first. If you do wish to ask her something and she has not initiated the conversation, you are to ask permission to speak before you go ahead with your question. Is that clear?"

"Yes, Mistress," Elizabeth replied, almost in a

devout whisper. Devon was pleased to note that the title came much easier and faster this time.

Pointedly, Devon looked over to the corner of her office. As she had expected, Elizabeth followed her glance. Hanging from a nail in the wall was a long, thin cane, which obviously had only one use: to discipline unruly students. Devon looked at her charge quickly and was impressed by what she saw. Elizabeth's cheeks were flushed and she seemed to come alive at the sight of the cruel instrument.

"You have noticed my cane," Devon said. Seeing that Elizabeth's bright blue eyes were still fixed on the cane. "Let me assure you, Miss Dunn, that we do not subscribe to the policies of some of the silly new freethinkers who believe that transgressions can be punished with a few kind words and a request that it not be repeated. We believe that a spared rod produces a spoiled student. I shall make allowances for new students such as yourself, until you become aware of our policies. but there is no second chance."

"Oh, no, Mistress!" Elizabeth blurted out. "If there are policies—"

Surprised, Devon stared at her new charge. Horrified that she had spoken out of place, Elizabeth dropped her eyes. "Please forgive me, Mistress," she said. "What I meant was—I meant—" She searched for something to say, then struck on an idea. "If there are policies that everyone must follow, Mistress, than I would not want special privileges. If I were not punished for my errors, the other girls might think poorly of me."

Devon could hardly believe her ears. This student was actually begging to be punished! The headmistress quickly realized that the elaborate schemes she used when breaking in new students to their private lessons might not even be necessary with this one. The thought made her feel almost weak, and she had to fight down an urge to rip off the girl's clothes and spank her sweet ass raw right there at her desk.

She smiled, breathing calmly to control herself. "A very noble idea, Miss Dunn," she agreed. "I shall keep that in mind. You are correct, of course. If a student receives preferential treatment it would naturally make the other schoolgirls jealous of her."

"Thank you, Mistress," Elizabeth said. Although she gave Devon her attention, she could not help sneaking quick glances at the thin cane that hung so menacingly on the wall.

"Now, as you are doubtless aware, our curriculum at the Whitfield Academy is similar to the studies you undertook at other schools," Devon said. "We will be teaching you languages, art, and physical exercise, which we believe is very beneficial to a student's health. We will also teach you household management, which will include monthly trips into town to study commerce. And, naturally, there are the equestrian skills."

Devon's calm voice struck Elizabeth like a white-hot shock. Her eyes went wide. Then she hid her face in her hands and sobbed loudly. "Oh, no, Mistress, please!" she begged. "I will take any classes, I will do anything else you require! But please, do not put me with the horses!"

"There is no question that you will learn dressage," Devon said calmly, although she had risen from her chair. "Every student studies it. As you yourself mentioned, you would not want the preferential treatment of abstaining from the class, would you?"

"Not horses! Not horses!" Elizabeth sobbed, and Devon could see that she was driving herself into hysterics.

Devon was now standing directly in front of the sobbing student, whose shoulders shook violently with the exertion of her crying. "You have no choice," Devon said. "You shall ride."

Elizabeth raised her head and screamed "No!" At the same moment, Devon's hand crashed upon her cheek with all the force the headmistress could muster. Elizabeth toppled from her chair and landed on the floor, the red imprint of her Mistress's hand on her cheek, her eyes filled with shock.

Calmly, Devon walked back to her desk. "That is merely a taste of what you will receive if you do not obey," she said. "I am the Mistress, and you are the submis—the student here," she added, catching herself. There would be plenty of time for Elizabeth to discover exactly how lowly her position at the Academy really was.

Elizabeth was still on the floor, almost in a trance. Slowly, she brought her hand up to her cheek and touched the red spot where she had been slapped. Then she ran her fingers over it, as if savoring the moment when Devon had struck.

"I did not ask you if you wished to learn to ride," Devon continued. "I told you that you would." She tugged on the bellpull, and very shortly there was a single light knock at the door. At a command from Devon, a young woman entered and, ignoring the student who was still sprawled on the floor, curtsied quickly to her Mistress and awaited instructions.

"Ask Mistress Briggs if she might join us," Devon said.

"Yes, Mistress," the young woman said, then turned and left. The door clicked behind her.

"You will also notice," Devon said, "that all of the Mistresses expect a small curtsy when approached by a student. Now get up off the floor and sit properly like a lady."

"Yes, Mistress," Elizabeth said and obeyed. Her mind was still digesting the remarkable events that had just taken place. She could hardly believe it. Was it possible that she finally had discovered the school that she had dreamed of, the teacher she had longed for all these years? Once again her hand went to her cheek and stayed there. Her skin still burned from the blow, and she basked in the feeling.

Devon said nothing more until Rebecca entered the room. "Mistress Briggs, this is our new student, Elizabeth," she said.

Elizabeth stood up and almost automatically dropped a curtsy to the riding instructor. Rebecca glanced over the girl's bowed head with a questioning glance at Devon. Devon smiled and nodded slightly, and Rebecca smiled also and regarded the young woman with a newfound interest.

She took a step toward Elizabeth, and the young woman froze. Rebecca had just come from the stable, and the unmistakable smell of horses was on her clothes. To her surprise, the composed and obedient young girl suddenly rushed to the other side of the room in terror and curled up in a ball in the corner.

"You see our problem," Devon said calmly. She caught a whiff of Rebecca's clothes and instantly realized the reason for Elizabeth's unorthodox behavior. "Do you remember the discussion we had about the student who would not go near horses? Obviously this is she."

She went over to the cowering student and none-too-gently pulled her up by her arm. "Fear is one thing, but you are simply being silly," she chastised. "There are no horses here. Now apologize to Mistress Briggs."

"I am sorry, Mistress," the girl said tearfully, and although she resumed her position before the tall, handsome instructor, every muscle was still poised for flight.

"Did Mistress Whitfield explain the rules of the Academy to you?" Rebecca demanded.

"Yes, Mistress," Elizabeth replied.

"They apply to everyone," Rebecca continued. "Let me assure you that if you do not obey them, you shall receive no quarter from me. I shall expect to see you at the stable with the other students tomorrow morning, and I shall accept no excuse if you are absent."

"Yes, Mistress," Elizabeth said sullenly.

"I believe it is now time for you to prepare for tea," Devon said. "There should be someone waiting at the end of the hall who will help you find your way."

"Yes, Mistress," Elizabeth said. Without looking at the riding instructor, and keeping as far away from her as possible, the young woman rushed for the safety of the hallway, closing the door firmly behind her.

"A most unusual student," Rebecca said.

"More so than you think," Devon said. "I truly believe we have acquired one who looks forward to receiving punishment as much as we enjoy administering it. Not only will she be receiving private lessons, but I also think she will commence them much sooner than we ever imagined."

Rebecca's hand strayed to her tit, and she absentmindedly tweaked the nipple as she thought about it. "A luscious concept," she said.

"It would be a shame to let it pass," Devon agreed, and once again she used the bellpull to summon a young woman.

The student knocked, entered and curtsied to both Mistresses, then waited silently for her command.

"Remove your clothes," Devon ordered.

The girl's expression was questioning, but she did not say anything and did not hesitate. Within moments her dress and petticoats were on the floor, and she stood before them naked, her large tits inviting and almost begging to be roughly squeezed. Rebecca obliged, and the young woman grimaced with pain as her tender flesh was pinched cruelly.

"Now, bend over the chair," Devon said. The young girl did so, leaning forward on her hands so that her back was straight and her ass smooth and ready. Devon walked over to the corner and picked up the cane that had intrigued poor Elizabeth so.

"Mistress, may I speak?" the young woman asked.

"You may."

"Please, Mistress, I do not question your actions, but have I done something to offend you or Mistress Briggs?"

"Oh, no, child," Devon said lightly. "In fact, you have done everything right."

"Thank you, Mistress." And the girl braced herself for what she knew was coming.

The cane whistled sweetly in the air, then struck flesh like a gunshot. The young girl groaned, and Rebecca and Devon admired the wire-thin, blood-red welt that it raised. It excited them more than they could imagine. Devon rained blow after blow on the tender buttocks, until Rebecca, flushed and hot, asked for the cane. She, too, struck over and over on the girl's asscheeks until her nasty desire was satisfied.

Devon gave the sobbing, trembling captive permission to move, and the poor girl's hand went to her bright red ass, touching the skin gently, as if to soothe it. On orders from her Mistress, she stood up stiffly, then gathered her clothes and rushed from the room, hoping that none would see her before she was able to dress.

"A fine performance," Devon said. "No one canes a young girl's bottom like you do."

"You have too much modesty," Rebecca said, putting her hands on the headmistress's neck and caressing the skin gently. "The sight of you punishing a slave sets my whole body aflame."

They kissed deeply, their tongues mingling, soft moans of pleasure escaping their lips. Devon's hand felt Rebecca's soft cunt through the folds of her long dress. Reaching down, Rebecca pulled up the fabric. She wore nothing over her private area, and Devon's fingers came away soaked with the sweet juices of her cunt. Rebecca pulled at the headmistress's skirts, and shortly her own hand was enjoying a delicious soaking of its own.

"Your sweet cavern is calling to me," Rebecca teased.

"Answer it, then," Devon replied.

They answered each other. Their mutual passion inflamed them, and they probed and rubbed each other's cunts, desperately seeking pleasure. Their kisses were now constant, their groans of delight louder and louder, their hands wet and slippery.

Devon reached her peak first, groaning and gasping, and she kept her fingers in the entrance to Rebecca's soft tunnel while her thumb traced the nub of flesh between those lovely downy lips. Within moments, Rebecca cried out and gushed all over Devon's fingers. She then took her own fingers, wet with the nectar from Devon's cunt, and slowly licked them clean until her lips glistened with her friend's rich wine.

Gradually they caught their breath and rearranged their skirts and hair. Rebecca still had a class to instruct, and Devon's attention was required by her paperwork, but they promised to meet later on to continue their passion and perhaps take one or two unsuspecting young women up to the discipline chamber for some exciting antics.

"You are sending this new student to me tomorrow, then?" Rebecca asked, pausing at the door.

"I am," Devon said.

"She will definitely require more attention than any other I have seen," Rebecca said. "What do you wish me to do with her?"

Devon looked up, smiled coldly, and glanced once more at the cane, now discarded on the top of her desk. "Your worst," she replied.

Leslie Cameron

THE WHISPER OF FANS

The gallery was filled with women. Ladies in lace and butches in dressy gray, young dykes in jeans with clean faces, and androgynous wraiths all came together to view the Gaia Gallery's latest show. The women milled about, talking with animation or in hushed reverent tones.

Smoke and music rushed out to embrace her as she pulled open the glass door. The walls were hung with paintings, photographs, and other two-dimensional art celebrating women's erotica. She paused by the reception desk and picked up a program.

Christina felt a hand brush her behind. Blushing, she turned, but there was no one near her. She looked for Adrien, but could not distinguish her from the throngs of women in dressy slacks and jeans. She decided to view the exhibit first and then network with the gallery owners, so that at least she would appear knowledgeable about their current show.

She walked at a slow museum pace past excited women clutching each other eagerly as they viewed the exhibits. Impassively, she regarded photographs of women embracing, women making love, and women celebrating love and life with each other. She blinked to clear her vision when one photograph tugged at her memories of Jyl. She moved on to the paintings, appreciative yet unmoved by their artful passion. Then, entering a small alcove, she paused.

The room was dim, hung with photographs in sepia tones and shades of gray. There was a sculpture in the room's center: a sprawling woman's form shaped in gray green stone. Her legs were planted on a bed of rough uncut rock, her heels just touching her buttocks. Her arms were upraised, clasped over her head, partially shading her face. The woman's profile could be seen in the space between forearm and shoulder. Unable to resist, Christina reached out and ran her hands over the woman's form.

The stone was cool and slippery, satin beneath her fingers. Christina found herself running her hands over the figure again and again with lighter and heavier touches. The rock warmed to her touch. She felt a corresponding warmth. This was erotic art. The sounds of the gallery dropped away. She walked around the piece possessively, viewing it from all sides, all angles. She found the title card. QUINN'S PASSION—NFS. Christina sighed. Not for sale. She touched the woman's figure again, it was still warm from her earlier touches.

Suddenly sensing that she was not alone, Christina looked up from the figure and saw a woman filling the alcove doorway. She blushed, pulling her hands back from the statue as if it burned her. Yet Christina did not step away; rather she looked at the stranger boldly approaching.

The woman was tall. Her hair curled around her face: a symphony of angles and planes framing small but incredibly expressive lips. Her legs whispered together as she moved. She was well built and returned Christina's stare with a sparkle in her eyes. Christina felt a responding smile tugging at the corners of her mouth. She waited for the woman to speak, urging herself to silence—her inside voices flinging out mindless cocktail conversation. But the woman appeared very comfortable in the silence and, without ever breaking eye contact with her, began to run her hands over the statue in an intimate manner.

Christina felt as if the woman were stroking her. She colored and took a small step backward. The woman stopped caressing the statue and cocked her head to one side inquisitively. Christina drew in a deep, ragged breath and stepped back up to the statue, placing her hands upon it boldly. The stone was hot where the woman had touched it. Hot like living flesh. Her lips curved involuntarily at the sensuousness of the warm stone beneath her fingers. The woman smiled in response.

Undercurrents of electricity ran between them like wildfire. Just as Christina longed to touch the stranger, the woman ran her fingers lightly over hers. Christina felt a jolt of excitement at this casual contact. Somehow their fingers met, wove together. They stood over the statue with their hands clasped. Just looking into her eyes, Christina felt that she knew a lot about this woman. She could see strength, boldness, a fresh sense of vitality that rocked her to the core. In turn she felt open, revealed under the woman's gaze—all her secrets already told. No need of shame or artifice.

Both of their lips parted, moved to speak, and silenced themselves in deference to the other. Fingers clasped tighter, the woman stepped around the sculpture.

"Tell me your name." Her voice was as soft as the velvet that caressed Christina's skin.

"Christina."

The woman smiled with only her eyes. She regarded her very intently, as if branding the name upon her form.

"In some ways it suits you." She added after some deliberation, "In other circumstances, I would name you differently."

Christina gazed raptly into her eyes, about to ask by what name this woman would call her and under what circumstances, when Adrien entered the alcove.

The presence of another person radically changed the atmosphere that had built up between them—the sensuality dissipated leaving them both flat and unmagical. Adrien looked from one to the other. She wore a puzzled frown.

"Christina?"

The other woman dropped her hands abruptly. With a murmured excuse, she left the alcove quickly. Adrien watched her retreat with a strange look upon her face. Christina gazed down at the statue and wondered idly if the stone still held the warmth of their joined hands.

"Chris?" Adrien asked again.

"Oh, I'm sorry. I didn't see you out there when I got here. Isn't this statue fantastic?" Christina babbled, the statue still holding her attention. She did not even notice that Adrien had forsaken her habitual jeans for dark slacks and a dressy sweater.

Adrien gave the rock a cursory glance, then returned her gaze to Christina.

"Yeah, it's great. Hey, where do you know Quinn from?"

"That's what it's called," she commented absently.

Confused, Adrien brushed her tousled hair artfully back from her forehead for the thousandth time, tucking it in place with a swift gesture. She peered at the statue's name card and then nodded.

"I didn't mean the statue, Chris. I meant the woman. That was Quinn herself," she muttered with exasperation.

"Oh," Christina murmured. Quinn. The woman was herself named. It suited her, perfectly—odd, unique, and very warm. She made no further comment as Adrien ushered her out into the throngs of women.

The noise of the crowd embraced her, yet she felt isolated, adrift. With her thoughts elsewhere, she spoke with the curator, the owner of the gallery, and several artists, conversing perfunctorily to each one about the Women's Collective. She made productive contacts, but all the while searched the crowds for the one face that had held her attention captive.

Once she caught a glimpse of the artist at the bar sipping a dark drink, intently looking at her. Quinn raised her glass in silent toast. It was Christina who first had to turn away, return to mundane conversation.

Later, Christina saw her laughing and strained to hear the notes, but the sounds eluded her. Adrien stayed close to her, prodding her into the conversations whenever possible and making it difficult for her to slip away and seek Quinn out. Finally Christina shouldered her way past Adrien and into the crowds with a simple "excuse me" and no explanation at all.

Almost immediately, it seemed, Quinn was at her shoulder. Her warm hand nestled in the small of Christina's back as she guided them gently toward the picture window of the gallery.

"Are you involved with her?"

Christina glanced back at Adrien.

"No. We work together, that's all. She has other ideas, but…" She trailed off, sensing there was no need to explain further—that all the rest of it really didn't matter now, might not ever matter again.

"Did she tell you who I am?" Quinn asked bluntly.

"Yes." The fact that Quinn had carved the stone woman seemed irrelevant now, compared to the energy that flowed between them, hot and prickly.

"Really?" She appeared amused for a moment, then took Christina's hands in her own.

"Say my name, Christina," she urged. "I want to hear how it falls from your lips, see what your mouth does with it, sense what lingers in the air after you've spoken." She gazed raptly into her eyes.

Christina could feel the reverberations of her own name in this woman's mouth, lingering erotically.

"Quinn." She said the name experimentally, as

one does with an unfamiliar, unsure word. "Quinn," she said, taking the name in and possessing it fully.

Quinn smiled with only her eyes. "What else do you know about me, Christina?"

"Only that—your name. And that you carved Quinn's Passion."

"There is much we need to learn about each other, then, isn't there?"

Christina nodded, again feeling uneasy. Quinn was playing a deeper game than she comprehended. There were recurring jolts of electricity between them. She felt charged just touching her hands.

"Come to tea?"

Christina gazed at her in wonderment.

"Any afternoon about four. Don't call, just come." Quinn spoke with subdued urgency. "Come. You move me, in mysterious ways, Christina." From a hidden pocket, she produced a small card bearing her address, edged neatly in black. Christina glanced at it for a moment before tucking it into her bag.

"I'll come."

"Good," Quinn replied.

Adrien sulked, the board of directors complained, and Christina was useless at work for the next week. She waited for Quinn to call. She pitted hope against hope in the dark house for two nights until she remembered that she had never given Quinn her number. Then she began to worry.

To just "come by." What boldness it required. "For tea." How innocuous, but it implied—what— that she was interested in Quinn? She had never felt so alive as when their hands had met and smoothed across the stone body.

Christina returned to the gallery to find that the statue had been retrieved by the artist. She was stunned. She wondered whether Quinn had taken it home to remind her of their first touch. She herself dreamed of it nightly, and the scenes she enacted with the stone maiden grew more erotic with each dream. She stood in the emptied alcove, for the first time really seeing the photographs on the wall—Quinn's work also.

Pictures of women—women enjoying darker pleasures than those depicted in the front rooms of the gallery. A woman being pleasured, her hair tossed artfully over her eyes in a mane of tousled curls; a woman gazing down at bound wrists, naked from the waist up. Photographs untitled, yet telling vivid stories of forbidden pursuits, exotic practices—all so subtly conveyed. Christina felt herself flush with excitement and apprehension. She looked at her watch; 3:15. She would have to hurry now.

Quinn pulled open the french door. It dragged on the carpet, rustling a soft protest. The room was bright, blinding white.

"There are some books on the table. Amuse yourself. I will return. Don't leave this room without me—understand?" Her voice followed Christina into the room. She nodded, turning only in time to see the glass curtains billow as the door sealed her in.

The room—more of a Victorian sun porch, really—was white. White curtains shot with yellow ribbon hung at the windows, while white sheers hung on the door separating this room from the rest of the large, dark house through which she had just come.

A few plants tried to interject color into the room and lay bleaching by the large screened windows that ran from floor to ceiling on all but one of the walls—the one with the french doors. She wondered what lay far beyond these doors, what secrets they concealed that required Quinn to guide her.

In her lacy cream dress, Christina felt like a Victorian lady surveying her domain, waiting to entertain guests and serve cups of fragile steaming tea. She regarded the willow-wood chair, its unruly branches lashed into shape with whitened rope. Despite the white cushion on its ample seat, it did not look comfortable. She sat anyway.

The table Quinn had pointed to was wrought-iron, enameled white and smooth. Three books lay upon it, framing a crystal dish of daffodils: a slim volume bound in gray leather that looked soft, like kid; a large hardback book with a white vinyl jacket; and a large oversized volume, which lay open, slightly apart from the others.

Ah, the books. "To amuse her," Quinn had said. She felt a little shiver run down her spine to settle between her legs. She glanced at the open volume, one page filled with a photograph of a woman bound, sunlight pouring over her as tangible as water. Her legs were spread-eagled, and the picture had captured the light dancing upon her. Christina could feel a throbbing begin within her, as if she, too, could feel the heat of the sun, opening lips, spreading warmth, fire licking along the taut limbs of the woman so exposed to the sun's caress. Her head was thrown back, obscuring whether her face was ecstatic or agonized. The page opposing it said merely "An Afternoon with Lisa." Moistening her lips, Christina reached out and turned the page.

Swelling curves of tanned buttocks spread across the page. The woman knelt, her lips visible, swollen and moist within the folds. Looking closer, Christina could see a fine tracery of marks running over each cheek in asymmetrical beauty. Its title, "Ann's Ass." She tightened her own cheeks, feeling the corresponding tension in her belly and deeper within, to catch and continue the pulse which had begun. Her hand reached out once more to turn the page.

At first blush, the image seemed to be a land-scape: a sandscape of mounded hills and shadowed valleys rolling away into a dark tangle of trees and brush. Seeking the woman within the form, Christina recognized the position. Hips elevated, far past what was comfortable, chin to chest, blood flowing down toward her face. And the woman's flesh: not only shadowed, but yes, bruised. There was a tension in the form, anticipation. Was it the lingering moments before her lover knelt to kiss the valley between those upraised legs, or the pause between blows? Either way, the tension was the same. She glanced at the title, "Julia Rising."

Christina's eyes fluttered closed, and she felt the heat within herself swell. She longed to touch herself, but wondered whether anyone might be watching. Swallowing hard against the rising desires these images provoked, she set the book aside reluctantly and picked up the small gray book. The leather felt soft and buttery in her fingers. For a moment, she imagined rubbing the book between her legs, feeling the softness, wetting the binding with her juices. Crossing her legs, she clutched her thighs together.

The binding bore no title, no scar for this soft hide. Opening to a page at random, Christina began to read. Blushes stained her cheeks, and she settled more deeply into her chair. Rising once, she tucked one foot underneath so that her heel pressed into her, providing a little friction as she rubbed herself against it.

The touch on her shoulder startled her so much that she jerked away reflexively.

"Come, come," Quinn said softly into her ear, her breath warming Christina's cheek. "It's only me." She laughed, amused at her own comment.

Christina looked up, her eyes glazed with remembered desire.

"How do you like our solarium?" Quinn asked.

"It's, uh, very warm."

"Ah, but is it the sun, or what you've been reading, my dear? Let's see." She took the book out of her hands and glanced at the page she had been reading. One dark eyebrow lifted in surprise.

"You like this passage?" she queried.

Christina nodded shyly. "I've never read anything like it."

Quinn cocked her head to one side, regarding her solemnly.

"'...when she is aching,'" she read aloud, "'her body covered in a fine sheen of sweat and her ass reddened from repeated blows, then cover your hand with honey and rub her crotch with firm, impersonal strokes. It is important that she not be directly stimulated at this time. Vary the intensity of the stroke, so that she will writhe and beg for a more direct touch. If she has been commanded to be still, punish appropriately for misbehavior in an area other than the area of concentration. The aim of this exercise is to refine her ability to transition from indirect stimulation to fierce stimulation and back again without release, thus prolonging the agony.' Do you wish me to continue?"

"Yes. Oh, yes," Christina murmured. Her head had lolled against Quinn's hand, which rested on the back of the chair.

"Stand up, then," Quinn directed.

Christina rose. Blood rushed to her belly, and she blushed at her own excitement, feeling vulnerable under her frank gaze. Quinn took the seat that she had vacated and, planting her feet wide apart, she leaned back into the chair.

"Kneel here." She indicated the space between her legs. "You may rest your head upon my thigh."

Christina complied. Her skirts whispered as she knelt. She leaned gingerly, her cheek scraping against the black denim of Quinn's jeans. Surreptitiously, she breathed in, tasting the womanly scent that flowed out toward her. Quinn smiled and grasped a handful of her hair, tugging her forward until she was off balance, unable to remain perched upon her knees. Her nose rested in the fold between Quinn's hip and thigh. Quinn did not release her, but relaxed her grip upon her hair. With her other hand, she raised the slim book and resumed reading out loud.

"'Make sure that she has been thoroughly honeyed before proceeding. Insert several fingers into her cunt at once, pressing upward. She should be more than receptive at this time. As she opens to you, insert more and more of your hand until you can fuck her easily with your whole hand.'"

Christina could feel a trembling begin in her legs from the strain of being so bent over and, to her shame, from the images that the words evoked. She began to move forward and was halted by Quinn's fist tightening upon her hair.

"Sit still, Christina, I am reading to you. Pay attention." She pulled her briefly against her crotch, pushing up with her hips so that Christina's face was buried between her legs for a moment.

Christina inhaled once deeply.

"Perhaps you are bored with the story?" Quinn's voice brimmed with a sarcasm she did not feel.

"No, it's not that," Christina began, her words muffled against the denim.

"How rude of me!" Quinn mimicked a polite hostess. "I invited you here for tea and haven't offered you a thing. Would you like some refreshment, my dear? Tea?"—her voice dropped low—"or honey?"

Christina's face displayed her torn emotions—longing and confusion at war inside her.

"Which is it to be? Do you want it?" Quinn growled softly.

The room felt very warm indeed. Christina caught herself breathing so shallowly that she seemed to pant.

"Do you want it all?"

"Yes," Christina whispered.

Quinn looked perplexed momentarily, then she grinned.

"Yes to tea?" she laughed. Christina looked away.

"Yes to honey? It's over there on the shelf. I need only send you to fetch it and we can begin."

Christina looked once more into her face. Quinn was no longer smiling and her eyes burned with a fierce intensity.

"Or yes to it all? Tell me. I can transform you into your darkest fears, your deepest secret desires. What do you choose?" She kept staring into her eyes in a way which made Christina feel dizzy and drunk all at once.

She thought to herself. So this is how it happens. I thought it would be different. But maybe the transition from real life to this realm of pure sensation is as simple as saying yes now. She heard herself say it. She saw emotions wash across Quinn's face, lingering in her eyes, a subtle pleasure.

"Yes." Christina tried the word again. It sounded the same in her ears, but what was this deliciously frightful sensation spreading through her—excitement or something darker?

Quinn rose, nudging her back onto her heels. Christina arched her head back to keep from nuzzling Quinn's crotch, which was inches from her face.

"Good," Quinn said with genuine pleasure.

"Your simple consent will do for now, but later we will form more complex—shall we say, bindings. Does that please you?"

She watched all the innocence and bashful emotions color Christina's cheeks, rendering her silent. Gripping Christina's hair, Quinn pulled her head back farther.

"I think the tea I promised will have to wait. I have other delicacies in mind for you at present."

Christina rose without complaint. Shyness constricted her throat so that she could not respond. Somehow she knew words were no longer necessary, anyway.

Quinn gathered Christina into her arms and held her for a moment. She could feel the fluttering of Christina's heart and her own wild response. She breathed in the soft scent of her hair—sweet wildflowers. Quinn's hands rested easily along her back, feeling the lacy fabric soft and fragile beneath her strong fingers. She placed the lightest of kisses onto Christina's hair and then tilted her head so that their eyes met, locked, held.

"I am glad that you came to me."

Christina nodded, unsure of what she meant, but happy within her arms.

"I will make this sweet between us," Quinn murmured as she lowered her mouth to Christina's, savoring the slight tremor that shuddered through her. Her lips parted, and she tasted the sweet, spicy flavor of Christina's mouth. Both of them breathed raggedly, shaken by the emotion which poured between them, molten as lava. Quinn drew back.

"If ever this is really too much for you, and you'll know what I mean soon enough, you may come here to the solarium." She looked around the room, as if seeing it with fresh eyes. "This is a peaceful room. You may be your own mistress here, and your wishes will be respected. If you need a break, well, we'll get to that later shall we?" She smiled, a glint of sinister wisdom in her eyes.

Christina smiled tentatively in response. Quinn descended once more for a sweet lingering kiss that set Christina's body on fire with the gentleness of it.

"Let's go," she whispered onto the softness of her lips.

Arm in arm, they left the solarium. Quinn led her through many hallways, past many closed doors.

Confused by the many turnings and passageways, Christina commented, "This house is bigger than it appears."

Quinn smiled at her brave sally but said nothing. Receiving no reply, she lapsed back into silence.

Quinn finally paused before a heavy door and eased it open. The door dragged, softly across deep plush burgundy carpet, opening into darkness.

Christina could make nothing out of the room which lay beyond as she stood in the doorway, squinting. Quinn tugged at her hand, and she followed her over the threshold into the dark.

"Wait here!" Quinn commanded, a little imperiously. She stalked off leaving her alone and unsupported in the center of the room.

For a moment, Christina could not see at all in the dimness. When Quinn left her side to vanish in the darkness, she stood her ground uneasily. She felt bright, white hot in expectation, yet trembling with nameless fear. She felt exposed, as her eyes could not yet see into the depths of the room. Her eyes began to adjust, and she glanced around, lingering when she saw the fireplace and the shadowed figures enacting a private drama before it.

There standing in front of the flames, a woman rested passively in the embrace of another. One was cast in shadow by the fire, but the other—ahhh... Christina caught her breath at her loveliness. The woman's hair tumbled over her shoulders in waves and ringlets of chestnut brown, stirred to honey by the flickering light. As she watched, the woman holding this hearth goddess reached from the darkness to smooth a gloved hand across the other woman's chest. It nestled and finally lost itself in the silken burgundy shirt that caught the firelight and refracted it back like a thousand twinkling stars.

Christina felt a jolt of desire shoot through her veins and set her loins to pulsing. What strange menagerie had she stumbled across? What uncharted territory of rites and ceremonies would Quinn lead her into?

She gazed at the woman for some indication of what she must be feeling as the cool leather brushed the soft skin of her breasts. Yet the woman only peered into the fire, her face clean of all emotions—almost frightening in its emptiness.

In the stillness of her concentration, Christina suddenly could hear Quinn talking softly to someone on the other side of the room, away from the drama. Reassured, she no longer felt exposed, the center of attention, but hidden, as if she were tucked away in some secret room observing without fear the women at the flames.

As she watched, the shadowed one reached her gloved hand up to smooth the lovely woman's throat, tilting her head back. The woman arched in response, leaning gently into the embrace. Withdrawing her hand from the silken folds of the blouse, the darkened woman held a small vial which sparkled, as crystal does when held to light. She raised her hand up to the porcelain skin of the other woman's face. The glass sparkled by the woman's mouth.

Oh, Christina mused, is this the draught to waken the sleeping princess? She watched as the woman tilted the vial, as if to perfume the one she held captive. The scent was almost visible; Christina imagined it aromatic, like some delicious elixir to stir the waxen beauty to life. She wanted to see the fragrance waft like the smoky tendrils of scent in a cartoon, drifting into the woman and waking her from her dreams.

The woman inhaled, her breasts rising slightly. In the deepening of her breath, she arched, arched and turned, turned and cried out. She stretched, becoming lean and alive in the other woman's shadowed arms. Her blouse shot a thousand sparkling motes of light dancing into the room, a shooting star incarnate. The woman stirred and kissed her captor with eager lips, pouting when the kiss was, at first, denied.

Christina watched in amazement at the transformation. The woman writhed, a dancing flame, turned to fire in an instant. She watched, spellbound, her own body pulsing with borrowed desire.

The woman fell back into the safety of her lover's arms, her face lost momentarily in her curtain of dark hair. Stretching sinuously, pulling upward, outward—fleeing her very form in a frenzied ballet of heated movement.

Christina jumped, as the now familiar touch was pressing softly into the small of her back. She turned almost reluctantly from the fire scene. She saw that Quinn carried a large ring of keys in her hand. A jailer's ring, she thought, her mind drifting to images of unspeakable acts. She could not meet Quinn's eyes.

Quinn saw the flush of her cheeks and looked over her shoulder to where Kaitlin still restrained

Sherry in her ecstasy, and was even now gathering her into her arms for more private tortures. She gazed evenly at Christina for a moment.

"You will not require anything like that to writhe for me, will you?" she whispered.

Christina looked away, her face stained a deeper red with embarrassment and promise. Quinn smiled softly at her easy blushes and thought with pleasure of the night to come.

Quinn extended her hand. Christina took it easily, without fear. Oh, if only she will face all I put before her with such easy grace, Quinn thought. Without another glance toward Kaitlin and her newest conquest, she led her from the room and deeper into the house.

Quinn led them through the house in a round-about fashion. Confusion about her surroundings should make her more pliable, Quinn smiled ironically. At last she directed her to climb the grand curving staircase.

"I want to watch you from behind," she replied in answer to the silent questions dancing in Christina's eyes.

Made self-conscious by her expression, Christina began to mount the stairs. Pausing at the first landing, she turned. In an instant, Quinn was at her elbow.

"I did not tell you to stop here!" A touch of menace colored Quinn's voice.

A shaft of anxiety overshadowed by her desire shot through Christina. Not for the first time she wondered just what she had consented to. What would Quinn evoke from her? How darkly did her desires run? She shuddered as she began again to ascend the staircase, thinking that Quinn seemed to know her better than she knew herself. As she climbed, her movements became more liquid, sensual, erotic, just knowing her every move was under Quinn's thoughtful gaze.

At the second landing, Quinn pointed down the long, bright hallway to the door at its end. Standing before it, she produced a key from the clutch that hung on her ring, reached past her to unlock the door, and opened it for her. The doorway opened up onto a steep staircase of polished golden boards. Quinn gestured and Christina began to climb once more. The stairs wound around three times. She began to pant with exertion. Yet Quinn rose steadily, relentlessly, behind her.

At the top of the stairs was yet another locked door. She stood to one side while Quinn reached to unlock it and nudge it open. The room was black. Darker than the others. Completely dark. Quinn gestured her inside.

The door latch dropped into place with a snap. There was no light of any sort. Christina turned, attempting to catch a glimpse of light from under the door, but she could see nothing. She felt blindfolded by the room itself. She reached up, touching her cheeks unconsciously, reassuring herself that her eyes were open—yet the room remained in darkness. Christina could hear her heart hammering in the silence, but she could not hear Quinn. Had she even come into the room with her?

"Quinn?" Her voice trembled. The familiar fear began to overtake her. Darkness. An unyielding curtain of infinite darkness. What did the room contain? What was that noise? The whisper of a sound, barely heard, possibly imagined. Christina's heart began to pound in earnest. Her mouth went dry. A sick feeling grew in her stomach and crawled up her spine. She began to shake, overwhelmed completely by the old familiar terror.

This was nothing like her nightly ritual at home—daring the dark. Swallowing her anxiety, Christina would walk purposefully through her shadowed rooms, holding the knowledge of each light switch's position like a talisman—ready to banish the darkness at her command, thus fooled into believing that she had mastered her fear.

Not even remembering now how many steps she had taken into the room, she reached out futiley. Her knees crumpled and she sank to the ground. Hot tears found their way, splashing, down her cheeks. She whimpered, a soft cry swallowed up by the dark. She began to rock herself.

The raspy striking of a match caught Christina's attention. She followed the sound and saw the match's weak light touch a wick and gather strength. A candle caught the match glow, and she could see its tapering length, and the lean fingers that curved around it. The darkness lessened where the candle flared, yet she could see no farther than a small orb around the candle itself. Her eyes remained riveted on the pool of light.

"Turn around," came a low and shadowy whisper. Unsure whether it was Quinn's voice, Christina merely shook her head. The fear was too strong, the dark too oppressive for her to relinquish this patch of light.

"Shall I blow out the candle?" the whisperer asked, raising the taper to perfectly formed feminine lips. Christina reached out reflexively. She still could not tell whether it was Quinn, but that no longer concerned her. Only the light did.

"No!" Christina cried. She turned slowly, sliding one knee, then another, around on the thick carpet so that she again faced the darkness. She could feel the light behind her—sense it, strained toward it with every fiber of her body. Yet where she now looked there was no light. There was silence behind her. The fear began to encroach upon her again. What was the woman doing? Was it Quinn? If not, where was she? Most importantly, had the candle been extinguished?

She dared to turn her head, attempting to catch a glimpse of the candle's light. Immediately the voice snaked out of the dark.

"Turn around," the whisperer hissed.

Christina complied, this time with no hesitation at all. She waited, a trembling fluttery feeling in her stomach. Tears threatened once more. Hours, minutes passed. She could no longer sense the passage of time with any accuracy. Once in a while, a soft sound issued from behind her. Although she desperately wanted to turn around, she remained still. Her eyes were wide, and she tried to focus on the unyielding darkness which alone remained unchangeable.

Emotions stormed through her: anger, helplessness, frustration, fear, apprehension. She felt tossed upon the darkness like a pebble flung about in the surf. Tears welled up in her eyes and she found herself crying again, tears of resignation. Christina yielded to the darkness.

Quinn watched by the flickering of the single flame. She had gauged Christina's reactions downstairs correctly. She was passionately afraid of the dark. Quinn smiled. What a simple way to begin, and how fortunate that she had obtained this room for them. She eased out of her sneakers silently, slid off her dark jeans, and donned black cotton leggings. Her shirt was next, sliding over her tanned shoulders with a whisper of cotton against flesh. She paused, frozen for a moment when Christina raised her head, listening. She relaxed as Christina slumped, her head bent, shoulders shaking once more with almost-silent tears.

Quinn gazed at her fondly, imagining the much louder cries she would be making soon. She buttoned on a gray silk blouse, then fastened a harness of worked black leather around her chest. She ran her fingers over the textures her garments made, pleased. The harness was mostly ornamental, but for Christina's innocent eyes she was sure the effect would be enough.

She opened the cabinet door so that the variety of leather thongs, whips, and other instruments of her craft was partially visible. Running her hands lightly over the different implements, she selected a burgundy riding crop. She touched it briefly, remembering the type of mark it left, the sound it made as it sliced the air and landed on yielding flesh. Thoughtfully, she replaced the crop and reached instead for a hand whip made of soft black suede. The leather slipped through her fingers like silk. She grinned as she snapped it onto the lowest ring of her vest. This was a much more intimate tool for a first initiation. Making a mental list of what else she needed, she checked once more on Christina, who still knelt crying softly in the darkness.

As Quinn brushed past the heavily weighted black velvet brocade curtains, which ringed the room, she shut her eyes tightly at the sudden glare. The tower room had been completely enclosed by the curtains to absorb all light within and from without. Outside, beyond the curtains, the afternoon sun flooded into the rounded room from the many windows. One afternoon they would play with the curtains drawn back, she decided, knowing instantly that the panoramic view from the dozen mullioned windows would evoke a strong reaction from Christina.

Quinn stepped into the adjacent bathroom and poured a glass of water into a goblet. She picked up a facecloth and then a feather from the vase. She smiled at her many reflections in the completely mirrored room. Here, too, they could play with the boundaries of Christina's shyness.

Quinn elbowed her way back through the curtains and returned to the cabinet, gazing briefly at Christina. She still knelt. Her sobs had subsided, and Quinn knew that she was now ripe for other games. The darkness had softened her, made her aware of the sensations she was capable of there in the dark. Quinn placed the goblet, feather, and cloth on a shelf of the cabinet and picked up sheepskin-lined wrist cuffs. She snapped the cuffs to another of the many rings on her vest and drew on her soft black gloves. She lit a few more candles, placing them in a branched candelabra, then walked silently over to where Christina knelt and crouched beside her.

Sensing her nearness, Christina turned and made out Quinn's profile in the quasi-darkness. She murmured incoherently and reached for her, grateful for her presence. Quinn caught glimpses of crystalline tears on her cheek. Gripping Christina's chin firmly, Quinn leaned in and tasted the salty tears, then released her. Christina fell back unsteady.

Quinn reached for and captured one of Christina's wrists within her hands. Christina flinched when Quinn unsnapped one of the wrist cuffs from her vest, the metal making a small clinking sound as the catch released. Christina's eyes never left the other woman's face as the soft cuff was fitted over her wrist and snugly laced closed. Quinn looked up to meet her eyes after tying the last knot and simply extended her now-empty hand. She hesitated, but Quinn's eyes compelled her. Finally she lay her bare wrist in her palm. As that wrist was bound, too, Christina sighed.

Quinn rose and reached her arm down to assist her. She looked at her outstretched arm and then stood on her own, refusing the help. She glanced toward the candles as she stood, seeing in their weak light the open cabinet. She caught her breath. Fear of a different sort altogether rushed in on her. Quinn smiled for the briefest of instants, her face smoothed cool and remote when Christina looked at her a moment later.

Knowing that Christina would follow, Quinn walked away. She squinted as she headed into the dark depths of the room, away from the light, searching for the reflection of wood columns in dim candle flickers. Finding them, she walked up to one of the columns and reached for the chain that hung there. She opened the hasp without looking as she watched Christina approach slowly. When she was within arm's reach, Quinn extended her hand.

Christina hesitated. She saw the chain in her hand. She saw the column. She looked at Quinn's vest for the first time and shuddered. It was an evil-looking harness of twisted leather and loops of metal cast here and there. At her hip danced a belt—or thong. It looked very ominous. A snapshot image of tracery lines across bare flesh popped into her mind and would not go away. She was afraid. Her heart began to pound.

"Give me your hand." Quinn's voice was soft and velvety. Christina looked at her, as a wild creature does when faced with the blinding light of an oncoming car's headlights.

"Give it to me," Quinn's voice became a little sharper. Christina lifted her arm. Instantly Quinn snapped the chain onto her cuff. Christina's eyes widened. Bound, she was free to feel her terror fully. The dark enfolded her, held her in the prison of her fears so that she could not tell what was fear and what was excitement. Of her own accord, she lifted her other arm. Quinn smiled, the briefest curving of lips in the darkness.

"Not just yet."

"Oh." Marveling, Christina wondered what was she to do, only partially bound. Half-held, half-restrained from herself, from the dark.

Quinn stepped up to her, impersonal, professional. Christina shuddered beneath her impassive gaze. At the first touch on the back of her neck, she felt her knees crumple. The trappings of this dance were harsh, but the reality appeared gentle, even tender. Her fears eased under Quinn's tender ministrations. She leaned lightly against her hand, delighting in the warmth of her fingers. One by one, Quinn eased each button out of its loop as the delicate cream lace blouse was undone. She pushed the blouse off Christina's shoulders, so that it hung by her wrist, the one that bound her to the column.

Quinn reached deftly around Christina, embracing her lightly, as she unzipped her slim skirt. Christina smiled as it fell to the floor. Quinn motioned her to step out of the pool of fabric, which she then tossed away into the darkness. Her warm fingers slid underneath the waistband of Christina's stockings. Slowly, tantalizingly, she eased them down her legs. Christina leaned back, feeling Quinn's warm breath first against her belly and then grazing against her thighs. Her desire grew in a sudden passion. She reached for Quinn's head to pull it in toward her crotch, at the last moment changing the gesture to stroke the top of her head, running her fingers lightly through her silky hair. Quinn made no response, merely removed her shoes and the tangled nylon stockings, casting them also into the darkness.

Although the room was warm, Christina shivered. Her blouse hung uselessly from her bound wrist and only the wisp of her camisole and her underwear shielded her from nakedness.

Quinn stood. She unsnapped Christina's bound wrist unexpectedly, and Christina stumbled as the tension released. Quinn snatched the blouse from her arm and had her bound again to the chain before she could even form a question. Quinn came to stand in front of her staring intently.

Christina could see only deep shadows where her eyes ought to be, but she knew that Quinn was looking at her. Tremors started in her belly when she reached out for her free arm. She moistened her lips as she placed her cuffed wrist in Quinn's palm. Quinn stepped to the side, drawing her arm with her. There was another column!

As Christina registered that she would be bound open, like this, facing the dark, unable to see or defend herself from whatever came from behind, she began to struggle. It was one thing to be bound, but to be made so exposed, so vulnerable and be unable to resist whatever Quinn might do to her struck her afresh. Part of her wanted Quinn to command her utterly, but she felt that she ought to resist. Her independent spirit demanded that she do so. To surrender without protest to Quinn's mesmerizing ways, why, she was half enchained already! She pulled her arm away, trying to jerk it from Quinn's grasp, but the grip held firm, having expected this reaction. Despite her struggles, Quinn snapped the link on the other cuff. And so she was bound for the first time.

Darkness rushed in upon her. Her arms tingled, held up and away from her body. Her nipples rose, whether in response to imagined cold or the fear that rolled over her, she could not tell. She stamped her foot, feeling ineffectual and silly without shoes to create the sound of her impatience. She shrugged, trying bravado. The darkness won. She sighed. She yearned for Quinn to touch her, kiss her, anything to divert her from the maelstrom in to which being bound threw her. Through her fear, a strange pulse had begun between her legs. She knew Quinn watched her; even standing back there in the darkness, Christina could feel Quinn's eyes upon her.

Suddenly Quinn stepped up from out of the darkness, as if she had been that close all the time. Christina turned towards her, pleading for her touch. Quinn's warm breath touched her throat, and Christina tilted her head, baring her neck. Desire built in her, aching.

From the innermost pocket of her vest, Quinn withdrew a knife. She opened it and raised it to shoulder height, so that Christina would know it was there. She saw the blade and cried out.

"No, please!" she begged, her voice dying in her throat.

Quinn placed her hand on the high part of Christina's chest, feeling her pulse beat wildly. She brought the knife close to her shoulder.

"Are you afraid?"

Christina gazed mesmerized at the knife and could only nod wordlessly. Fear and something much more intense drove her now.

Quinn merely smiled. She lifted the spaghetti strap of Christina's camisole and cut it, first on one side and then the other. The straps fell down, lashing her breasts with the lightest of touches. Her nipples tightened in response. Quinn then reached to cut the sides of her underwear and they hung briefly suspended between her thighs. Christina parted her legs just a little, and the cloth fell to the ground. The camisole still hung suspended by the swelling of her breasts. Quinn reached out and tugged at the hem of the flimsy garment, easing it down past her breasts, over her stomach and hips, to fall in a silky pool at her feet.

Christina stood naked. Her skin was hypersensitive, and she could feel whispery breezes that touched and enticed her into a heightened awareness of her body. She closed her eyes and let her head fall back, pulling lightly on the chains that bound her. Shifting, she placed more of her weight upon them. She was helpless. She was completely naked. And Quinn just stood there. What could possibly happen next? She shivered with delicious excitement, for once forgetting that she still faced the dark.

Quinn called to her from the darkness. She opened her eyes.

"Spread your legs."

Christina shuddered but obeyed, widening her stance a little. Her nether lips flushed and swelled, wetness warming her all over. Touch me, she begged silently.

"Wider," Quinn encouraged her. She unfastened her hand whip softly, so as not to break Christina's reverie, prodding her upper thigh when she did not respond immediately.

"No, no, no. That's not the way to behave." she admonished.

Seeing the thong in Quinn's hand, a tremor of nameless dread ran through Christina as she realized the inevitable. She pulled at the chains in earnest, trying to increase the distance between Quinn and herself.

"Please," she begged, unsure if she was pleading for release or for Quinn to begin.

"What?" Quinn asked absently. She let the soft leather brush against the smoothness of Christina's inner thigh. Christina squirmed, pulling the chains taut, then sank onto them. Walking behind her, Quinn trailed the softest part of the whip down Christina's back. She first arched away then leaned toward the leather's soft stroking. Quinn came to stand beside her and feathered her chest lightly with the silken tongue of the lash. Christina moaned and stirred a little in her bonds. Her breathing grew rapid, and her eyes fell shut once more. She was lost in her body.

"You like this, don't you?" Quinn asked, more to keep her tied to the moment and the sound of her voice than for any real response.

Christina looked at her, drugged, desire coloring her face. For her this might have been enough, but for Quinn the game had only just begun.

"Did you spread your legs as I asked?"

Christina merely looked at her, feeling the kiss of the leather brush against the soft skin of her breasts. As the lash was withdrawn, she strained toward it.

"Did you?"

"No, yes. Yes," she breathed, not caring what she said.

"Shall I continue?"

"Oh, yes," Christina sighed. She closed her eyes, surrendering. Quinn watched her for a moment, a smile played over her features. Eyes glinting, she raised her whip hand.

Cast through the air, the suede fell silently, unexpected, to land with a soft smack on

Christina's behind. She strained forward, pulling with all her might away from the blow. She cried out wordlessly with the shock of it, the unexpected sting after the feathery touches that had gone before.

Quinn let fall another blow, a little harder than the first. She smiled as the leather connected with Christina's ass. The resounding crack had not really hurt her, nor would it really mark her, as the crop might have done. This whip was perfect for her. Quinn cast the velvety leather tongue again and again in an easy rhythm over Christina's backside, until it began to appear flushed in the dim candlelight.

Christina danced away from each blow, maneuvering as if she could avoid the next one, and then the next. She cried out softly at first, ashamed of the part of her that wanted to wail and scream with the agonizing flicks Quinn laid on her behind. As she grew more sensitive and the blows did not end, but seemed to grow sharper, she moaned. She cried. Then she pleaded.

Quinn continued to whip her, the little blows landing one after another on first one cheek, then the other. No matter how Christina tried to evade them, regardless of how prettily she begged, no matter what she promised, the blows still fell upon her. Finally she cried out. Her voice split the darkness and then was swallowed up by it. She shrieked. The soft rain of lashes continued.

Her behind was on fire. Her legs ached and she strained and strained to evade the blows. She cried in frustration knowing escape was impossible, that Quinn could continue to do this as long as she wanted, and she had no choice in the matter.

Quinn paused. Christina's rump was a pretty shade of deep red. Any more lashes, even this gently, might mar or bruise. She was as yet too virginal for darker marks yielded by more permanent sports. Still, Quinn knew that sitting for the next day or so would bring these moments immediately back to her. That was enough. She was ready for something stronger. Quinn contemplated just how far to push her.

Christina hung her head down, tears streaming down her cheeks. Her arms strained against the chains' tension as she leaned forward, grateful for the respite. Her body wanted to remain tense, knowing that Quinn could not be finished with her, some secret part hoping she was not. All the tears, the raging out of control, had stirred her profoundly and she knew that she was very wet. She had just scratched the surface of a wealth of emotions she was unaware she possessed. Quinn could take her all the way into her self—this hidden self—and back out again. She did not want it to be over just yet.

And it wasn't. A delicious, almost burning sensation began on her behind. Was it a touch? Or the memory of the small leather thong that Quinn

had used on her so mercilessly? The touch continued. It began to arouse her and make her want to
jump away at the same time. She strained to turn
her head over her shoulder to see what was touching her.

Quinn trailed a long ostrich feather over her
warmed skin. Where the tiny feathery fingers
touched, Christina felt the warmth and echoes of
the lash. Quinn reached out and placed a gloved
hand upon her reddened asscheek. She tightened
her cheeks and tried to jerk away. Quinn pinched
her flesh and she moaned, openmouthed, surrendering to the hot flush of emotion that stormed
through her, washed over her, and left her helpless
once more.

Quinn released her. Christina stood, her legs
barely supporting her, hanging onto the chains
with her hands. Her lower lips opened wet; she was
aching to be touched, stroked, perhaps filled. She
turned slightly, presenting her behind.

"No, no, no," Quinn said, refusing to touch her.

Christina ran her tongue over her lips as if to
ease the aching in her loins, scraping their fullness
with eager teeth, then running her tongue again
and again over the sensitized flesh. Her eyes fluttered closed.

Quinn ducked under her arm, coming to stand
in front of her. Christina's face was flushed, her
mouth open and inviting, a few wet tracks still ran
down her face. Quinn raised the little whip once

more and gently snapped the tongue of it across her heaving chest. The lash caught both of her nipples, and Christina jerked up and away from its sting. Quinn met her shocked eyes and deliberately raised the whip again.

"No." Christina begged.

The soft leather whisked through the air and landed full on soft breast flesh. She moaned. The lash snaked out again, again, and again. Each blow much softer than before, but enough to redden, to sting, and to arouse her tremendously as she writhed away from them and the intense look in Quinn's eyes.

Christina suddenly realized that she no longer feared the lash so much. After the sting there would come a rush of warmth, a tingling that found its way to her belly. Quinn withheld the lash, but she moaned anyway. Her body was on fire, each blow rushing blood to her chest.

Christina's arms stretched out forever, pulling and sending warm fire down into her heart. Her legs felt taut, so she spread them wide, then pressed them close, squeezing her thighs together, relishing the sudden pressure against her lips and her soft hidden hood. She could feel herself swollen open, slick and soft from perspiration and desire. She pulsed, beating in time rhythmically with her pounding heart. Her head felt like it was floating, so light. No thoughts, no worries, only the endless round of sensations flowing into her. She lolled her head onto one shoulder and looked at Quinn, her lips curved enticingly.

"Touch me."

Quinn smiled. "No," she replied, her voice soft as a breath.

"Please," Christina begged.

Quinn reached out and with one gloved finger traced a circle around one rosy nipple. Christina moaned and her hips came forward reluctantly. The sensations coursed from her breast down to her toes. She nudged against Quinn's still-outstretched hand. The touch was too harsh, and she recoiled in a brief agony of blinding sensation.

Quinn stroked the sore breast again, plumping it, seducing her back into pleasure from pain's border. Christina gave a guttural openmouthed cry as pleasure rushed through her once more. Quinn placed both hands on her hips and urged her to be motionless.

"Be still now." she commanded.

Christina tried, but the fire racing from her buttocks to her breasts and lingering in her moist crotch made her move against her own volition. She must move, must keep the little bursts of pleasure, pain, coursing through her. She needed it now; she wanted more. She looked at Quinn and tried to rub her hips against her, but Quinn stepped back. She whimpered in frustration.

"Be still!"

Wavering between desire and impatience,

Christina struggled languorously in her bonds. Quinn reached up for her hair and grasped a handful lightly.

"I warned you," she growled. She raised the soft leather whip once more and with the butt of it, worked Christina's legs apart. Finally she kicked them apart with her foot. When Christina tried to clamp her thighs around the whip's butt, Quinn laughed and propped her booted foot against her bare foot. Then she began flicking Christina's inner thighs with the soft leather. No more than the gentlest of slaps a lover's hair makes when she tosses it from side to side against her lover's flesh.

Christina drooped in her chains, struggling to get the buttery soft tongue of the thong to catch her netherlips, to make the light contact stroke her wet sex. As time after time the lash missed its mark, she growled in frustration.

The taps became the slightest bit stronger, little bites into her skin. She began to writhe as the heat reached her. Her face flushed and her breathing changed as she surrendered completely to it. The lash stroked her and she danced with it, first moving away, then leaning into it, moving her hips in a vain plea for release. Her face was a deep red and she panted openly, sobbing Quinn's name. Her soft cries filled the darkness until she was begging for her lover's touch in continuous refrain of open, shameless desire.

Finally Quinn clipped the whip back onto her

vest and, with her still-gloved hand, she slid her fingers between Christina's burning thighs, which started to close almost immediately around her hand.

"Keep them wide, or I'll stop."

Christina froze at the sound of her voice. "Stop? Ah, please, don't," she whimpered.

Quinn's hand slipped back and forth easily, gliding in between Christina's moist folds. She searched with her forefinger, and when Christina arched and cried out in ecstasy, Quinn ran her finger lightly over and over, and over her.

She tucked two fingers inside and pressed up, pulling forward lightly, massaging her from within, all the while rubbing her continuously with the other hand.

As Quinn worked her, Christina flung herself against her hands. She bent her knees and pumped against Quinn's firm touch. Then shuddering, pounding waves of pleasure flowed from her toes to her clit and all the way to the top of her head. A funny burning sensation began in the soles of her feet and her palms, an itchy burning. She tossed her head back, stretching herself out—a taut bowstring pulled to a quivering standstill by Quinn's hands and fingers. The darkness could not contain her suddenly and she rent the sky in showers of golden sparks. Christina melted, liquid in Quinn's hands, pressing her cunt into her in slow, steady thrusts.

"Ah," she crooned.

Quinn removed her fingers slowly, easing them away from her. As she pulled out, she could feel Christina still clamping down upon her, her walls beating against her fingertips, keeping time with her heart. She sagged, spent. Her arms strained against the chains as she hung limply.

Quinn brushed Christina's hair back from her moist and glistening face and kissed her softly on the temple. Christina sighed with pleasure.

"I'm going to blindfold you now." Quinn whispered into her ear. Christina made a moue of protest, but it was a feeble attempt. Her head lolled against her shoulder, then her eyes fluttered shut.

Quinn walked over to the cabinet and set the whip in a basket on the bottom, for cleaning. She peeled off her gloves and tossed them into the basket also. From one of the cabinet's many drawers she withdrew a silk blindfold. Flushed with her own excitement, she rubbed the silk briefly against her cheek.

Christina pouted when the silk slipped over her eyes, cooling and soothing her fevered flesh. Quinn unhooked her wrist cuffs from the chains, then massaged her shoulders and arms until the blood had rushed into them fully.

Christina groaned softly during her ministrations but did not pull away. She stood with her head bowed, arms to her sides, flushed with sweat and light bruising. The blindfold humbled her, kept her inside herself, pulsing in the darkness that now enfolded her like a welcome cloak. The fear was far off, but not worth considering with the present trembling in her buttocks, her breasts which still tingled from Quinn's touch, and her moist center, warm now. Content. She stood pliant, graceful in her absolute surrender to sensation.

Quinn finger-combed Christina's hair. She felt impossibly pleased at the way Christina bent and leaned in the ecstasy of even such a little touch. She then playfully tugged the soft thatch of hair that nestled between Christina's legs.

"Oh, yes." her captive sighed.

Quinn chuckled softly and clipped her wrists together so that they hung in front of her, limp, fingers curling in toward her crotch. Then she tugged at her wrists, smiling when Christina stumbled as she first walked towards her.

"Come along now," she urged softly. She blew out the candles and then led them from the room, down the stairs.

Christina stumbled along in darkness, her feet tingling, her cheeks flushing with twinges of half pain, half pleasure with each step. Then, carpet, thick like the black room, her toes dug in with pleasure, curling happily. They walked. She heard voices, dimly, far off behind her dark satin mask. She disregarded them, feeling slight breezes against her naked flesh. Quinn would take care of her.

Quinn led her down the main upstairs hallway and into a large bathroom. She tugged and positioned her so that she was poised above the toilet.

"Sit," she commanded.

Christina sat, her mouth forming a little O when she felt the cold plastic seat.

"I never...," she whispered.

"You will now." Quinn smiled. She propped one leg up on the tub wall and rubbing her fingers along the sole of her foot, sighing with pleasure.

Christina felt her stomach muscles tighten with embarrassment and shame. She had no idea whether she was being watched. She held herself rigidly. A moment later, her muscles gave out, worn from her exertions, and she emptied herself, face flaming. When she was done, she lifted her hands uselessly and then dropped them back into her lap.

"You'll have to let me go," she said in a small voice.

"I'll have to?" Quinn questioned mockingly.

"Yes. Please?"

"Oh, no."

Christina trembled and blushed all over when Quinn pulled her up and wiped her delicately with toilet paper, fore and aft. Her nipples tightened and she shook with little tremors from the indignity of it as the toilet flushed behind her. She stood there, beet red, and listened to Quinn's footsteps cross the room.

Quinn ran the tub half-full of warm water. She stirred a few drops of scented oil into the waters and then tested the heat. When it was fragrant and gently steaming, she led Christina over to it and gently lowered her into the tub. She raised her arms above her head and clipped them to the ring that hung down from the ceiling for that purpose.

Quinn bathed her all over. Washing her tenderly and rinsing her off with streams of warm water from the hand held water jet. She massaged Christina's sore muscles and swished the water around at her crotch playfully. Then she made her stand up and toweled her dry with a fluffy black towel from the rack.

Christina had returned to her dreamy state and leaned into Quinn's hands with wanton abandon. After drying carefully between each of her toes, Quinn unhooked her from the bathing ring and led her down the hall, rosy and clean, to one of the guest rooms.

Quinn settled her into the high feather bed, unhooking her wrists, but leaving them bound in the sheepskin cuffs.

"You are not to touch yourself. Do you understand?"

Christina nodded sleepily into the pillow. Quinn reached underneath her hair and untied the blindfold. She placed a soft kiss on her lips.

"Sleep sweetly," she murmured. Christina's lips formed soft words in response, but she was already asleep. Her lips curved in an easy welcoming smile.

Quinn smiled tenderly. Christina was so easy. So responsive. Her lips pouted in sleep, still full with desire even while slumbering. Quinn felt a hot flash in her loins and inhaled deeply to calm herself. Not yet, not yet. Tomorrow, perhaps.

She padded silently from the room and shut the door behind her. She turned the old skeleton key in the lock and made her way down the grand curving staircase and into the dining room.

❧

They began the first run, as it was sometimes called by the denizens of the household. For many of those who came into the house as guests, it was their first experience with public nakedness. Even for women familiar with women's festivals, who were comfortable being partially or completely unclothed, it was unnerving to be completely naked around fully dressed women who exuded power as the women of this particular household did. For Christina, this was the first time she had been naked outside of the privacy of her bedroom.

Christina tried to match her steps to Quinn's long-legged pace. At first she gave no thought to the other occupants of the house; yet, when she passed one of the open doorways on the second level, still breathless from her descent from the tower room, she saw a woman garbed in black leather regarding her with amusement. She blushed beet red from top to toe and could not meet the woman's eyes as she hurried past. The woman's appraising stare haunted her as she scurried down the main staircase after Quinn. Quinn did not pause for her, not once.

Christina wondered why she could not seem to stop herself, but half-ran to keep up with her, even though she was mortally embarrassed by her naked state. She thought how easy it would be to slip into the bedroom she had used the night before and take out another of the satin robes she had seen hanging in the wardrobe. If she could find which room it was, she thought ironically. Quinn would be displeased with her—the thought insinuated itself into her mind.

No, she thought. I can bear this. I do not want her to be angry with me. She hurried to catch up.

Quinn once more led her through the many hallways of the immense restored Victorian mansion. She avoided the breakfast room and the large-group play areas, and stuck to the halls where Christina might see only a few of the house mistresses. She personally did not like the tradition of a first run and made it a point of honor to make the run as brief as possible.

Yet she smiled when she saw Kaitlin ministering to Sherry and immediately led Christina in their direction. She had seemed drawn to Sherry last night. It would be interesting to see her reactions to their daylight play.

Christina dogged Quinn's steps. Despite her attempts to catch up, Quinn always seemed four to five paces ahead of her, turning the corner just before her. As she rounded the latest turning, Christina stopped abruptly. Dumfounded.

The lovely brunette woman, who had appeared to turn to flame in her lover's arms, stood before her. Her eyes were bright with tears, and she no longer resembled the drugged princess of the night before. She was bound with her arms above her head, stretched taut to a chain that hung from the high ceiling. Glancing around quickly, Christina saw that Quinn and the woman's lover from the night before stood talking together by the windows of this vaulted room.

It looked like a music room, Christina decided, seeing a piano and guitar discarded in one corner. But there were other elements in the room that made it disturbing. The chain against which the brunette woman struggled futilely, for example, and an old leather chair that might have been for dentistry—or something more barbaric. A multitude of chairs occupied one side of the room. Christina shuddered. Public displays of private acts flashed through her mind.

Quinn beckoned to her. Then, when she did not see her, she called out, "Christina, come here."

Quinn's voice bit into her thoughts like a whip.

Christina started. She walked over and stood next to Quinn. The woman with Quinn watched her every step with a hunger in her eyes that was unmistakable. Christina shivered inwardly; she would not want to be left alone with this woman.

Quinn reached for her and curved her hand around the back of her neck, guiding her to kneel upon the floor in a flood of sunlight.

"This is Christina, Kaitlin." Quinn said in a proprietary manner.

Christina flushed with pleasure that Quinn would use such a warm possessive tone about her.

Kaitlin bent down to turn her head up to face her. "Christina?" Kaitlin asked in the formality of introduction.

Christina responded automatically. "Kaitlin?"

Kaitlin drew back her arm and backhanded Christina hard across the cheek. She lost her balance and fell sideways. She came up on her knees swiftly, her hands clenching into fists. Her face was stained from the blow. Quinn placed a restraining hand upon her shoulder.

"Lesson number two: you must address Kaitlin as 'Mistress' or 'Mistress Kaitlin.'"

Christina looked up at Quinn, feeling betrayed. She would allow this Kaitlin-woman to strike her? Christina was dazed by the unreality of it all. She was already having difficulty admitting that she did not mind it much when Quinn struck her with loving intentions, but this woman had really hit her. She rubbed at the sore place on her cheek and opened her mouth to protest, but she was silenced by Quinn's next words.

"Let's try this again, shall we?" Quinn chided her lightly.

Christina steamed. Quinn was speaking as if she had done something wrong, not Kaitlin. Or Mistress Kaitlin, she thought sarcastically.

Kaitlin again gripped her face, tugging against Christina's reluctance to face her.

She refused to meet Kaitlin's eyes, but cast her eyes down, sullen and uncooperative.

"Christina?" Kaitlin asked again, her voice no different than before, sweetly neutral. Christina remained silent. Quinn nudged her softly with her booted foot. Christina tried to wrench her head free, but Kaitlin held her fast.

"Mistress," she spat out at last. Her voice was laden with sarcasm.

Kaitlin released her, smiling, and took a few steps away from them. She lit a cigarette and took a deep drag, looking over at the bound woman.

Quinn crouched down beside her. "You were not polite just now, Christina. I expected more from you," she said sorrowfully. "We will have to discuss courtesy later," she promised with malice in her voice.

Christina shuddered. In this place, courtesy meant God-knew-what. She bit her tongue and tried to overcome her anger. Quinn looked withdrawn and distant. She felt as if some spark had died within Quinn and hoped that it was not of her doing. Conflicting emotions waged a private war within her. She reached out, pausing, before laying a hand on her knee.

"I am sorry," she murmured. Quinn allowed the briefest curving of her lips to light her face before she rose.

"We have been very rude," she announced. Kaitlin turned back toward them with a shrug.

"No, I insist. Christina and I will think of something to make it up to you, won't we?" Quinn addressed her last remark to Christina, who looked away and said nothing. Quinn placed her hand lightly on her hair.

Kaitlin smiled openly at Christina's continued ill humor. "Let me put her up." She indicated the chain upon which Sherry hung.

Quinn shook her head silently. She believed that Christina would not find Kaitlin's pastimes to her taste, but she would know for sure soon enough. She knew herself to be adept at reading pleasure levels in others; it should be especially easy, given Christina's transparent desires. She would be able to determine immediately whether she showed the slightest interest in the harsh games. Kaitlin would require little persuasion to show off before a new girl.

"Show us what you're up to with Sherry." Quinn urged. "We'll find some way to make our rudeness up to you before the weekend's over," she promised.

Christina looked over at the woman named Sherry, fuming over Quinn's words. It was easier to think about Sherry before she knew her name. Suddenly she wondered what she did for a living, how she lived, how could she allow Kaitlin to humiliate her publicly in this way.

Sherry opened her tear-reddened eyes and looked at her, as if sensing her eyes upon her. Kaitlin drew near. Sherry's eyes closed, and her head dropped wearily between her shoulders.

Kaitlin took another drag on her cigarette and then held the burning end of it close to Sherry's swelling breast. Sherry cried out and pulled away.

Christina gasped and Quinn's hand tightened upon her hair. Kaitlin grabbed hold of Sherry and swung her back into place. As Sherry turned she could see a welter of small red spots on her buttocks. Christina shuddered and turned away, sickened.

Quinn murmured softly to her. "Sherry has consented to this. She enjoys it. Much as you enjoyed last night, despite your tears and protestations."

Christina gazed at Quinn, searching her face to see if she indeed spoke the truth. Quinn did not waver, but met her glance steadily. Christina shuddered.

"I'd never, I—it's awful," she hissed, very upset.

"Then we won't," Quinn responded flatly. She

smiled down at her and quipped, "Besides, I don't smoke."

Christina smiled in spite of herself, enraptured once again by the fire returning to Quinn's eyes. They locked glances, drowning in each other's eyes.

A scream split the silence. Sherry writhed and moaned on her chain. Kaitlin stood by calmly, watching her distress. A small red mark flowered on Sherry's breast.

Christina shuddered but could not look away as Sherry opened her eyes and begged Kaitlin for release. Just so had she begged Quinn. The way she held herself, it was the same way that she had stood when desire had transcended all, bringing pleasure. She was confused. How could pain bring pleasure? Suddenly conscious of her own cheeks burning from the constant pressure of her heels, she knew vividly that pain indeed could bring pleasure.

Kaitlin kept Sherry waiting until the fire of the burn had subsided. Then she stroked her burned flesh. She kissed Sherry as she moved ecstatically under her caresses. Her gestures were loving, tender. She drew her cigarette close to Sherry's skin, warming it.

"Yes, please."

From where she sat, Christina could hear Sherry beg. A moment later, she screamed again with abandon, her voice filling the music room.

Christina turned her eyes away, unable to imagine that this lovely woman wanted to be burned, scarred, tortured in this fashion. It sickened her. Quinn stroked the top of her head lightly. She looked back reluctantly at the couple.

Kaitlin had put the cigarette in her mouth and was stroking Sherry from behind. Sherry stood on her tiptoes and swung freely into her caress, moaning with pleasure.

"Come," Quinn said softly, urging Christina to her feet. "Let's leave them to their pleasure."

Christina could not drag her eyes from them as they left the room. Quinn set off down the hall, and once again Christina had to hurry to keep pace. Sherry's ecstatic face and piercing screams haunted her, as she wondered what she herself might beg for in the coming hours.

Quinn paused once in the dark back hall and took Christina into her arms for a sudden kiss, moist and sweet with tenderness and promise. Christina melted into her arms, gentled and reassured. When she would have spoken, Quinn lay a finger across her lips.

"It's forbidden," Quinn murmured into her ear. She then released Christina and set off through the house once more at breakneck pace. Christina trailed after her.

Quinn led her to the kitchen. The room was large

and bright, full of gleaming white appliances. The counters were white marble, littered with canisters of every shape and size and jars full of cookies. Spicy, sweet aromas filled the air. The hum of the dishwasher at first blocked out the sound of wood on flesh.

A large woman dressed all in white stood by a dressing board wielding a small paddle-shaped cutting board. She applied it with resounding smacks on the naked bottom of a lithe black woman who flinched as each blow landed, but did not make a sound. The black woman wore an apron which covered her from breast to thigh, and nothing else.

Quinn laughed softly as she entered the kitchen. The woman in white turned around, her face wreathed in smiles, genial and friendly.

"Don't tell me," Quinn gurgled. "Chocolate-chip cookies." The woman laughed and nodded.

"Damn if I can keep her away from 'em." She smacked the black woman's behind once more. "Get up there now." She ordered the young woman.

Christina could not help staring, the woman was lovely, her skin a beautiful shade of milk chocolate. She clambered up on the marble-topped dressing board, gasping a little as her tender flesh touched the cold stone. The chef grabbed a cucumber from the kitchen table and thrust it at her.

"Well?" she snapped. "Lie down. Get to it."

The young black woman lay down upon the table, wincing a little as her back and thighs came into contact with more of the marble's cold surface. She moved the apron to one side and placed the cucumber between her legs.

Quinn chuckled as she looked at Christina, staring openmouthed as the young woman inserted the cucumber inside and began to thrust it back and forth while she touched herself with obvious pleasure.

"Nan, this is Christina." Quinn introduced her to the woman in white.

Christina reluctantly tore her eyes away from the sideboard, where the woman had begun to writhe, heedless of her audience, and looked appraisingly at the woman in white.

The woman called Nan appeared to be in her fifties, with short dykey hair that had turned salt-and-pepper with age. On closer inspection, her jacket and pants were the garb habitual to chefs. Her face was round and full, and she rested her hands easily on her ample hips. Her smile lines were creased deeply into her face.

Christina could see at a glance that Nan's approach was completely different than either Kaitlin or Quinn's. Where they both were serious, exuding power and mystery, Nan seemed full of humor. She seemed to regard the woman lying on the table touching herself as part of a big joke.

"Mistress Nan." Christina acknowledged softly,

deciding that she liked the looks of her. Nan beamed.

"Now, she has manners!" Nan chortled to Quinn. "When will you give her kitchen duty?"

Quinn smiled absently as she gazed around the room. "Not for a little while yet I think," she replied. "Besides, it looks like you have your hands full, at present."

Nan laughed and walked closer to Christina. She looked to Quinn, seeking approval, then reached out to take Christina's breasts in her hands. She squeezed them, pinching, like testing a melon for ripeness. Christina winced a little, but said nothing. Nan then ran her hands over her belly and thighs, slipping one hand unexpectedly between. Christina gasped.

"Now, now," Nan admonished, kneading her flesh roughly.

Against her will, Christina felt herself warming to this woman. Her lips flushed, and moisture seeped out to wet Nan's fingers. She moistened her lips and glanced over at the young black woman. The woman was still sliding the cucumber in and out. Her body glistened with a light sheen of sweat as she worked herself on the cold marble. She could see the flash of her long fingers as they dipped between her legs, and felt Nan's fingers playing on her own soft nethermouth. She felt a tremor of pleasure run through her, and she pushed herself against Nan's hand. Nan continued to stroke her, her fingers playing in and around her lips, teasing, opening her up, making her pant, hungry for more.

Quinn watched for a moment then walked to the sideboard to watch the young black woman more closely. The woman opened her eyes, sensing her presence. She uttered a soft wordless cry of pleasure.

Quinn turned away. "Christina," she called, "come here, please."

Christina started to step away from Nan, from her gently stroking fingers, but Nan suddenly hooked her fingers inside her and tugged urgently. She cried out, closing her eyes, still once more.

"Christina!" Quinn called again, more sharply.

Nan withdrew her fingers just as rapidly as she had entered and stepped back, watching Christina lurch off balance ungracefully. She laughed again, deeply and gutturally. Christina shuddered once all over and walked toward Quinn. Nan followed.

Quinn watched, a sardonic smile on her lips. Christina was flushed. Her nipples had ripened to hard points of pleasure. She walked lightly, as if the soles of her feet were too sensitive to touch the cool tile floor. Quinn pointed at the dark-skinned woman.

"Robin made your breakfast tray." she said conversationally.

Robin opened her eyes briefly and moaned as she continued to stroke herself. Christina watched in fascination.

"Thank her for your breakfast, Christina." Quinn said softly.

Christina darted a glance at Quinn. She opened and closed her mouth, realizing that words were not what was wanted of her. Quinn pointed at Robin's wet crotch, into which the dark green cucumber moved slickly. She sighed helplessly. Quinn raised one eyebrow.

I don't even know her, Christina thought. Her hesitation was brief; Quinn's eyes compelled her. Her body tingled, and she moved to the edge of the sideboard as if in a dream. She leaned in between Robin's spread legs. The wet, musky scent of the woman rose up to meet her. Robin's hands had not stopped moving over her soft wet lips, and Christina watched for a moment before reaching out to capture her hands and push them away. Robin whimpered in frustration.

Christina blew a soft warm breath over Robin's wet flesh. She smiled as the woman rose up off the marble in response. She placed a soft kiss on her inner thigh, avoiding the cucumber which jutted obscenely out of her. She took hold of the vegetable and began to pump it steadily in and out. Robin rose and bucked beneath her. Christina placed her other hand on her belly to hold her hips to the table and leaned in.

Soft tongue on dark rich skin. Robin gasped at the first touch of her tongue. She tasted her, sampling her sweetness. A vegetarian, probably, she thought as her tongue began to lap Robin's lips, teasing her gently. Robin cried out her pleasure.

Christina worked the cucumber in and out, building an irresistible rhythm for her to match. She could feel Robin's pulse in her mouth as it beat strongly against her tongue. She lost herself in the other woman's pleasure. Her own lips opened, gaping empty, pulsing strongly herself. Opening and closing on emptiness.

"Sweet temperament." Nan commented. Quinn nodded, her eyes fixed on Christina's nether-mouth, which peeped out between her cheeks as she stood bent over Robin. She was wet. Good, she thought.

"I'll need a lunch basket," she murmured. Nan grunted.

"You want everything Quinn. Breakfast in bed, picnic lunches. Why do I put up with you?" she grumbled.

"Because I'm good in bed." Quinn replied seriously, her voice rich with promise. She turned and stared into Nan's eyes. Nan blushed and turned away.

"That's right—don't play fair." she muttered.

"I never do." Quinn smiled, a cruel twist of her lips, and turned back to Robin and Christina. Nan looked searchingly at Quinn for a moment, then snorted with frustration. She ambled to the sink and began putting lunch together.

Christina was crouched low over Robin's belly, her arm stroking back and forth, nudging her own breasts. Quinn could hear the soft, wet sounds of her mouth against Robin's lips. The two women rocked together in an easy rhythm.

When Robin came, it was in great pulsing waves, bucking herself against Christina's teeth and lips, bearing down upon the cucumber with her strong muscles. Christina rode it out, continuing to stroke her as the last throbbing eased into soft contractions and she sighed contentedly. She opened her eyes and smiled.

Christina smiled back, her mouth wet and gleaming in the light.

"Thanks for breakfast," she whispered. Robin chuckled softly and closed her eyes. She eased the cucumber from her and held it, warm, in her hand. Robin whimpered when she withdrew.

"Robin, fuck Christina for me, will you?" Quinn asked, her words falling like stones into the stillness of the room.

Shocked, Christina turned to her. Her face was neutral, impassive. She shook her head slowly from side to side. "No," she mouthed.

Quinn looked at her and said nothing.

"Sure." Robin said softly from the table. She sat up gingerly and slid down. Then she patted the table invitingly and waited for Christina to climb up.

"Christina!" Quinn warned.

Christina felt as if she was going to cry. She

wiped her still wet mouth with the back of her hand and stood there undecided. Part of her wanted to be touched very badly, but not by a stranger. She wanted Quinn. She looked at Robin, smiling tenderly at her, still rapt in her own afterglow.

"Now, Christina," Quinn urged gently.

Reluctantly, Christina set the soft, wet cucumber down on the table. She backed against the side edge and, using both arms to prop herself up, slipped up onto the cool marble. She gasped at the shock, goose bumps covering her. Robin lifted her legs for her, forcing her to lie down, spreading her legs wide. Christina bent her legs, resting her feet on the table, letting them absorb most of the cold. Her back wanted to lift away from the cold stone, and she felt shivers of expectation and fear run through her.

Quinn took the cucumber from the table and tossed it across the room toward the sink. Nan looked up as it fell onto the porcelain.

"We'll need something for Robin to play with, if you please, Nan," Quinn requested.

Nan reached into a drawer and withdrew a marble pestle; long, rounded, and very cold to the touch. She held it up for her inspection.

Quinn shook her head, smiling. "Another time."

"Here, then." Nan said, tossing her another washed cucumber, trimmed smooth.

Quinn caught it easily. "Not quite what I had in mind," she murmured.

Nan began to sputter as Quinn pulled a knife from her pocket and began to carve the top ridge of the cucumber. After she had made several ridges and gouges in the fruit, she passed it to Robin with a smile. "That's better."

Robin sensed dangerous undercurrents between Nan and Quinn. She took the proffered cucumber and held it briefly between her hands to warm it.

Seeing Robin appear suddenly between her legs, Christina squirmed.

Robin smiled reassuringly, then bent down and took Christina in her mouth. Without preliminaries, without hesitation. She lapped at her wetness with her broad, flat tongue and, with a sudden gentle thrust, urged the cucumber inside Christina.

Christina moaned. Shocked by her own excitement, she clapped her hand over her mouth. Quinn smiled.

Robin moved the cucumber back and forth, setting up an urgent rhythm that had Christina's ass slapping against the marble as she moved to keep the pace. Christina opened, wide and wet, closing down on the cucumber with sudden tight contractions. Then Robin touched her. Her fingers flew fast and sure, moving lightly across her hooded softness, teasing and tormenting her as she tried to do both, feel the fullness within her and the electric sensations of Robin's fingers outside.

Robin bent low and brushed Christina's moist folds with her soft, full lips. She reached out her arm to smooth the skin of her belly, stroking upward. Then she rubbed her palm over Christina's breast, pushing her back down onto the stone as she rose up in pleasure. Her lips and tongue stroked her, back and forth, darting in and around in a titillating dance of erotic tension. Christina moaned.

Nan came up to stand beside Quinn, a basket in her hand. They watched together as Christina rose and fell against Robin's hands. Her skin had turned a rosy pink, and her body gleamed.

Christina cried out as Robin kissed her. She bit her hand. She arched her hips against the rhythm of her thrusts until her back could feel the strain. She forgot that Quinn watched, forgot about everything except the warm touch between her legs, the softness of Robin's mouth upon her, and the achy feeling of her breast where she teased her. She could feel the pulsing beginning within her, steady beats that raced with her heart and surrounded her in an oncoming flood of warm wet sensation. She arched, eagerly on the edge.

"That's enough." Quinn said softly.

Robin withdrew quickly, shaking her head apologetically. Christina had been so close, poor thing.

Christina cried out, frustrated. She opened her eyes reproachfully.

"Lunch is ready." Quinn said. "Let's go." She turned and took the basket from Nan, who was beaming from ear to ear.

Dazed, Christina sat up. She watched Quinn stride out the back door and out to the lawn.

"Get going, girl." Nan prodded. "That one doesn't like to be kept waiting."

Disoriented, Christina looked from Nan to Robin and back again. Then she slid from the sideboard and hurried from the house. Wetness snaked trails down her thighs as she began to run.

Valentina Cilescu
MISTRESS MINE

Sophia sighed on her prison bed and rubbed herself to a sad and solitary orgasm. It was no consolation for her lost life, her lost innocence. She wondered sorrowfully where Emily was now. And she shuddered as she thought of Mademoiselle Malin, who had brought such turmoil and darkness into their innocent lives. Would she ever be free of the memories that haunted her?

Footsteps sounded in the tiled corridor outside the cell, and the grille in the door slid back. A round, brutish face peered in.

"Prisoner Cranleigh—visitor for you. Smarten yourself up now, you disgusting little slut—this is a respectable lady!"

Sophia got to her feet, smoothing the folds of

her coarse gown as best she could. She was bewildered. Who could possibly have come to visit her? All those she knew either vilified her or were too afraid to come near for fear of soiling their good names.

The door swung open, and the fat wardress came in, keys clanking on her belt and an expression of grim disapproval on her face.

"Behave yourself, Cranleigh, or you'll get no more privileges like this." She turned to someone behind her. "I'll give you an hour with her, madam. I'll be right outside. If she gives you any trouble, just call to me, and I'll sort her out—don't you worry."

A moment later, the stocky form of the wardress was replaced by the figure of another, very different woman.

A glimpse of crimson satin announced her arrival, and Sophia gasped as the woman swept into the cell and watched the door close behind her. She was tall and slender, but with a swelling bosom that sent lust coursing through Sophia's veins. Her breasts seemed molded into the black-and-crimson bodice, tailored so finely that Sophia imagined she could make out the outline of the woman's nipples, thrusting against the taut, sheer fabric.

The woman stood contemplating Sophia for a few moments, then took off her black calfskin gloves. Her hands were white, slender, and beautifully manicured—the hands not only of a highborn lady, but of a sensualist, thought Sophia, intrigued.

"Sit down, Sophia. We have little time, and I am not a patient woman."

The woman sat down rather disdainfully on one of the rickety wooden chairs, and lifted her veil. She was an ash-blonde, with glossy hair and fine features, and the naturally scarlet lips that drove other women mad with envy. Her eyes were a piercing icy blue.

Sophia sank down onto the other chair, feeling suddenly lumpish and inadequate beside this chic temptress who had already set her pulse racing. Her voice trembled as she spoke.

"Why have you come to see me? Do you have a message for me from my family?"

The scarlet-lipped temptress smiled; it was a cynical, hard smile that made Sophia shiver—not only with distaste, but with a guilty, unwilling pleasure. For it was a smile that reminded her irresistibly of Mademoiselle Malin.

"I am not here to offer you empty platitudes," the woman continued. "Nor am I here simply to listen to your foolish prattle. No, I am here to offer you practical assistance—should you choose to accept it."

The woman looked down at her slender white hands, folded neatly in her lap, and smoothed the black calfskin gloves with subtle fingers. She was evidently in no hurry to reveal her secret.

"I—I don't understand. How can you help me? Can you get me out of this place?" Sophia sank back onto the wooden chair. "No. Of course you cannot. None can save me. And it is through my own foolishness that I am incarcerated in this terrible dungeon." Ashamed, she felt a teardrop gather at the corner of her eye, unbidden, and spill out onto her pale, perfect cheek.

"You are a sentimental creature," observed the woman, not without humor. "It is not difficult to see how you have found yourself in this difficult situation. But in answer to your question: Yes, perhaps I can help you to gain your freedom. I have influential friends in high places who might perhaps be swayed to grant you mercy, should I speak in your favor."

Sophia could hardly believe what she was hearing. She felt as though she were in some fantastical dream. The woman's voice droned in her head, faraway and unreal, and for a moment she thought she might faint. Reality was slipping away.... The next thing she knew, she felt strong hands lifting her up, helping her back onto the chair. She looked down and saw the woman's slender ringed hand on her bosom, massaging the warmth back into her. She gasped with pleasure at the sudden, brutal caress, her nipples stiffening instantly. It had been so long since a woman had touched her so....

Too soon, the woman took her hand away. Sophia felt bereft.

"What must I do if you are to help me?"

"You must be totally honest with me, my child."

"Honest—about what?"

"About your life, Sophia. About the events which brought you here. I want to know everything."

Sophia's head spun. She felt ashamed. She could not—would not!—tell a perfect stranger of the strange, dark love which had driven her to her own destruction and to that of her beloved cousin Emily. And yet, if she did not tell her story to this woman, she would go away and leave her to her fate. She stared at the woman, dumbstruck.

"What is your name?" she whispered.

"You may call me Miranda," replied the woman. "Miranda, the worker of miracles." And she laughed humorlessly. "Now, tell me, Sophia— however did you come to write this work of scandal and sensation?" She opened the velvet bag she carried and took out a copy of the banned novel, *Mistress Mine*. Sophia blushed crimson as Miranda opened the book and began to read:

"'I parted her arse-cheeks with brutal caresses and set about thrusting my questing tongue into the very depths of her shame. She writhed and moaned beneath my caresses; but I knew her cries were all of pleasure.' It is indeed a work of salacious mastery, my dear. One can understand how the Lord Chamberlain might view it in a dim light. But tell me, my dear: how did you come to write it? Wherever did you find the knowledge to pen such delicious filth?"

Sophia stammered out the lie, trying desperately not to look into the deep, dark eyes of the woman in the crimson dress.

"My father...sent us to London to live with our aunt for a while. While we were in town, we undertook good works among the fallen women of the East End. At one of the refuges, I met a young woman of good family who had fallen into bad ways. She told me that strange woman had robbed her of her innocence. One night she told me her story. Foolish thing that I am, I was fascinated by her tale. I could not get it out of my head. And, little by little, I began to wonder if I might not tell her tale to the world, as a warning to others—"

The stinging blow on her cheek made her cry out in pain and astonishment. Miranda was standing over her, the black kid glove still raised, as though threatening a second onslaught.

"Idiot!" she hissed, and Sophia felt the anger bubbling out of the woman like molten lava. "Did I not command you to tell me the truth?"

"I—I have told you all I know. I—"

The second blow was much harder than the first, and Sophia felt her face burning red with discomfort and shame.

"Liar!" Miranda reached into her bag, took out something small and metallic, and cast it onto the table. It glinted in the flickering gaslight. "Does that refresh your memory?"

The blood drained out of Sophia's burning

cheeks, and she trembled as she looked down at the two silver nipple rings lying on the table. Of course she remembered them. Had they not once adorned her dear, sweet, cousin Emily's breasts? She looked up at Miranda, shocked and afraid. How could she have come by the rings? How could she know so much about the secret life of Miss Sophia Cranleigh?

"Who...? And why...?"

"No more questions, Sophia. There are things which it is better you do not know. Believe me, Miss Cranleigh. I am your last chance of freedom. If you refuse to tell me the truth of your story, I shall abandon you to your fate in this godforsaken place.

"There are some wicked and lascivious women in this prison, Sophia, and men also—men who could easily take from you what you would never willingly give."

Sophia shuddered, sick to her stomach with the thought of the fate that might await her.

Miranda settled herself down on her chair once more and ran the fingers of the black glove over her palm.

"Begin your tale, Sophia. And this time, you must tell me everything—every terrible, shameful detail. Your freedom depends on it, Sophia Cranleigh!"

One day Mademoiselle Malin announced that we were to practice our needlecraft. I groaned inwardly, for I have never been more than an indifferent seamstress, and I resigned myself to endless hours of tedious embroidery.

Needless to say, we were greatly taken aback when Mademoiselle Malin opened a large carved chest and took out a jumble of black and shiny leather strips. Emily picked up a few of the strips and looked at Mademoiselle Malin, bemused.

"What is this to be, Mademoiselle? Is it a harness for a horse?"

Mademoiselle gave a dry, humorless laugh.

"It is indeed a harness, my pretty little simpleton. But it is not for a horse."

We were both puzzled by now, and I confess I was more than a little uneasy. Already Mademoiselle had shown herself to have a cruel and unnatural disposition, and I feared what she might have planned for us. But what choice did we have but to obey? Even our dear Miss Aycliffe had been hard-pressed to believe the fantastical tales we had told her of our "education" at the hands of the mysterious Mademoiselle. Our hurts alone had told the truth of our tales....

"Remove your clothes, Emily. All of them. You shall be our dressmaker's model. Shall that not be a pretty game for a pretty girl to play?"

Mademoiselle Malin ran her black-gloved finger under Emily's pretty pert chin, and I saw her quiver—was it with apprehension, or with the apprehension of pleasure? I felt jealous indignation surge through me.

"Yes, Mademoiselle." Emily's voice was quiet and obedient as she began undressing for her mistress. In a few moments, she was naked before us both, her nipples erect in the cool breeze from the open window.

"Stand absolutely still, Emily," commanded Mademoiselle Malin. "Or I may hurt you." She opened a workbox and took out a paper of wickedly sharp pins, thick and strong enough to penetrate soft leather.

"Hand me a strip of leather, Sophia."

I did so and was rewarded with a stroke of the cane across my delicate breasts.

"A *long* strip, you foolish creature. Long enough to extend from shoulder to thigh and back again."

It was not until the fourth or fifth strip that I realized what we were making: a curious little harness for Emily's body. A harness which consisted of strips running across the breastbone and between the thighs, exposing the breasts and throwing into relief the almost-naked swell of Emily's pubis.

"Turn around," instructed Mademoiselle, and Emily pirouetted prettily. I gasped with ill-concealed lust as I saw how the leather straps crisscrossed her back and disappeared between her velvety arse-cheeks, forcing them apart and exposing the secret amber rosebud of her arsehole—a playground where even I, little innocent that I was, had never yet dared venture. Why, the two of us were no more than pretty nymphs, curious yet virginal, whose exploration of each other's bodies had not yet gone beyond the first, faltering steps. Already, Mademoiselle Malin had shown us that there was a whole new, undiscovered country still waiting to be explored. Would we dare explore it?

"Sophia—I wish you to practice your needlecraft skills upon this pretty garment," Mademoiselle commanded, putting away her pins. "And for each wrong or inelegant stitch, you shall receive a little discomfort, by way of correction."

The sharp point of the pin entered the bare flesh of my arm so suddenly that there was a moment of numbness before I realized the pain. I gasped and clutched at my arm. There was a flush of deep crimson on my white flesh. And Mademoiselle Malin was smiling at me, as though she could read my thoughts and knew that, deep in my heart, I craved the pain that she was only too willing to bestow.

With trembling fingers, I set about sewing the harness in place. There were too, too many straps, too many fiddlesome pieces to hold in place and bind together. Fine and supple though the leather was, it was too thick for my needle to pass through easily, and about halfway through my task, the needle snapped in two.

"Imbecile!" thundered Mademoiselle Malin. "Is this how you handle delicate work like this?"

She pushed me away from Emily and, as I stood trembling before her, she took hold of my high-necked bodice and tore it open, stripping down the fabric until I was naked to the waist. Then she took one of her pins and showed it to me as it glistened in the morning sunlight. I shrank away, but she seized my arm and drew me closer to her. Her lips were parted, and her breath smelt of sweet violets. I felt like a cornered animal, caught in a poacher's trap. All the power of movement had gone out of me.

"A little discomfort," hissed Mademoiselle. In the next second, I felt the most terrible, searing pain arcing through my body like a sudden surge of electricity. I looked down and saw the pin piercing my right nipple; the trickle of blood running down my breast. The pain took my breath away, and I saw darkness at the edges of my vision, closing in on me in welcome oblivion. I staggered and fell, but Mademoiselle Malin was not going to permit me an easy way out of my punishment. A pitcher-ful of cold water brought me to my senses and had me gasping my way back to consciousness.

When I was fully myself again, I saw that Mademoiselle had removed the pin from my nipple, and I watched her draw it across her lips, leaving a smear of deep crimson. As I stared in disbelief, she ran the tip of her tongue over her lips, devouring my blood with obvious relish.

"Now you know the penalty for disobedience, *chérie*," she breathed. "Perhaps you will be more careful this time."

Still trembling from the shock, I completed the task of sewing the leather harness onto poor sweet Emily, who was still standing obediently and unmoving before me, though I caught sight of a telltale tear in the corner of her eye.

When I had finished I drew back, and Mademoiselle Malin inspected my work with a critical eye. My heart sank as she found one stitch a little larger than the others. Would she torture me again? And was that feeling in the pit of my stomach merely fear, or something more dreadful, more perverse?

"It is a fair effort, for one so young and inexperienced," she concluded. But mark me well: I shall expect more of your future efforts." She turned her attentions to Emily. "You may turn round now, *ma chérie*."

My desire for Emily knew no bounds as I gazed once more upon the adolescent promise of her youthful body. I longed to bury my face in her mossy triangle, but Mademoiselle's stern gaze forbade any such intimacies.

For Mademoiselle had intimacies of her own in mind....

As I looked on in jealous hatred, Mademoiselle Malin put out her hand to touch my darling Emily's breasts, firm and juicy as young apples as they thrust forward from their prison of glossy black leather. She stroked Emily's nipples gently, and Emily gave an involuntary groan of pleasure as her nipples grew stiff and rubbery.

Mademoiselle's intimacies grew more explicit, more outrageous. She forced Emily's legs apart and thrust a finger between her slender thighs. At first she confined herself to toying with Emily's cunny-lips; but suddenly she slid her finger in much farther, and Emily gave a little cry of pain.

"Bon, très bon," Mademoiselle murmured to herself, and—removing a slippery index finger from my cousin's cunt—she turned toward me. "Your cousin is a little slut in the making, Sophia. And a born lover of pain. She will no doubt enjoy it thoroughly when her first real woman relieves her of this tiresome maidenhead." She gave me an ironic smile. "It is a poor lover indeed, Sophia, who leaves her mistress's maidenhead intact! But, as it turns out, your childish reserve will suit my purposes well."

I understood nothing of all this; for, as I have told you, all we knew of our bodies came from our timorous experiments. Even in the pretty games that Miss Aycliffe had taught us, we had never dared explore the tight, wet tunnel that opened into the very heart of our womanhood.

Mademoiselle Malin left me alone with Emily in the schoolroom, and we clung together for comfort, though we knew our teacher would not approve of such puerile indiscipline.

"Oh, Sophia," sobbed Emily, her head on my shoulder and her bosom soft and yielding against my flesh. "What are we to do?"

"What can we do but do as Mademoiselle commands us?" I replied with a hint of bitterness. It had not escaped my notice how easily Emily had fallen in with Mademoiselle Malin's wishes. Nor had I failed to see how my cousin's eager nipples had sprung to attention at Mademoiselle's skillful touch. But inwardly my jealous heart was breaking, for I feared the loss of my dear cousin to this other mistress, far more skilled than I, whose curious demands brought with them their own piquant brand of pleasure....

The door to the schoolroom swung open, and Emily and I sprang apart like guilty children.

"More disobedience!" hissed Mademoiselle Malin, flexing the malacca cane between leather-gloved fingers. "Are you so eager to feel my displeasure once again?"

But we could not reply, for we were both gazing speechlessly at our Mademoiselle, our mistress....

In truth, I had never seen anything to compare with the firm, naked flesh of Mademoiselle Malin. She had taken off the sober black silk gown, and now she stood before us on towering spike-heeled black boots, mirror smooth and tight-laced to the knee. Her nakedness was adorned and embellished by wasp-waisted stays in black lace, rigidly boned to accentuate her bosom and reduce her waist to a tiny circle. I gasped as I gazed upon this vision—and it seemed that the figure before me was no mortal woman, but some goddess of lust from the very pits of Hell, the tip of her pink tongue moistening her full crimson lips as she drew the tip of the cane across my naked breasts.

But my gaze was drawn not to her face, but to the secret triangle between her thighs. Strapped to her pubis with leather thongs and buckles, a smooth baton of polished ebony thrust out from Mademoiselle Malin's profusion of black curls. Innocent though I was, I suddenly realized what her intentions were; and I wanted desperately to run away, to flee from the threat of womanhood.

Her violet eyes seemed to bore deep into my soul, and terror sent the sweat trickling down into the furrow between my naked breasts.

What was this emotion which overwhelmed me and made my cunt drip fragrant moisture?

"Come, Sophia. I have a gift for you. A gift of pain...and pleasure."

❦

Mademoiselle Malin had spoken of Emily's initiation into womanhood, and all my fears had been for her. I had not thought for a moment that she would turn her attentions to me. I was unprepared, incapable of resisting her lust. And oh, I confess it to you now, for already I have sunk to the depths of shame...yes, I admit that in the depths of my soul I longed to feel Mademoiselle's cruel fingers on my soft flesh, opening up the secret folds of my cunt to take her pleasure.

My pleasure, also...

Emily watched in alarm as Mademoiselle Malin forced me to my hands and knees on the cold stone floor and ripped off what remained of my school dress, leaving me clad only in my coarse cotton drawers—and they afforded me neither modesty nor protection from my mistress's inexorable will.

The malacca cane bit into the flesh of my back and backside, but I knew that I must not cry out, or it would be the worse for me. Again and again my back arched to meet the stinging blows, and I grew half-delirious with pain, my fingernails scraping desperately at the unyielding stone of the floor until the flesh was raw and tender.

"This is how I break a mettlesome filly," panted Mademoiselle Malin, breathless with exertion. "For much as I love a spirited steed, she must sacrifice her own will to the service of my lusts. Only when she acknowledges me as her mistress does she become deserving of gratification."

A curious thing began to happen. After a while, I became incapable of distinguishing between the individual blows of the cane, though I still heard its rhythmic swishing as she brought it down upon my poor, martyred flesh. Little by little, the pain seemed to ebb away, to be replaced by an insidious creeping warmth that turned my pain to an exquisitely pleasurable torment....

"Submit to me, steed!" cried Mademoiselle Malin, bringing the cane down with demonic ferocity. And, through the red mist of my pain, I glimpsed the grail of my pleasure, and—no longer understanding what was happening to me—I gave a long, sobbing cry:

"Yes, yes!..."

In that moment, Mademoiselle Malin fell upon me, wrenching apart my torn arse-cheeks. I screamed with terror and pain as a smooth, relentless hardness thrust its way between the soft folds of my cunt. In a single brutal thrust, the ebony dildo was inside me, tearing through the tough membrane of my maidenhead and showing me for the first time what pleasure it is to be ridden by another woman. Mademoiselle Malin rode me as she would some highbred mare, recklessly and ruthlessly, with no thought for my terror or the tenderness of my martyred flesh.

And she was wise in her cruelty, for with each new thrust I felt the growing power of pleasure within me. My clitoris was throbbing now, yearning for the touch of a lover's kiss. I thought of Emily's soft wet tongue, teasing my erect bud with gentle strokes of its muscular tip, and could have wept for frustrated desire.

And then I felt Mademoiselle Malin's leather-gloved finger on my cunt, forcing its way between my love-lips and seeking out the burning, throbbing heart of my guilty desire. In a single ungentle stroke, she brought me to the brink of orgasm and held me there for what seemed an eternity.

At last she released me from my torment, and I leaped forward into the cold, bright sunlight of pleasure—a pleasure so intense that it was the most terrible, the most delicious agony; falling, falling, falling until at last the final spasms of my cunt ebbed away, leaving me trembling and defeated upon the stone floor of the schoolroom. Consciousness was draining away from me...And then I felt hands turning me onto my back, cold water being forced between my lips.

When I opened my eyes, Mademoiselle Malin was standing astride me, the ebony dildo in her hands like a battle trophy. It was glistening with a wetness that I knew must be my mingled fluids. I felt confused, afraid—was I ashamed or angry or elated? I could no longer tell. This new dark world of pleasure was so alien to me, so frightening. And my enjoyment of it was more terrifying still.

Mademoiselle Malin's violet eyes were jewel-bright, the pupils hugely dilated with lust.

"Kneel, slave. Kneel and suck my pussy."

I needed no further bidding. Scrambling to my knees in spite of the pain of my hurts, I planted a passionate kiss upon Mademoiselle's luxuriant black bush.

"Mistress," I breathed. "Mistress mine..."

Over the days that followed, Mademoiselle Malin's behavior both puzzled and unsettled us. No doubt that was exactly as she wished.

Having conquered and enslaved me to her lust, she wanted to toy with me for a little while, to ensure my continued obedience by depriving me of that which I wanted more than anything else: the dark, forbidden gift of pleasure which she alone could bestow.

Emily and I grew fearful. Our mistress's treatment of us began to display marked differences. Was she trying to divide us, to set us against each other, simply for the perverse joy of seeing our pain? Or had she some other, more sinister purposes in mind for us? Emily she now handled with extraordinary delicacy, primping and preening her like some exotic cage-bird, prized for its rare and fragile beauty. It was as though Mademoiselle Malin had recognized some great value in Emily and was now protecting her as one would protect any other costly investment.

As for me, Mademoiselle Malin had very different ideas of my worth. Emily might be a priceless jewel, to be polished and pampered for some unknown purpose—but my own value was rather less evident. Mademoiselle Malin found fault with me at every turn, as though craving each opportunity to vent her anger upon me. She beat me frequently; and, from time to time, whenever I showed signs of resentment or rebellion, she renewed my allegiance to her with further glimpses of her own dark world of pleasure.

With each day that passed, Emily and I became further enslaved to Mademoiselle Malin, for she fulfilled deep needs within us. Emily she won over with honey-coated menace. Terrified of retribution and eager for approval, Emily swiftly became the embodiment of sweet subservience. Mademoiselle Malin began dressing her up like a doll, accentuating the cherubic prettiness of her face and form with tight, diaphanous muslins which made my heart race and my cunt drip with unsatisfied lust.

But no matter what I did, it seemed that Mademoiselle Malin would find fault with me. Her carefully judged cruelty had precisely the effect she desired: Each day I grew more fascinated by her, more desperate to gain her approval…or, if not her approval, the gift of her sex.

Our lessons became stranger and stranger. Emily's slightest efforts—however inadequate— were praised to the skies, while my displays of cleverness were derided, my failures punished mercilessly. If I dared protest the injustice of my treatment, I was whipped and chained to the wall.

My cruel mistress knew exactly what punishment would cause me the greatest hurt: not physical wounds (for already she had judged how the lash excited my lusts), but the pain of witnessing my dear cousin giving my mistress the pleasure which I craved to give her. And yet she never laid a finger upon Emily's sweet maiden body. Try as I might, I could not puzzle out this inequality of treatment, which filled me with a terrible, angry lust. I vowed that I would find out the reasons behind Mademoiselle Malin's curious behavior.

I was often forced to lie on the cold stone floor while Emily performed pretty acts of pleasure upon Mademoiselle Malin's magnificent body. How I seethed with suppressed passion as I watched my dear coz burying her face in the forest of her mistress's pubic curls, sucking and licking at her pussy as she had so often done with mine. I felt a jealous rage, for I could see the pleasure on Mademoiselle Malin's face. And I could not even relieve my own frustrations, for my coldhearted mistress had chained my hands behind me, leaving me to squirm in distress on the unyielding stone.

One sultry afternoon, Mademoiselle Malin decided to set about the important business of teaching us etiquette. After all, had my Papa not wished us to be turned into respectable young ladies? I remember the ironic smile that played about our mistress's luscious scarlet lips as she talked to us of "respectability" and "good behavior." Her powerful, sleek body was encased in a tight-laced corset which framed her breasts and buttocks to perfection, the midnight-black lace setting off the creamy whiteness of her flesh. Her long, slender legs were encased in black silk stockings, and she wore black gloves of soft, supple leather to the elbow.

Diamond rings glittered on her fingers.

But the glossy black triangle between her thighs —the triangle of delicious curls which I longed to taste and smell—was, like her creamy buttocks, completely naked. She must have known how desperately I would long to touch her there—to plant kisses on her glorious womanhood—for I could see her watching me slyly out of the corner of her eye.

"Today," she announced to us as we stood in the dining room of her cottage, "you shall learn how to serve properly at table. Every young lady of quality needs to know how to...satisfy her guests' needs and wishes."

She gave us a meaningful glance and indicated a tray of wine, coffee, and sweetmeats on the polished dresser.

"You shall each serve me in turn," she directed. And she settled herself at the head of the table. She turned to me. "You may begin, Sophia. Bring me a glass of claret."

I approached the tray of wine and was plunged immediately into confusion. There were several crystal decanters upon the tray, all filled to the brim with dark red wine. Which was the claret? I was not well versed in wine, for we were not a wealthy family, and my father believed that young ladies should be shielded from the pleasures of the flesh, lest their "natural weakness of spirit" be overcome by sensual delight, ending in inevitable moral disaster. The consequence of this philosophy was that I could no more tell a claret from a burgundy than I could climb the Himalayas.

I glanced at Mademoiselle Malin, but her face betrayed no clue. What was I to do? I knew that if I asked for advice, I would be punished, so there was nothing for it. I must make my choice and take my chances with my mistress's wrath. Taking my courage in both hands, I selected one of the decanters and poured wine into a fine fluted glass. This I placed on a silver salver, and carried it across to where Mademoiselle Malin was sitting.

"Your wine, Mademoiselle."

My heart was pounding, and I thought I might faint with terror. But Mademoiselle Malin took a sip from the glass and smiled.

"It is a good claret, Sophia."

I could hardly believe my good fortune. I had selected the correct wine, and I was being praised!

"Thank you, mistress." I could feel myself blushing with pleasure.

Mademoiselle Malin was holding the glass up to the light.

"What is this, Sophia?" Her voice was suddenly stern.

My heart sank.

"What, mistress?"

"There is a fingermark upon the glass!" Rage was in her voice now, as she turned her magnificent, terrible violet eyes on me. "How dare you serve wine to me without first polishing the glass!"

She threw the glass of wine at me, and its contents spilled all over the front of my white summer frock, like a great garish splash of heart's blood. The glass fell to the carpeted floor and rolled away, under the table.

"I—I am sorry, mistress. I did not think—"

Emily opened her mouth to defend me, but Mademoiselle's angry glance commanded her to silence. I stared, wide-eyed and suddenly afraid.

Mademoiselle Malin was on her feet now, advancing toward me with inexorable slow steps. I wanted to back away, but I knew that if I fled it would be the worse for me.

She was standing before me, towering above me; her leather-gloved fingers were under my chin, forcing me to look up into her flashing eyes.

"You never think, do you, Sophia? Never think of my needs. And see—what have you done to your dress? You have spilled wine all over the fine white muslin. Such a careless, feckless, headstrong minx. You are a thoughtless slut, Sophia Cranleigh."

"Yes, mistress," I whispered, my face now red with shame.

"What are you, Sophia?"

"I am...a thoughtless slut, mistress."

"Louder, Sophia. Emily and I cannot hear you."

Anger surged through me, and I wrenched my chin free from Mademoiselle Malin's iron grasp. What right had this woman to enslave my soul and body? I would not let her! I opened my mouth and shouted defiantly at the top of my voice:

"I am a thoughtless, careless, shameless slut!"

The slap across my cheek was so violent that it sent me reeling across the room, stumbling against the sideboard and falling to the ground, dizzy and sick. When I opened my eyes and looked up, Mademoiselle Malin was standing over me, her eyes narrowed and filled with an unearthly fire.

"You may think you have the better of me, Sophia Cranleigh," she hissed. "But I shall beat the spirit out of you—you may be very certain of that. And now I think you shall have an opportunity to cool your hot temper. I have work to do with Emily."

She tore off my white dress and drawers and lashed my hands roughly behind my back. The rough hempen cords bit into my wrists, but I dared not protest as Mademoiselle Malin dragged me across the room and tied me to an iron ring in the wall as one might tether an unruly beast.

Then she settled herself back on her chair, and turned her attentions to Emily, who was trembling and pale with fear. Her eyes were moist with tears, and I knew the terrible pain she must be feeling as she looked upon my torment.

"I am thirsty, Emily," Mademoiselle announced. "Bring me a glass of claret."

In her confusion and fear, Emily selected the wrong decanter of wine. I tried to signal the mistake to her, but she did not understand my frantic glances, and poured the wrong wine into a crystal glass, which she then carried across to her mistress.

"Your claret, mistress."

Mademoiselle Malin cast me a meaningful glance as she picked up the glass and took a long sip from it.

"This is not claret, Emily, but it is an excellent burgundy. You have done well in selecting the better wine."

My eyes must have been like saucers. How could Mademoiselle Malin be so unjust? How could she so blatantly use one rule for me and one for my cousin Emily? I knew that if I had selected the wrong wine, I would have been beaten soundly. And her wrath over the unpolished glass had been no more than a feeble excuse—Emily had not observed any such niceties, yet here she was, being praised! There was a smile on Mademoiselle's cruel lips—doubtless she was greatly enjoying the delicious piquancy of the situation...and, most especially, my sufferings.

She stroked Emily's bare arm with her gloved hand, and Emily shivered with apprehension.

"For your cleverness, *chère enfant,* you shall lick

out my pussy," she announced. "Kneel between my thighs. I wish you to pleasure me."

My heart ached with frustrated desire as I watched my dear cousin scramble obediently under the table. From my position, belly-down on the cold floor, I was in an ideal position to see Mademoiselle Malin slide apart her thighs to admit her young worshipper's blonde head. I felt physically sick with jealousy and longing.

"Pull apart the lips of my quim, Emily. Yes, that's it. Now put your finger into my hole—feel how tight and wet it is. I want you to keep your finger there while you lick my clitty."

"Yes, mistress," Emily breathed. Her face disappeared into the musky pleasure-garden between Mademoiselle's beautiful creamy thighs.

The moments that followed were a torment to me, for my own clitty was throbbing with unsatisfied desire—and the sight of my darling cousin pleasuring my hard-hearted mistress served only to inflame my lust to an unbearable degree. As I watched, Mademoiselle Malin grew more and more excited; her gloved hands were cradling Emily's head, and her fingers tightened, tightened as her breathing grew more rapid and hoarse.

"Lick me harder, faster—fuck me with your finger. Yes, yes, yes!"

With a great groan of pleasure, Mademoiselle threw back her head and surrendered her great spirit to the helplessness of orgasm—her only weakness. When Emily emerged from beneath the table, I saw that her lips were dripping with the fragrant juices of Mademoiselle Malin's abundant pleasure. How I longed to kiss them from her lips!...

That afternoon I could do no right, but Emily could do no wrong. And, in the evening, Mademoiselle Malin announced that I had performed so badly that I must remain at the cottage all night, as a further punishment. Emily returned alone to the rectory, commanded by Mademoiselle to tell my father that I was unwell and would return on the following day.

Emily left in floods of tears, and I spent several solitary hours in the schoolroom, naked and bruised from the assaults on my body during the afternoon's lessons. Chained to the wall, I gazed through the window at the gathering dusk. Did Mademoiselle Malin intend to leave me here all night, cold and alone?

I must have slipped into sleep, for I awoke suddenly to a small sound in the room. It was the hiss of a whip, cutting through the air.

Opening my eyes, I looked round to see a figure in the gloom: the tall silhouette of a woman, naked save for a tight leather basque and high-heeled boots.

"Mistress!" I gasped, and struggled to my knees before her, though the heavy collar and chain about my neck almost squeezed the breath from me.

"The day belongs to your cousin Emily," whispered Mademoiselle. "But the night belongs to you, Sophia...for you and I are both creatures of the darkness. Already I can feel the blackness in your soul, taste the taint of guilty pleasure, oozing out of your every pore. Surrender to me, Sophia— surrender to the pleasure of pain!"

She unchained me from the wall and led me like a docile beast into her bedroom. I had never been in there before, for she kept the door locked securely. It was a dark and forbidding place, with a bare stone floor and whitewashed walls. All the furniture had a spartan feel to it, for it was all made of rough wood, painted black. At the foot of the bed stood a prie-dieu. The kneeling portion was furnished with the most terrifying rusty spikes and nails. I understood now why I had sometimes seen small, bloody scars on Mademoiselle's creamy-white knees...

In the center of the room was a hard wooden bench with manacles and cuffs for the ankles. But a few feet from the wall stood a curious frame of rough wooden laths, nailed together in the form of a letter X. Afraid but deeply, deeply excited, I allowed myself to be strapped to this fearsome contraption, beyond imagining what was to happen to me next. All I cared about now was the fact that Mademoiselle Malin had chosen me; that my transgressions had brought me to this room, alone at last with the mistress who terrified but fascinated me. I hated and despised her, and yet, her cruelest blow would be as soft and delicious to me as any angel's kiss.

The shape of the frame was such that it threw the prisoner's breasts into relief and, in forcing apart the legs, opened up the treasures of cunt and arse. There was room between the frame and the wall for a body to pass, and so it was that my tormentor had me completely at her mercy. The next thing I knew, a leather gag was being forced into my mouth, half-choking me.

Evidently, Mademoiselle Malin did not wish anyone to hear my cries.

"See, *ma chère* Sophia—see what a beautiful gift I have brought you." She lifted it to my eyes, which widened in sudden fear.

The bullwhip was an exquisite implement of torture: fully six feet long, with an intricate handle of plaited leather and silver thread. I gazed at it with a mixture of fascination and terror. There was something so beautiful, so perfect about the bull-whip; and it occurred to me that perhaps the pain it inflicted would also be beautiful and perfect....

The first stroke of the whip across my buttocks made me howl with anguish; but the leather gag stifled my cries. Tears poured down my cheeks, and my poor, martyred body tried desperately to twist and turn in an attempt to evade the next blow, and the next.

But the leather straps held me fast, and Mademoiselle Malin's aim was true. Each new blow fell with a fresh intensity, bringing with it new and novel nuances of pain. The pain became my whole world—my only goal to live through it; to prove to my mistress that I was worthy of the angry pain of her love.

"Feel my caresses, *chèrie,*" hissed Mademoiselle Malin. "Feel how my love for you burns...."

I was almost delirious with pain, yet inwardly I was rejoicing, for my detested, adored mistress was lavishing her burning caresses upon my unworthy body. My only thought was to be strong enough to bear the pain, to prove to Mademoiselle Malin that I was worthy of this most exquisite of pleasures. Mademoiselle Malin's favor had become all to me.

She was highly skilled with the lash, and my flesh opened up to her like a flower. I felt the moist warmth of my wounds reopening and trickling over my martyred flesh. It felt delicious, like a lover's kiss. And, as my head spun, the burning began to fade to a wonderful exotic warmth. My cunt dripped with desire, my own juices mingling with the rivulets of sweat from my back and buttocks.

With a deft flick, Mademoiselle Malin sent the tip of the bullwhip darting like a serpent's tongue between my arse-cheeks, biting into the secret furrow. Half-dazed though I was, I felt this new pain like a fiery arrow piercing my delicate flesh, and I cried out with pain. But the gag stifled my cries. Tears flowed down my cheeks, and I sobbed with anguish as the lash fell again and again on my poor arsehole, like the stings of a thousand hornets.

Finally I could take no more. The insidious warmth of sinful pleasure cradled me like a mother's arms; and, swooning from the pain, I slumped in my bonds, quite unable to resist my tormentor's wicked demands.

The biting pain of the bullwhip faded away, and I became aware of a new and novel torment. Mademoiselle Malin was standing before me now, her creamy-white breasts stiff-nippled and but a hairbreadth from my yearning lips. How I longed to kiss those rubbery nipples, to roll them around on my tongue and bite upon them; but the gag kept me from such delights. And Mademoiselle had very different plans for me.

Suddenly I felt a terrible, searing pain and, looking down, I saw that my mistress had placed heavy metal clamps upon my nipples. Cruel, serrated teeth were biting into my sensitive flesh; and, for a moment, I feared I would be unable to bear the dreadful hurt. More burning pain, and I realized that my cruel mistress had also placed clips upon my love-lips, spreading my labia wide so that every secret of my poor bruised body was revealed.

I was in torment—twisting and turning on the

X-frame; quite unable to free myself and lacking the will to resist or to cry out. For, in the depths of my soul, this was what I wanted: the dark, infinitely pleasurable pain of utter possession. I was at last hers, and she—whose pleasure craved my submission—was just as much mine.

I was scarcely aware of the glittering blade as Mademoiselle cut through the bonds that held me and caught my body as it fell. Her strong, brutal hands upon my wounded flesh brought me back to my senses, and I sobbed into my gag as she dragged me across the room to the wooden bench.

I prayed that she would fuck me—fuck me as she had that hot afternoon in the schoolroom. The memory of her surrogate prick in my cunt made me groan with anticipated pleasure.

Her smell was all around me: heavy, musky— the scent of pleasure that will not be denied. If she would not fuck me, perhaps she would allow me to lick out her quim, as I had seen my cousin Emily do. Perhaps I would at last be allowed to taste the honey-sweet cunt-juice which I knew must flow abundantly from between those two plump love- lips.

But Mademoiselle Malin threw me forward onto the hard wooden bench. I winced as splinters pierced my tender flesh. The heavy metal clips scraped on the rough wooden surface, twisting and pinching my nipples and love-lips. Such love was indeed hard to bear....

Mademoiselle Malin inserted my wrists into metal cuffs at the head of the bench and snapped the cuffs shut, but she left my legs free. The collar and chain about my neck were also fastened to the bench, ensuring my compliance. To my surprise, she unfastened the gag.

"I want you to scream your pain and pleasure into the darkness of night," she breathed. "And no one will hear your cries—no one but I."

The pain was sudden and sharp, and I gave a little gasp.

"Just a fingernail, *chèrie*—to open up the way for me."

I squirmed at the torment; but no matter what I did, I was unable to escape Mademoiselle Malin's sharp-nailed finger, toying with the delicate membrane of my arsehole.

"No!" I cried, shame and desire mingling.

But it was too late. Already Mademoiselle Malin's finger was inside me, forcing its way past my forbidden gateway, opening me up to her pleasure—and my own. I blushed crimson as she toyed with this, my most intimate of places, the last bastion of my girlish purity and prudishness. But a second finger was inside my cunt, and already my resistance was ebbing away.

"Foolish slut!" Mademoiselle Malin exclaimed. "How will you ever succeed in society as long as you are so infernally prudish? Submit to me, or it shall be the worse for you!"

How could I do other than submit? For already my pleasure was intense. And when I felt the dildo pressing against my delicate membrane, I knew my arsehole would yield joyfully to this new intruder. I wanted it desperately, desperately...

"I want to hear you beg for it," Mademoiselle Malin hissed, removing her finger and tormenting my arsehole with the tip of the dildo.

"Yes, yes, please!" I cried.

"Beg me—beg me to fuck you in the arse."

"Fuck me, fuck me..."

"Beg me."

"Fuck me in the arse, mistress, I beg of you!"

I was sobbing with frustrated desire as Mademoiselle Malin finally yielded to my pleas. The dildo was hard, smooth and massive. I screamed in agony as it thrust mercilessly into me, opening up my secret places to this brutal invasion. She fucked me with consummate skill, and the clips on my nipples and cunt scraped against the wooden bench, losing me in a world of unbearable sensations. Truly, truly I submitted to this terrible, wonderful mistress who took my darkest shame and turned it into the most exquisite pleasure.

Her finger on my clitty did not tease but commanded my orgasm. At last I gave a terrible cry of abandonment and surrendered to the tyranny of her will. My cunt tensed in a mighty spasm of ecstasy, and my arse clenched about the smooth ebony dildo.

The orgasm was so intense that I thought I might die of such brutal pleasure. When at last I opened my eyes, Mademoiselle Malin was standing at the head of the bench, a smile of satisfaction on her face.

"Very good, Sophia. We shall make a passable young lady of you yet. But now you shall thank me for your pleasure. And if you do not satisfy me completely, you shall pay for it dearly...."

Parting her thighs, she pulled me toward her and opened up her love-lips with her skillful fingers. Tearful with gratitude, I dived into the forest of her womanhood and prayed that the moment would never end....

Aarona Griffin
PASSAGE

Moonlight pierced the window and bathed her bed in a foggy passion of shadow and light. Nina pushed off her covers, moving her body into the pattern of moonlight. Stretching her legs out, arms overhead, she grasped the wooden headboard, watching the fingertips of light caress her smooth body as she arched and twisted slowly, eyes following the shadows and patterns. A photograph of a woman, barely clothed, wearing only chaps of smooth black leather and holding a whip, hung pinned to the wall over Nina's bed. A dark-skinned woman standing, legs parted, deep brown eyes dramatically lit—burning the fury of her sensuality into the camera lens. Nina sighed, her body aching in the moonlight that touched her, but whose touch she could not feel. Her eyes found the eyes in the photograph. The woman seemed to look back at her. Nina's imagination raced in a fantasy begun many nights before: the woman live, not at the restaurant where Nina, not daring to speak to her, saw her every day. No, here, in Nina's room, glistening naked in the moonlight: whip raised, eyes able to see Nina's passion, her need; Nina's body moving now in a rhythm that began each night, over and over...a thin veil of sweat forming between her creamy white breasts, along her belly, her body pulsating as she slipped her fingers down to meet the fire that raged between her legs...the liquid desire that flowed now, slippery and wanting as she arched, thrusting, and building... building....

Nina didn't notice when a figure appeared in the hallway, paused, then disappeared quickly.

When she opened her eyes at last, the figure was gone. She was lost in the beauty of the photograph, both hands tracing patterns along Carrie's body, caught as it was in a state of heat. Nina began panting as she recalled the ache of her body's need, the need that throbbed even now, the long nights that had led her here. All she had been able to focus on every night over the passing months, was this secret aching. Never before had Nina fantasized about a real person, someone she had actually seen. But this woman had something sparkling—and wicked—that captured Nina completely.

In truth, after almost a year and a half now, Nina had almost begun to like the single life. She'd regained her pride and her strength, so she thought. She'd decided that women were not for her really, that it had just been a phase; chance that it had happened at all. She'd been seeing men again: gentle, beautiful, feminist men with nice smiles and smooth, lithe bodies. They wooed her with flowers and other gifts. They respected her. So nice. Nina liked them, although she couldn't really talk to any of them, not about anything too heavy. Still, she thought it was enough, that *nice* was okay for a while. It made her family happy and eased the stress of daily living. She could be seen walking hand in hand with them on the streets, and there was acceptance everywhere. It was easy, noncommittal.

But then suddenly there was Carrie. She'd seen her once on the street, accidentally almost plowing right into her. The woman had smiled, not sweetly or warmly, and yet not exactly in a snide or rude way, either. Her eyes blazed as Nina had never seen before. She saw her again at the café, where the only words exchanged were about Nina's order. And yet that night Carrie's presence began to fill her room, her night dreams, and soon after, her days, as well, making concentration at work a virtually impossibly task.

Nina began morning rituals of tea and muffins at the café, sometimes a full breakfast, always sitting at the same table by the window. The woman always tended to her on the days she worked, leaning over to set down the cup, her loose blouse billowing ever so slightly, seductively exposing just the teasing curve of caramel breast, her name detailed across the pocket—CARRIE— then turning away, snug black pants over a tight round ass and muscular thighs, neatly tucked into black leather boots. Curves and strength and sexuality that mesmerized Nina.

Now with her cheek to the photograph, Nina could imagine Carrie's taste on her tongue, suddenly aware of her desire in a real and tangible way, wanting to feel the woman's skin under her nails, fingers on her body; wanting to search and explore hidden places, not just a fantasy. Nina hugged the wall, dreamily rolling over her shoulder, head against the hard surface, now facing the center of the room, her back against the huge photograph.

She opened her eyes slowly. Four leather-clad figures, all silhouettes, filled the three archways that led from the room. Nina cried out in surprise, suddenly trapped, both hands now behind her, ready to push away and run, but there was nowhere to run. An overwhelming instinct to bolt overtook her, her adrenaline pumping, eyes searching for a way out but finding no escape. She stood frozen against the wall, face flushed, heart beating like that of a race horse.

"I know your face," one of the figures said. "I see you in the café almost every morning. What is your name?"

It was Carrie. Nina knew her voice.

"Nina. My name is Nina. I, um, I'm sorry...I...I got lost," she replied lamely, immediately cringing at her own idiocy. *Beautiful, now she's sure to want you madly,* she chastised herself silently.

"You followed me down here," Carrie challenged.

"I..." Nina paused this time, considering her response. "Yes, I'm sorry. I didn't know this place existed. I...I wanted to talk to you."

"Why didn't you talk to me at the café? You always sit and drink tea, eat breakfast. I wait on you. You watch me. What do you want?"

Nina tried to make out the woman's face in the dimness. But Carrie's smooth brown skin was in shadow.

"I want...*you,*" Nina answered in almost a whisper, surprised at hearing her own voice actually saying this, speaking the truth so candidly to Carrie, and in front of all these people.

There was a tense pause before Carrie spoke.

"Leave us, please," she said to the silent,

motionless figures. "Lock up. And bring tea. I'll be in soon."

They all exchanged smiles that Nina could not see. Two disappeared down the second hallway, one down the first. Carrie entered the room through the central archway.

She approached the wardrobe, her back to Nina, looking in at its contents.

"You have something of mine?"

Nina didn't remember she was holding the gloves at first. Then, faltering, she answered her.

"Bring them here, please."

Nina floated to her, entranced. The room seemed to go on forever, slowly stretching out before her as she walked and walked. From one corridor, another woman appeared with a tea tray. She set it down and left the room. Nina handed the gloves to Carrie, who took them slowly, golden brown eyes meeting hers as Carrie ran the leather over Nina's hands.

"You like the photograph?" she asked Nina, her gaze still burning into the startled blue sea of Nina's eyes.

"Yes," Nina answered, staring back as if hypnotized, a little frightened. The room was spinning ever so slightly.

"Tell me what you like about it."

They talked about the photograph: Carrie asking questions and serving tea, Nina answering. Nina began to relax a little. Carrie smiled at her, a low flame still burning in her eyes. They remained standing. And while they continued talking, Carrie after slipping on the gloves, undid the shackles on the wall. She circled Nina as she asked her questions. Nina tried to answer, distracted and perspiring as Carrie came in close behind her, their bodies almost touching.

"And what do you think the women in the photograph are feeling?" Carrie asked as she reached around Nina's waist and began unbuttoning her jeans. Nina froze. But, amazing herself, she did not stop her.

"Passion," she answered, her voice husky and excited, betraying her calm exterior; her head now leaning ever so slightly back, eyes closing, dark curls falling back away from her face.

Carrie left Nina's jeans loose and moved her leather-clad hands up along Nina's belly over the cotton of the white poet's shirt, unbuttoning the tiny buttons one by one, feeling the silk of Nina's bra beneath the cotton, then slipping the blouse slowly over the woman's creamy shoulders. With a quick glance towards the archways, Nina allowed her. Swiftly Carrie unhooked the white lace push-up bra that held Nina's beautiful, full breasts captive. Instinctively Nina reached up to cover her suddenly exposed chest. Carrie gently pried Nina's hands away, lowering them to her sides.

"Beautiful," Carrie whispered to Nina, running the palms of her large hands over the pink, hard tips of Nina's breasts as they stood at attention in the dim rose light. From behind her, Carrie could not see Nina blush, only that the woman stood still, quietly, surrendering. Carrie slipped the woman's black jeans over the curve of her hips and slowly down the length of her legs; Nina stepped out of them shyly, still not stopping her. Silky black hair graced the smooth porcelain of her toned legs. The dark bush of her pubic hair was barely visible beneath the white satin of her bikini panties. A creamy wetness dampened the crotch, causing them to stick snugly against the swell of Nina's lips. Carrie moved around to Nina's front, her eyes devouring the tease of those wet panties; then, looking into Nina's eyes, she ran one long, slim finger over the wet satin, over the swollen wetness of her labia, pushing just ever so slightly against the entrance to Nina's pulsing body.

Nina sucked in her breath, suppressing a moan of pleasure, her hands in fists at her side, dizzy from the contact...*so close*. Her face was hot with embarrassment, her excitement so apparent, her body already flowing like a river. She held her breath until Carrie moved away, reaching for Nina's hand as she did. Nina, who hadn't realized her hands were in fists, self-consciously relaxed them. Carrie led her across the room to restraints secured in the wall to their left.

Nina did not look at her captor, allowing herself to be led, feeling as if she were really lying in her bed at home, that this was all just a continuation of her fantasy, a dream, unreal—not actually happening at all.

The shackles clanged a bit as Carrie fastened them around her ankles. The sudden cold of the smooth metal on her warm body shocked Nina back into the reality of her situation. As if suddenly awakened, she watched through wide eyes as Carrie secured Nina's body to the wall.

Nina, she thought, *how far will you go? This is real, you can't wake up and escape!*

The logical, safe side raged at her to stop. The other side, born in the deepest part of the night, of her midnight self, this other side blossoming now, ravenous from the long wait, the unfulfilled nights past, begged her to continue, Nina remained silent, tensed and thrashing in her mind for control, but unable to stop the wanting.

Carrie's hands left the ankle restraints and followed the pattern of Nina's calves, inner thighs, hips, up, up, over her stomach, onto her breasts. Nina drew in her breath, eyes half-mast. Carrie took Nina's hands in hers and raised them above Nina's head, securing the wrists in the cold metal restraints. With one hand behind Nina's head, Carrie pulled the woman toward her and kissed her deeply, her tongue finding Nina's, moving in smoothly, then out again, tasting, teasing. Nina's body blazed, a torch lit, engulfed by flame, dangerous. *She wanted to touch her, too.* Nina ached to touch the woman, not believing what was happening, where she was, what she was feeling.

As they kissed, Carrie loosened the black silk robe she'd been wearing. It slid from her shoulders to the floor. At last, Nina opened her eyes. Carrie stood before her dressed only in slick black leather chaps, tailored and detailed with designs, the outline of strong, muscled legs visible beneath this second skin, the V of her silky black pubic hair framed by the arc of leather. A black leather belt scooped low over one hip, a whip resting at its lowest point. A gold ring circled one toe. Nina's eyes devoured the woman's beauty, eyes traveling back up to Carrie's breasts. They were smooth and firm, just over a nice-sized handful each, exactly as Nina had pictured them, sloping sensuously to aroused nipples that stood out, a slightly darker brown, with a small gold ring pierced through one.

She hadn't imagined that—the piercing—had never seen anything pierced on a body other than earlobes. Nina wondered if it hurt; she was quite certain it would be painful on her own, larger breasts. Instinctively she tried to reach down and shield her chest, as if the pain were real. But the shackles prevented her, and she ended up yanking her wrist, frustrated.

Suddenly Carrie pulled away. The cruel *whoosh!* of the whip slit the air as she let loose on Nina's soft skin—once, twice, then again—startling the woman out of her reverie and into the agony of the moment. A welt rose across her body.

"No!" Nina cried out, shocked and confused. *What had she done?* "Stop! Let me out of these, please!"

Carrie smiled. Nina had not panicked, but she was somewhat afraid—surprised, perhaps, by the reality of pain. She winced, then relaxed her features in a rush of pleasure and stubborn strength: the face of a willful child.

Nina composed herself and looked at the woman straight on. Anger and attitude overcame her; she was suddenly furious at her powerlessness. At the same time, she felt her body betraying her, accepting the challenge of more, even desiring more, wanting to extend the limits; all the blood in her body went rushing down over her breasts, through her belly, between her legs. Her muscles flexed, ready to accept a dare.

"You've been deceptive, Nina. Isn't this what you've been wanting all this time? Otherwise, why did you follow me? You know about the rumors, the photographs." She paused, observing the woman. "You can't accept it yet—I see that. I see it in your eyes. This is no photograph, Nina. This is real. Touch me."

Carrie almost whispered the final words as she approached Nina, laying her body against the other woman's, breast to breast, pinning her against the wall. She tilted her head back, neck exposed. Nina's mouth opened, caressed the incredibly smooth skin with her tongue, kissing Carrie's warm flesh, up over her sloping jaw and high cheekbones, searching for lips and tongue. Nina's body almost hung from the bindings that held her hands aloft over her head and rendered them useless, no longer a part of her eager body. Thwarted, she forced her mouth against Carrie's, aching for a real kiss.

Carrie sighed, having enjoyed everything up to that moment. She drew back in a flash, away from Nina's aggressive mouth, out of her reach, one hand squeezing Nina's cheeks in a disciplinary action. She spoke slowly, deliberately, jaws tight.

"You don't do that. Ever. You are never to make a move unless I order it, Nina. That is not your place. You are here on my terms. That beating was a demonstration."

Nina had been leaning toward Carrie, her hands gripping the shackles that held them. Now, in a rush of confusion and anger, she tried to pull away and out of Carrie's grip. But Carrie was strong, and Nina was at a disadvantage. Carrie waited for Nina to stop fighting back.

"Perhaps I'm misled in my interpretation," she said gently, loosening her grip. The women stood face to face, each studying the other's.

Carrie stood back from Nina, eyes lazily traveling over her silky body. Carrie could feel her own caramel flesh responding to this woman's porcelain form, to her innocence. She approached her again, eased her body up close against Nina's. They leaned against the wall, Carrie sliding a leg up between Nina's, feeling the heat of her, the wetness of her pubic hair. Nina sighed, accepting the other's weight, her own dangling body tingling and pulsing at the touch.

"I'll let you go, if that's really what you want. I'm not a rapist and I don't dislike you. We've developed a sort of silent relationship over the months, yes? But it must be your true choice."

She is beautiful, Carrie thought for the hundredth time, running a hand through Nina's thick, dark hair, envisioning what could be. *I don't really want her to go.*

She stopped seducing for a moment, controlled herself, stepped back a bit. She smoothed Nina's hair, waiting for a reply. Nina's light blue eyes gazed at Carrie, then down at the floor. Breathing was difficult. Her body kept recalling the feel of Carrie's hands and lips on her startled skin. She tried to think clearly. Why had she come? *Really, Nina, what is it you want here?* she asked herself. She looked up at the photograph, beyond Carrie on the wall to her right. A red light illuminated it dimly, creating an unusual effect: as if giving life to the subjects.

"I'll leave you here for a moment," Nina heard her say. "You're here now; you decide. But once you do, you're either out or in, *all the way.*"

She smiled at Nina, not wickedly at all, but honestly, with obvious passion.

"I'll be back," Carrie continued, moving a strand of hair out of her eyes. Then, picking up her robe as she turned, she disappeared.

⚜

Carrie, bent down at Nina's ankles, finished releasing Nina from the restraints. As Nina felt the last restraint loosened, she stood up, away from the bed, and waited instinctively for Carrie's next move.

"Go now," she was told. "Go to the door and wait."

Carrie's eyes followed her; she was full of a thousand feelings, but kept in check the deepest flame. Nina's energy pulled at her, and she found it very hard to resist, to let her go alone.

Nina moved away without looking at Carrie, eyes focused on the beautiful, carved wood door ahead of her. As she neared it, she stopped, waited.

After a moment the door opened toward her. Two masked figures waited at the threshold. Nina looked them over. One, holding the now-familiar leash, moved forward to secure it to her collar. Nina held her chin high, heard the click of metal on metal, lowered her gaze to level, and waited. The other figure approached, swung a satin-and-velvet cape over Nina's shoulders to cover her nude, but shackled, figure. The last things Nina saw were those leather-clad arms swooping up toward her once more. Then everything disappeared into darkness beneath the familiar soft leather blindfold, and she was led, carefully, out of the room.

Beneath her feet, thick carpeting muffled the sound of their footsteps. If not for the gentle, sporadic tug at her collar, Nina could have been walking alone down some silent tunnel. Figures and colors bent and twisted before her sightless eyes, flashes of light in her mind, memories of childhood gone mad: a moving tunnel rolling like a barrel as she tried to crawl through it; the smell of urine in funhouse corners; moving stairs that suddenly disappeared beneath her feet; the fear of darkness; the strange waiting in an empty house of mirrors; rolling pins spinning as she slid down them; everything moving around her...only young Nina standing in the middle now, trapped, watching the breathing room like a spy in the lungs of a sphinx.

The images flashed by her in the silent darkness; her breath quickened. She didn't notice that she had almost stopped moving until the collar at her neck was gently tugged forward, vaulting her out of her daymare, nightmare. She concentrated now only on the present, on moving her feet, one in front of the other.

As she turned yet another corner, the party stopped. Nina felt a hand on her shoulder. A door opened and air thick with steam and soft perfumed scents wafted through. Nina sniffed the air, felt the moisture on her face, envisioned a long, hot bath in a sunken tub in her dream bathroom.

The cape loosened at her neck, then slipped from her shoulders. She was led by the leash through a doorway and into the steamy air. The sound of water flowing, gentle waterfall sounds, mixed with the sound of soft voices murmuring some indecipherable words nearby. The shackles at Nina's feet fell away from her ankles. At her sides soft hands moved her arms for a moment, then were busy at her wrists. Then those shackles, too, fell away. Only her collar, connected to the leash, remained. She stood naked, the blindfold still in place. A gentle tug on the leash and Nina moved forward, amused by the fact that she no longer felt embarrassed by her nakedness in the presence of others.

Not down this far, she thought, *not in this place.*

It was somehow liberating—a strange sense of safety in this world of surprises, unknowns. There was knowledge in the ways of controlled power and passion; knowledge of how to play hard without permanent damage.

Suddenly light filled Nina's sight as the blindfold slipped away. She raised her arm to shield her eyes. As they adjusted, she found herself in a beautiful black-and-cream marbled room. Small hollows in the walls housed thick, brightly burning candles. Beautiful, full, emerald green plants hung from the ceiling by black chains—ferns, ivies, strange exotic-looking others. Steam curled up from a large, round bath sunk deep into the floor. A small stone waterfall brought water out of the wall, down over the stones in sensual patterns and into the tub. It seemed that the water was constantly renewed because it wasn't overflowing or changing its level. "How wonderful," Nina sighed, her body relaxing already.

Flower petals floated gently on the water in the bath, and the soft scent of rose and lavender filled the huge bathing room. Classical music, barely a suggestion, weaved its way around the new visitors.

A narrow archway led to a much smaller room far across from her, and Nina could see a black marble toilet through the doorway. Hooks on chains hung on the walls around her at different levels. Along the wall to her far right, a sleek black marble shower head arched away from the wall, a large, wide circle at its end. Two other shower heads came out from the walls at lower levels, arching around from the sides.

Lots of water! Nina thought. *Enough for a party of bathers!*

There was no curtain, no boundary. The entire

floor was black-and-cream marble and fanned out in a huge half-moon away from the wall. The floor sank slowly down toward a drain below the fixture. Two shining black handles stood waiting in the middle of the wall a few feet above the drain. Mirrored tiles mixed with marble on the wall and allowed for an interesting view for the bathing party.

Nearby, a clear glass case housed assorted items for various pleasures and disciplines, as well as bars of soap in shiny black and red wrappings.

Before Nina had a chance to take in any more of the room, she was led by her leash to the waiting bath. Her collar and leash were temporarily removed, while a new plastic collar was secured around her neck. Then, three steps down and she was sunk to her shoulders. She closed her eyes, sinking further into the luxurious heat, the water soaking through to the sorest parts of her body, releasing all the pain and tension.

As she turned her head, sighing, she opened her eyes again to find that her assistants had retired. Light chains surrounded by plastic covers extended from her collar out to two separate points, securing her to the floor on either side, but leaving room for her to swim freely in the huge tub. Steam rose up from the surface in swirling clouds. Nina smiled and spread out her body, floating among the flower petals. Then she took a breath, closed her eyes and immersed herself completely in the soft, scented water.

After a while her assistants returned. The heat of the tub, the continuous tumbling of the waterfall, and the soft melody of classical strings had lulled Nina almost to sleep. She lay with her head back against the side of the tub, lips parted slightly, body held gently in the water, pink breasts just breaking the surface.

"She's pretty," a woman's voice whispered.

"Mmm," came a soft reply.

"I hate to wake her," came the first voice.

"Hush," a third and harsher voice added. "No talking."

Two of the three women approached the tub and knelt beside Nina, stirring her from her restful oblivion. She opened her eyes and looked into the faces of her assistants.

"Hello," she said, her voice husky with surprise.

The women smiled hello but did not speak. Both were clothed in slick bathing suits, the fabric like second skins: one burgundy, one sea green, cut like cycling shorts along gently muscled thighs, but slung very low in the back and coming up from the shorts as only widish suspenders in front, barely covering their breasts. They both wore their hair short and slicked back from their striking faces. Nina smiled, pleased with the view.

The two women slipped into the tub on either side of her and began washing her, lathering her hair and body, raising her up to the surface of the water as needed. She watched them for a while, their movements smooth and graceful, nipples poking out against the thin fabric of their outfits, skin shining with wetness.

"What are your names?" Nina asked quietly. But neither woman answered. As it was obvious her assistants would not be conversing with her, Nina decided to just enjoy the attention and closed her eyes, giving herself completely to their hands. They caressed and kneaded her skin and muscles, neck, shoulders, breasts. One of the women dove beneath her as she floated, resurfacing between her feet, soaping and massaging her feet, calves, up to her knees, thighs. She opened her eyes, surprised as the woman's hands made their way up to her pubic hair, lathering and caressing, fingers dancing lightly down over her lips, along the soft, sensitive skin of her vulva and down. Nina sighed, her sense of touch focused like a laser at the meeting points of the women's hands on her skin. Her body began tingling, aroused and yet still completely relaxed, barely breathing. *It's heaven; it must be heaven to which I've been delivered,* she sighed silently to herself.

After the washing, a woman standing watchful at the door brought the bathing party to a close, clapping her hands twice, startling Nina.

"We will return after a short time," the woman said. "Enjoy your bath."

Nina silently nodded in response, watching as her two assistants emerged, dripping, from the tub;

they disappeared for a moment through another doorway and returned with towels in hand. After a quick dry-off, they followed the other woman obediently and silently out of the bathing room. The doors closed quietly behind them.

Nina again closed her eyes, letting out a long sigh, basking in the heat of the water and the memory of the women's hands on her skin. She didn't notice when the doors again slipped quietly open and a figure entered the bath chamber. She didn't notice, either, when the figure moved quickly to the display case, took a few items from the shelves and moved as silently as a huntress through the steamy room toward Nina...slipping like a water snake into the tub on the side farthest from her.

Mozart was playing, filling the room with strings and horns. Nina sighed, relaxed and floating, let go of the side of the tub and floated out into the middle, the plastic restraints allowing her plenty of room, her dark hair swirling around her head like a mermaid's crown.

Suddenly she felt an oh-so-gentle touch on the inside of her thigh. She opened her eyes to see what it was, and to her great surprise found a woman moving in slowly through the mist, up between her open legs, wearing only white string-bikini bottoms. Nina cried out, suddenly heavy in the water and splashing.

"Ssshhh," Kate whispered, putting a finger

against Nina's mouth. "It's okay, it's just me, sshh..."

She smiled at Nina, coming in close, and motioned toward the door.

"No one knows I'm here but one, and she's my friend. Don't worry."

Nina allowed Kate to lay her on her back again, floating her. Then Kate disappeared underwater for a moment, resurfacing between Nina's legs, parting them gently, moving in close enough to lick the soft skin of her hip as it broke the surface of the water.

Nina drew in her breath but did not move. Kate's eyes met hers as her pink tongue explored the curve of Nina's hipbone, moving seductively toward the curl of dark pubic hair against soft, light skin.

"Kate," Nina whispered.

Kate's eyes smiled, her tongue now dangerously close to where Nina's body was awakening.

"How did you get in?" she pressed. "What if you get caught?" Her voice was tinged with worry, but she was filled with the pleasure of Kate's tongue on her body and the adrenaline rush of danger.

Kate pushed Nina's legs down into the water as she slid in close against her, eyes aglow, pressing her naked skin against Nina's, her hands holding the woman's beautiful, passionate face as their mouths met in a deep and probing kiss, tongues teasing and searching.

At last, Kate sighed to herself; her whole body was sighing, full of pleasure, full of the sweet taste of Nina's mouth. She held Nina's jaw, one hand on either side, feeling the push and pull of their kiss beneath her touch.

Nina wrapped her arms around the woman's narrow shoulders, pulling her in tight. Their bodies slid against each other in the steamy wetness of the tub: Kate rubbing her small breasts against Nina's soft and full ones; her hands searching along every inch of Nina's body; legs caressing soft, downy-haired legs; hands on curves, hips; Nina's hands discovering the smoothness of Kate's petite figure, so pale; the strength of her lithe back, slim legs and arms...both women completely immersed in the physical sensations of their exploration.

The hot breath of the two women mixed sensuously with the steam heat, rising in tendrils and swirls, aroused and furious. A sudden whirring sound made Nina jump, pull back from the kiss, guilty and nervous as a child. The water around them began to froth and churn, adding to their own touch a thousand fingers, reaching for their bodies, touching, pulling back. Nina's face was surprised and worried as she looked around quickly. But Kate just giggled and wrapped her arms around Nina's neck, pulling her in and kissing her again.

"I hit the button on the way over to the tub,"

she whispered impishly, arching against Nina's body, coaxing Nina back into the passion. Nina obliged, sliding out of her grasp, kissing along the creamy white skin of Kate's elegant neck, collarbone, and down to suck the tips of Kate's nipples, hard as pearls. She sucked gently, then harder as Kate arched into her mouth. A silver ring hung from the other nipple. Nina eyed it as she sucked, harder now until Kate drew in her breath, on the edge of pain. Taking as much of Kate's breast into her mouth as she could, Nina created a pleasurable suction, gently pulling back into a kiss on the tip of Kate's nipple. She kissed a path from one breast to the other, sliding her tongue into the center of the silver ring when she arrived. Experimenting, Nina pulled gently on it, circling her tongue around the cold metal.

"Oh, yes," Kate said, "harder, please...."

Kate's voice brought a creamy heat to Nina's body, a wet desire that escaped from the channel between her lower lips, her clit responding in turn, swelling, pulsing with the increasing beat of her heart. She closed her eyes, feeling the ripples of desire wash over her as she stuck out her tongue and flicked the tip of Kate's nipple, continuing to pull on the ring with her lips, harder, harder, as Kate wished, until the woman cried out, her hands out at her sides, grasping the air, her face tight with concentration and the intensifying pain. Nina pulled a moment longer, squeezing Kate's other nipple gently with her fingers, then slowly eased up, kissing Kate's tortured nipple sweetly, then covering both breasts in a flurry of kisses. Kate sunk her hands into Nina's wet hair, pulling her head in close against her chest. In the water the lightness of Kate's form allowed Nina to raise her up with one arm, lay her back on the surface of the churning water. Kate spread out her arms, stretching out her body and smiling with pleasure. Music beat through the room. Nina slid one arm under the small of Kate's back, lifting her hips up clear of the water, attempting to remove the woman's bikini bottoms. To her surprise they melted away under her touch! She stared in shock at Kate, who was grinning.

"Edibles!" she laughed. Nina smiled, familiar with the garments but hardly expecting them at this moment. "I wasn't sure they'd last long enough in this water for you to find them!" They both laughed over the roar of the water and the music, and Nina lifted Kate's hips up out of the water once again, holding her body in her arms, guiding the woman's pink, open sex into her mouth. Kate lay her head back on the water.

"Oh, yes," she purred, her wet hair swirling in soft black tips around her face underwater; her hair was baby blond under her armpits, barely visible. "Mmmmm, yes...."

Nina stroked the woman with her tongue, feeling the hardness of Kate's swelling clit against her mouth, plunging her tongue into the woman's deep river, tasting her as Kate wrapped her legs around Nina, pulling her in deeper and harder against her heated body. Nina went wild, her tongue dancing and singing to the music of a snake charmer as Kate's body arched and fed her, daring her to take her.

"Give me something inside," Kate instructed, her face aglow with passion and desire, smiling her thanks. Kate took one of her fingers and slipped it in her mouth, then out, demonstrating. Nina's eyes ate her alive as she watched. She slipped two of her own fingers into her mouth, out, then slid them gently between the open lips of Kate's body, feeling the wet slickness surround her fingers, muscles contracting around her, pulling her in, slipping in a third as Kate instructed.

"Ooohh, yeah...." Kate moaned in pleasure as Nina bent back to tease at the slippery opening of her body, fingers busy touching the sensitive places inside as her tongue once again found its course on the surface. Kate was loose and wild with her pleasure, crying out and moaning, stroking Nina with her words of praise and desire, her breathing quickening.

"Mmmmm, oh yes, so good. Nina, yes, right there, oohhhhh, take me, take me away...."

Nina worried momentarily about Kate's cries being heard beyond the closed doors, but her attention was quickly pulled back to the task at hand; her mouth full of the woman's taste, Nina's hands moved in and out, in and out with her fingers, as deep as she could go, then out again. Her tongue produced a constant vibration of pleasure on the button of Kate's desire.

Kate's body was alive with the pulse of her blood, rushing and pounding through her, straight to the meeting point of Nina's lips and her own, below.

"Oh, yes, take me, Nina, right there, right there, oh don't stop...." Kate held her breath for a moment as Nina worked her furiously, concentrating, then suddenly let out her breath in a wave of sound. "Aaaaaaahhhhhh!"

Kate arched desperately into Nina's mouth as her body contracted around Nina's fingers, tensing and expanding with orgasmic pleasure; her muscles flexed as she released the volcano, pumping in spasms of pleasure around Nina's fingers again and again and again. Her scream filled the room. Nina stayed against her, laying her tongue ever so lightly against Kate's oversensitive clit, bringing wave after wave of contraction and release, waves of pleasure that threatened to explode Kate.

Nina rose slowly from between Kate's open legs, sliding her fingers gently out of the deep, hot cavern of Kate's body; a final contraction of pleasure rippled around her fingers just before they emerged, victorious, the slippery juices coating her fingers and mixing with the restless water around them. She ran her hands up Kate's sides, pulling her in toward her, sucking one hard nipple into her mouth, sucking harder and shaking her head like an animal. Kate cried out in pain and pleasure, roughly pulling Nina up into her arms and into a ravenous kiss. They wrapped their bodies around each other, lost in the steamy heat of the water and their passion.

"Oh, touch me, please, touch me, Kate....," Nina whispered, nibbling Kate's ear, teasing with her tongue, her excited breathing coaxing the woman into motion.

Kate leaned down and put her lips to Nina's neck, hands strong against Nina's shoulders, sturdy back, sucking the flesh into her mouth. Nina breathed heavily, leaning her head back, exposing her soft neck for Kate to feed upon. The painful pleasure of Kate's sucking mouth and nibbling teeth excited Nina beyond control. She pulled at the woman's hair, clawed gently at her back, but did not speak.

Kate finally freed her from her bite and smiled into the woman's shadowed eyes, a curtain of desire blocking out everything beyond their bodies; Nina was now deep in the zone where words and wishes escape, unconsidered, all thoughts forgotten but one.

Nina fell into Kate's mouth: a frenzied kiss of need and passion. Kate kissed her back wildly, feeding off her energy, lifting her in the water and moving Nina against the wide steps of the tub that held her body easily. Music boomed like a heartbeat through the room, the water still restless and alive. Kate left Nina at the steps for a very brief moment, stepping quickly out of the water; then climbing from across the room. Nina watched her, confused, her head spinning. Kate held something in her hand. Nina tried to see what it was through the fog of her impassioned sight.

Slipping quickly back into the steaming hot tub, Kate eased up between Nina's legs, opening them, pushing slightly with her body until Nina was snug against the side of the pool, leaning over to kiss her beautiful shining lips. Nina kissed her back softly but firmly, gave herself up to Kate's touch, to her will; gave up trying to see what it was she was holding and lay her head back against the side of the tub.

"Yeah, that's right, relax, let me lead." Kate whispered the words, mesmerizing Nina into a state of surrender. She slid over Nina's body like a beautiful water sprite, causing tiny electric explosions at every touch. One hand stroked Nina's mound, scratching and pulling gently at her pubic hair; Nina's lower lips were swollen and shining with desire, her pink clit peeking out from amid the dark forest of hair, beckoning. Nina tried one last time to lift her head to see what Kate was holding, what she was going to do to her; but Kate's hand rose and gently motioned her back down. Nina lowered her head, floating on the water again, uncertain, every nerve focused on Kate's next move.

Kate held Nina's body just above the water, her mouth now touching the edges of the woman's sex, teasing around her clit but not on it until Nina arched into her mouth.

"Don't tease me, Kate, touch me! Give it to me now!" she demanded, unraveled in her state of need. "C'mon...." she begged.

Kate smiled her approval, then wrapped her warm lips around Nina's tiny, hard shaft and sucked, gently at first, coaxing the woman's pleasure. Then she ran her tongue along the wetness of Nina's opening, darting in, out, running a finger down further and caressing the sensitive skin around Nina's rear entrance, between the firm cheeks of her ass.

Nina moaned as Kate's tongue teased the front, her finger stroking the back. Kate's touch on her anus felt so good, so exciting; but Nina flushed deeply with embarrassment, although it was now a weaker shyness, most certainly. Kate whispered words of assurance: how beautiful, how good Nina felt, how sexy....

She sighed, relaxed and let it go—all her old hang-ups, embarrassments—let Kate take her along the corridors of new pleasures.

And just as Nina began to relax against Kate's touch from behind, her passion building now, she felt something firm teasing from behind, where fingers were just seconds before, teasing the ultra-sensitive skin into arousal. Overcome with excitement, Nina thought nothing of it. Her body flooded with a throbbing heat under the woman's intense mouth; the soft tongue and lips building her higher and higher toward climax. Nina's body was pulsing and shivering now, focused only on the sensation between her legs, deep inside her, pounding, dripping sex.

As orgasm built inside her like a bomb, Nina suddenly felt the firmness that was caressing from behind enter her, breaking through the barrier of her ass, slowly, then slipping in easily and sending shock waves of penetrating pleasure and pain ripping through her body, one after another. Nina cried out, shocked.

"Oh, God, yes! Oh, Kate! Aaahh!" Nina's voice was wild and high now, laced with an edge of pain that aroused Kate and intensified her movements. Kate's mouth stormed over the woman, seducing and coaxing, keeping the passion building at a frantic pace as she took Nina further, further toward the edge, toward a deeper satisfaction, melting the pain into complete pleasure.

Nina cried out as if she would burst, the pressure now intense, a balloon too full of air but still being blown into at an alarming rate; she was on the verge, taut and pushing at all barriers. Sensation raced through her entire body. She grasped the side of the tub with both hands, head back against the marble, body outstretched, as Kate fed from her, giving back to her, now slipping two fingers between her hungry lips, igniting fireworks deep inside, the muscles of her sex sucking Kate in as she filled her, filled her from all sides.

In a crash of ecstasy, Nina blew like dynamite, exploded like a balloon pricked in slow motion, muscles contracting in front, behind, clit throbbing hard, a rage of release, still filled completely as her body pushed and pulled, pushed and pulled, unable to breath, to see, mouth open, face contorted with the intensity of orgasm. Nina's entire body pounded out the beat of her heart.

Slowing now, Kate's tongue caressed the final shock waves of pleasure through Nina's body.

"No more! Stop! Aaahhhh...stop, please...."

In this raw state of release, Nina's body could take no more. She pulled up and away from Kate's now gentle mouth; the woman's fingers slipped free and gently removed the plug from Nina's still active body. Nina's cries echoed through the chamber as the motion caused more waves of pleasure, more contractions, her blood rushing through her veins still; she was feeling light-headed and ethereal, not quite grounded yet. She lay on her back on the marble floor, which was amazingly warm, letting her feet drip into the steaming bath. Sweat and water dripped down her face; she turned onto her side, tears filling her eyes.

Kate pulled herself out of the tub and went to Nina, taking the woman in her arms and cradling her. Nina closed her eyes, still breathing hard, her body still responsive, emotions raw. Tears streamed down her face.

"What is it, Nina?" Kate asked, stroking the woman's face, moving her hair out of her eyes. "What?" She waited for Nina to speak, rocking her. Nina lay in her arms and held her back, then slowly moved up to kiss the woman's lips, sat up a bit and held Kate's face, smiling now, her eyes wet but her whole face shining.

"It's just that I've never felt such pleasure before, such complete, intense passion and fire like that. Thank you," she finished, kissing Kate again.

Kate laughed a bubbly laugh and hugged Nina.

"You're nuts!" she teased. "Absolutely crazy!"

They both laughed, slipping back into the tub and holding each other, petting and floating together. Kate's eyes were bright as diamonds as she looked at Nina's face, eyes, lips, and soft skin. Nina smiled and they hugged a long, soft, sensual hug.

"Listen, I have to go," Kate said after a short time. "Your two helpers will return in a couple of minutes, and I can't be here. It's our secret." She leaned forward and laid a passionate kiss on Nina's lips. "Thanks for a wonderful bath," she said impishly, winking.

Then she rose from the tub, disappeared for a

minute, and returned with a fluffy towel. Quickly she wrapped it around herself, and with a little wave, slipped through the door and was gone.

The jets turned off as if of their own accord. Nina looked around to see who had turned them off, but no one was in the room with her that she could see. Bach now played from the sound system, piano and gentle strings.

What the...? she wondered, but didn't bother to finish her question, or worry any further. She felt too good for worry. She laughed out loud, a soft laugh of childish delight, high on the joy of passion consummated, of having a forbidden secret now to keep, something wild and exciting and dangerous. She hugged herself and spun around once, falling back into the water, eyes closed, blowing bubbles as she disappeared into the depths.

Moments later the doors opened, and her attendants returned. They took her from the tub, dried and blow-dried, brushed and shined, scented and lotioned her, all under the supervision of the third woman's watchful eye. She wore leather and stood silently in the doorway.

Dark, shiny curls fell around Nina's face and onto her powder-dusted shoulders. She sat naked as they inspected their work. No hint of modesty or shyness occurred to her. She was beginning to understand the universality of the human body, the beauty of its display. And by the time the women were quite finished with her, she felt as if she might have become, at last, a totally new person.

She smiled warmly at her assistants, who finished their work and went to stand beside the watching woman, never meeting Nina's eyes.

"The mistress will see you now," the leader said. The other two women took items from her and moved to Nina's side, removing the plastic collar and affixing the leather one and all four shackles. They draped a warm black-and-burgundy cape over her shoulders, blindfolded her, and led her from the room.

Alison Tyler
THE BLUE ROSE

The Blue Rose: Rules and Regulations

1. Always address your elders with the respectful title of "Mistress." Always answer properly when spoken to.
2. Proper hygiene must be enforced at all times. This means keeping the body well cleaned, well shaved, and sweet-smelling. Panties will be worn to bed every night—this will be enforced by spot checking.
3. Hair must be brushed 100 times every morning and evening.
4. There will be no swearing or vulgarity permitted inside or outside the Blue Rose. Proper ladies do not keep company with those who swear.
5. Self-indulgence will not be tolerated.
6. Tardiness will not be tolerated.
7. Little sisters are under the care of their elders. They are to consider themselves "owned" by their big sisters. They will not indulge themselves with each other.
8. Elders have the right to educate, discipline, or punish any younger sister for her own benefit.
9. Teatime and dinner will be attended by all girls, unless a written excuse is requested from a headmistress ahead of time.
10. Chores will be performed daily. There will be no exceptions, without a written excuse.

Jasmine's Confession
In which I meet my Juliet

I went from attic pleasures to basement drudgery, so fast that it made my head spin, sending my thoughts rattling around in my brain without making a single connection. She stood me up, my lovely Mistress, my beautiful Domina. She stood me up and kissed away my tears of pleasure. Then she told me to go downstairs to clean up and prepare myself for the evening's festivities.

I followed her orders, although it was still early in the afternoon, and I bathed again, washing *myself* this time, slowly scrubbing, soaking, losing myself in the warm caress of the water. The bath was so relaxing, and I luxuriated in the feel of the smooth porcelain beneath me, the tile still cool above the waterline. Then, breaking into the delight of my afternoon leisure, there was a knock on the door, and Corrine's voice called, "Cassie! I need you in here—now!"

I dried myself as quickly as possible, dressed in the same clothes from the attic exploration, and entered our bedroom. There she stood, like a haughty queen, pointing to a pile of laundry on the bed: dresses in every shade, every style—the red Chinese silk robe, the gold ball gown.

"You're to wash these and hang them in the basement to dry," she told me. "They're your gift from Mistress Justine, but all of them want cleaning."

I nodded to her and curtsied low, to show my respect, and then gathered the clothing in my arms and waited for her to tell me where to go. "Jasmine will show you," Corrine said. "She has her own washing up to do."

Jasmine was a new pledge, like myself, but she had already lived in the house for three weeks and knew the routine better than I did. I found her at the stairwell, waiting for me, her eyes lingering over my dusty dress, the still-wet curls in my hair. She didn't ask what I had been up to or laugh; she simply regarded me with her wide-set brown eyes and then motioned for me to follow her.

We walked down the flight of steps and around the corner to the hall. Here she pulled a small key on a chain from her pocket and opened the door, taking care to flick on the light switch before heading down the steep wooden staircase. Each step creaked, like the stairs in a horror film, but the basement itself was well-lit and clean, much less dusty than the attic room. I carried my bundle of clothes to the bottom step and looked around. Directly in front of us stood a washing machine and dryer, both modern, which Jasmine quickly told me was for sheets and towels only. To the side were a pair of old-fashioned washtubs, washboards, and the like. A clothesline ran the full length of the long room.

In one corner stood a bed and a wooden cupboard that was closed and locked. There were restraints on the bed—as there had been on the examination table—thin leather restraints. Jasmine caught me staring, but did not bother to explain their use.

"Here," she said simply, setting her dresses on a nearby table and then separating my washload into piles. "These colors together, and these. The whites over here." As she worked, I watched her, taking in her long brown hair and the tortoiseshell band that pulled it off her face. She had an intense look as she worked, concentrating, feeling each material and judging the type of water it could stand: hot, medium, cold. Then she filled the tubs and told me to start.

We scrubbed away together, in silence, with me stealing occasional glances her way. I wondered whether she was mad at me, whether I had done something to offend her. I had not yet spoken to her, but I wondered if she were angered by the attention to me from Mistress Justine. (Perhaps all the girls were.)

Finally, when I could handle the silent treatment no longer, I spoke.

"Do you like it here? Living at the Blue Rose, I mean, not working in the basement."

"Oh, yes," she sighed. Then she smiled at me, her face lighting up. Instantly I realized that her silence had been from shyness—not anger—and I felt so ignorant for not having recognized something that was so true in myself. Shyness, silence, fright.

"Who is your big sister?" I asked, hoping to draw her out further.

"Nora." When she realized that I could not match a face to the name, she continued, "She is the tall one, with the short blonde hair. She wore a light purple dress last night. Lavender, really, with antique lace at the collar and the cuffs."

I still looked blank. Jasmine continued, "You might not have noticed, I guess." And I blushed, recalling the rigors of the previous evening, the blur of the faces in the gallery before the blindfold was fitted over my eyes.

"No," I said. "I don't recall. Is she nice?"

"Very," Jasmine said, and then smiled broadly, "At least, she's kind to me, if not always to the rest of the sisters. She is known for her temper—Naomi told me that—but I have worked hard not to disappoint her."

I nodded at that. I knew that power of wanting to please. Only the day before, I had been overwhelmed with a desire to throw myself at the feet of Mistress Justine. And that very morning, I had felt a wave of devotion wash over me as I brought my Mistress Corrine to orgasm among our tousled bedclothes.

"She is not too happy with me just now, though," Jasmine continued, and I caught the flush in her own cheeks, a blush of embarrassment that I was also familiar with in myself. I wondered if all pledges were instructed in lessons that brought forth such rosy-hued responses, and I hoped that when I became an elder, I would outgrow my childish blushes.

"Why?" I asked, not sure whether it was polite to do so, but wanting to know, regardless of proper etiquette. "What have you done?"

"*Not* done, really," she said, ringing out the first of her dresses and bringing it to the clothesline to hang. She took two wooden clips from a basket nearby and fastened the long white dress to the line. I watched as it swayed gently, the breeze coming in from two high-up windows, windows that must appear at ground level in the garden. I thought about Mistress Emily up there, working away among her glorious roses, and then I thought of my own Mistress Corrine, who had been chosen for garden duty with her.

"I am..." Jasmine began, her haunted voice

recapturing my attention. "I am…" And then she turned away from me, obviously unable to meet my gaze while she spoke. "I am not very adept at *receiving* her." I hardly caught the last bit, her voice had gone so soft, so thin. I wasn't sure exactly what she meant by it, though I had a vague idea. She came back to her basin then, and continued washing a dress of pale blue.

"What do you mean?" I managed to ask, hoping not to frighten her with my question.

"I am not able to receive the pleasure she talks of."

"Can you not climax?" I asked, feeling rather bold, perhaps by my ability to come so easily. "Is that what you mean?"

Jasmine did not answer, but she nodded so forcefully that a few wisps of her mahogany hair slipped free from her barrette and fell over her forehead. She seemed glad for this, as it partially hid her fiery cheeks from me. "That's it," she whispered finally. "That's what I mean."

"Have you never?" I pressed her for information. I had finished my own dress and got up to hang it by hers on the line. My distance from her seemed to make it easier for her to reveal herself to me.

"No…never with another."

"But by yourself?" I did not look at her while I asked this, but instead looked over at the bed, at the dark leather of the restraints, at the plastic sheet that fitted the mattress. Self-indulgence was forbidden, but she knew I wouldn't tell on her. (*Is that what this bed is for?* I wondered. *For punishing those who touch themselves in the dark curtain of privacy brought on by the night...?*)

"Only once," she admitted, and I turned then and saw her staring directly at me, almost defiantly. "Only one time," she repeated. When I waited for her to continue, she said, "After watching you, last night," and I understood her previous silence even more. I could feel her eyes on me, delving into me, begging I knew not what from me.

And, shamefully, I could see the bed in my mind's eye, could picture her tied to it while I worked her, while I nestled between her gentle thighs and worked her as Mistress Corrine had taught me, as Mistress Justine had showed me. I could feel how much pleasure it would give me to bring her to that point where her breathing would go ragged, where her small hands would ball into fists, where her mind would betray her and her mouth would open and let out all of her hidden desires. How I longed to know her desires!

I came back to her and sat close by her side. "Does she know?" I asked, realizing that this was the most important thing to sweet Jasmine. "Does Nora know what you did?"

"She guessed," Jasmine whispered. "She touched me *there* in bed and I quivered, my body all tingly, my...my..." She couldn't say it, couldn't say any word for it. I wanted to help her.

"Your pussy?" I asked and she nodded. *Her sweet, tender cunt...*

"On fire," she said, softer still. "I couldn't hide it. Nothing had made me feel like that—the watching, I mean. There were other girls before you, of course, other pledges this September, and myself, as well—all fastened to that table, all examined for the pleasure of our headmistresses, though they don't call it that. But, Cassandra, nothing has ever had such an effect on me." She paused to catch her breath, but before I could respond, she went on, "And I've read and read. Which is why they accepted me, I think. I know all of it. I mean, I *know*. I understand what is supposed to happen, but it just never has..."

I was surprised by the flood of words that escaped her, but I didn't interrupt.

"...I know all of the stories, and all of the lessons and rules and everything. And I can make her feel good—Nora, that is—and my Mistresses, of course. And I behave, even when I am punished. I can take it—do you know what I mean? They didn't think I would be able to take it; they thought I would break."

I could tell that she was proud of this fact, but her voice grew even softer as she continued, "Cassandra, I have never, never been able to feel it, to feel what it said in the books, the waves of it, the...fire of it, like silk, somehow."

Now she stopped and looked at me. "Nora said I

should be ashamed, that I should not have touched myself in that way, should not have indulged myself without her permission. And after all that she has done to try to make me...to try to help me. But, deep inside, I think she is happy for me, also, and wants to try again between us to see if I am now 'cured.' To see if it will happen every time now."

"But why?" I managed to break in. "Why was it me? What was it that you saw?" I couldn't imagine, couldn't come up with a satisfactory answer.

"Oh, Cassie." Suddenly she grinned and grabbed my hand. "You have no idea how you looked, while they poked and prodded and worked you. You were so embarrassed, but it overpowered you, and you let it. You released to them, you...*submitted*." She sighed. "It was beautiful."

I stared at her, not seeing, trying to picture myself as she said. In the center of that hateful table, their hands on me, their...toys, tools, fingers, all for the pleasure of the headmistresses and the cluster of girls, the group in the gallery. I could not imagine it as she described it—my tensed body, the way I tossed my hair, the slap of Mistress Corrine's hand on my naked skin—that it was a beautiful spectacle.

As if she knew what I was thinking, Jasmine insisted, "But it was...it was lovely, like you cannot possibly dream of. You released for them, Cassie. You let them do what they would with you, and they made you..." Again she stumbled. "It made you climax. I watched your body, the emotions running through you, the will to keep control but inability to do so. And then when you finally let it happen—*oh, Cassie, you cannot know*. It was truly beautiful, and I found myself squirming on the seat in the gallery, dying for a release, the release that you were having. I wanted to submit as you were submitting. I wanted to feel the beauty of it, the necessity of it. And when they let us go to our rooms, I headed directly to the bath and took care of that need, the burning there, rubbing, rubbing until it happened. And finally I understood what it was all about."

Another torrent of words from this shy sprite of a girl, and this one left her out of breath, desperate to make me understand. Instead of answering her, I bent forward and kissed her open mouth, just softly, letting her know that I *did* understand, that I did know how it felt, the first time, when the need builds up and makes the yearning unstoppable. I understood and I kissed her to let her know.

And she kissed me back.

And that is when the door opened and her Mistress Nora came down the stairs.

We were quick to part, and I was sure that she had not seen us, that the two swaying dresses had blocked her view of our indiscretion. At least, that's what I hoped.

She walked slowly down the stairs, lifting her

long pale-yellow dress up and away from her feet. Her dress made her look a bit like a walking daffodil, with the petal-soft panels of its skirt, along with her short swirl of hair and delicately limbed body. I watched her walk toward us, and I suddenly placed her from the living room the night before. Tall and willowy, her blonde hair cut in a bob just to her chin, her expression cold and somewhat frightening, not kind at all. She looked to me like a fairy-tale queen, a beautiful creature with a vile and blackened heart. She wore pearl drop earrings and a silver band on her middle finger, but no other jewelry. Her shoes were ballet flats of a satiny fabric, and the way she walked made me think that she might actually be a trained ballerina.

"Cassandra." She reached for my hand to help me stand. "I don't think we've properly met." There was a filament of gold burning within her light brown eyes, and I understood that she was jealous of me, jealous of the fact that I had excited her lover, when she herself had failed to do so. She regarded Jasmine, who had also stood and curtsied quickly before her Mistress, and then she turned those angry eyes back on me.

"You've made quite an impression on my little sister, haven't you?" she asked.

I stammered, not knowing how to answer. Jasmine looked at me, pleading with her eyes. I wasn't to know anything about her indiscretion, and I could not think how I was to respond. And inside myself, all I could think was that this was not a "kind" Mistress, as Jasmine had said. This was a woman ruled by a dark and envious soul.

"What do you mean, Mistress?" I finally managed to ask. "In what way?"

"Your spectacle last night." Nora's eyes were drilling holes into me. "The little show you put on during your examination." I felt her hatred burn me, and I wanted to grow angry myself, to tell her that I had no control over the events of the previous evening. In another life, in another world, I would have been able to speak back to her, to say all the things I was feeling. But, in this new life with its new rules, I simply bowed my head and said, "If I have offended you, Mistress, I am sorry for it." The words did not ring true to either of us—I was not able to conceal my contempt for her.

"No," she said, lifting my chin with one hand and forcing me to meet her eyes, "You are not sorry. Your voice tells me that. But I can assure you, young lady, you will be sorry for it, and soon enough."

She looked at the pile of washing on the floor, the dresses that Jasmine and I still had left to do.

"Finish up here, you two, and then meet me in the library." She headed back to the steps, but paused at the top. "*Before* tonight's festivities...do you understand?"

We both nodded at the same time, and said contritely, "Yes, Mistress."

"Good. I'll be waiting for you. Don't keep me too long."

Then she closed the door on us, plunging us back into silence. I saw the tears in Jasmine's eyes, tears for having angered her Mistress.

"What will she do?" I hurried to dip the next dress into the tub and began scrubbing.

"Give us a spanking," I suppose, Jasmine murmured. "Nothing too harsh, since she is not your big sister, and it is only your second day here. But a spanking, for sure."

I felt a tingle in the pit of my stomach at the word, and I thought again of Cici and her morning's punishment.

"We must hurry," Jasmine said when she saw I had gone daydreamy. "We don't have much time. We don't want to make her wait any longer than necessary—believe me, Cassie."

I followed her lead, working faster through the pile of dresses. But in my head I was lost, Nora's voice echoing, "You'll soon be sorry." And then Jasmine's: "A spanking, I suppose."

A spanking.

Lindsay Welsh

A VICTORIAN ROMANCE

Dearest Alicia,

Such a time of wonder for me, and of change! You know about all which I set forth in my last letter to you; and as Madelaine had said, I went to my bedchamber that night, but sleep was not to be mine. How could it be, when my head was so filled with the events that had transpired!

I recalled her tender kisses, and the touch of her fingers upon my naked bosom, and how natural it was to me when she undressed me, and joined me upon her bed. And as the moon rose in the clear night sky outside my window, so did my passion rise within me, and I knew finally that this was what I was meant to be. A "lesbian" was the word she had used, and indeed, if that be the name then that is what I am. You, dear Alicia, are the first to know.

As I thought about Madelaine, once again that delicious hot feeling crept in between my legs, with its prickly warmth and its relentless pressure aching to be relieved. I hardly knew what I was doing, for soon I found that my hand had made its own way down to that place, and my fingers were busy there. Alicia, I had never done such a thing in my life, but it felt so good to touch myself. I was warm, and my fingers came away wet, with such a nectar upon them that was an unusual but welcome perfume to my nostrils. I was not exactly sure what I was doing, but I did know to touch myself where the pleasure felt strongest; and soon I was breathing hard just as I had done when Madelaine's fingers tarried in that very same spot.

There was one place that was supreme in its pleasure, a very fleshy little button that made me gasp whenever it was touched. Of course I paid especial attention to this particular item, and rubbed it at first gently, and then much more firmly; and even as I did, I could not stop myself from moving, for my hips pushed against my fingers almost independently of me. I could not stop writhing at my own touch, as unbelievable as that sounds, for it awakened in me desires that I did not know I had the power to produce. And then all of it peaked together as it had when Madelaine had touched me, and I gasped and cried out with the joy I had given to myself; and my arms tingled and my whole body swooned at the momentum of the pleasure released from this warm, moist spot between my lower limbs. I was wet with perspiration, and gasping for air, and as I calmed down and relaxed into that sweet feather bed I knew that nothing would ever be the same for me again, now that I had begun to unlock the secrets of this body I had unknowingly occupied yet had also ignored for so many years.

I would urge you, Alicia, to try this for yourself, to lie back in your bed and understand the feelings that you are capable of creating with only your little hand and your imagination. It is such a lovely thing to do to oneself, and I am not at all ashamed to admit to you, my dearest friend, that I enjoyed the special sensations not once but thrice that night, and finally fell asleep just before dawn, knowing that I could never be the same again. I could love myself, I could love other women, and my journey was just beginning!

Finally a knock came at the door; it was the maid, informing me that my breakfast would be laid out very soon if I cared to take it. She assisted me in dressing, and I noticed that I had been allowed to sleep much later, for it was almost eight o'clock. I then followed her into the dining room; but to my surprise, my Aunt Lydia and Madame Killey were not there; there were only two places set at the large table; and at one of those places sat Madelaine.

I went into the room, and Madelaine got up, and kissed me sweetly upon my forehead. "I am so happy to see you this morning," she said, and I admitted that I was thrilled also by her presence in the room; and at this news, she dispensed with her proper decorum and hugged me heartily to her. I could feel her lips upon my hair and I reveled in the touch of her arms about me, and I hugged her back with as much sincerity as she had shown to me.

We sat down, and our coffee was brought to us—strong but containing a large portion of warm milk, in the style that the French prefer—and then a loaf of crusty new bread, and cheese and fruit, and other delicacies for us to dine upon. But we did very little eating, and much talking, for there was so much to discuss and I was glad that she was there to speak with me.

She looked at me, and smiled, and asked almost shyly, "Did you have much to think about last night, Elaine?"

Of course I had to tell her all that had happened to me, what my decision was and how it had been made; and I even let the word slip from my lips, for I told her that the term I had learned from her—"lesbian"—would truly now apply to me as well, for I knew that this was the path I wished to pursue. Then I spoke in a low voice, and I knew my cheeks were a rich scarlet when I told her of how my hand had found its way to the area she had so lovingly caressed, and that my fingers had done for me what her hand also had done—but Alicia, as you are my witness, my cheeks were not red from shame but from excitement, for there was no disgust associated with my actions, but only complete happiness that I had finally discovered what had escaped me for so long.

Madelaine was glad for me as well, and she admitted that she had not thought I might experiment in such a way so quickly, yet she was excited that I had done so on my own. "Most women go through life as prisoners of their very own bodies," she said. "They see their bodies as things that must be fed, and bathed, and which offer them nothing in return but a means to walk around!" she laughed. "Many women, unhappily, go from the cradle to the grave not realizing that their bodies are capable of producing such pleasure, for they have not been informed of this, and they are ignorant and even afraid to touch themselves, for they have been told that it is not proper or clean. What nonsense! Why would a woman spend her entire life this way, when she can know such joy and desire as we do? How can it be sinful, when it is so obvious that we were created with such a capability? This is why I am so happy for you, Elaine. Never again will you live a life of boredom, of repressed desire, of frustration, for the door has been opened for you, and you have decided to step outside of it!"

We finished our breakfast, and were drinking our last cups of milky coffee, when I asked Madelaine where my Auntie and her friend were.

"They have gone off by themselves today," Mad-elaine said. "They wished for me to come to you and they thought it best if they were to leave us alone. They understand that this can be a difficult time, and they decided to pursue their own interests today, independent of ourselves."

I am afraid my jaw dropped open at this point, Alicia, and I must have looked unusual with my eyes wide open. "Then," I said in barely a whisper, "they know all that has transpired between us?"

Madelaine took my hand in her warm fingers, and stroked my arm lovingly. "Indeed they do," she said. "Do not be shocked, dear Elaine, for it was their idea that I come to you, and introduce you to these joys. Your Auntie loves you so very much, and wants the best for you; and she knows me well, and knows that I would never push or frighten someone into something they do not want, or force them to go against their own desires; my way is to show young women what is available to them, and let them decide for themselves if it is the way they will choose. I am happy to say that you did so, and your Auntie is glad of this as well, for it would break her heart should you be one of those women who go through life without a single pleasure, with no enjoyment at all."

"Then Auntie is—" I could not finish the

sentence, for although this had gone through my mind a number of times throughout the night, it was still difficult to fully comprehend in the bright light of morning, with my beloved Madelaine by my side.

"She is, and Madame Killey also," Madelaine said. "She asked me to tell this to you, if you so inquired, for she thought it might be easier coming from a friend, and not your Mother's sister whom you have known as your Auntie all of your life. Your Auntie has cast off the bonds that strangle so many of our sisters, and force them into a drab existence. She has many friends, many dear friends who love her as much as any could, myself among them, and you will meet a number of them upon this trip. I am only so happy that I could be the first."

She then took me into her arms, and I almost overflowed with emotion at that point, Alicia, with all that had been revealed to me. I was so happy for my Auntie, that she indeed knew of the pleasures which I had received the previous day. I was thrilled that Madelaine had told me, and her honesty along with her obvious affection for me touched me deeply. Finally, I was overjoyed that my Auntie would not keep her life a secret from me, but would insist that I share in the ways she knew so well, and that she had found for me a teacher as kind and loving as Madelaine to initiate me into her secret world.

"Madelaine," I said, "yesterday you told me

that there were many ways that women could love each other. You showed me one; I discovered another upon my own. Am I to believe that these two methods are all that are available to us?"

"Definitely not," she smiled, and she got up and took my hand; and together we went through the long hallways toward the bedchamber I had slept in that night. You know, Alicia, that once a truth is made evident, then all of the suspicions surrounding it become as clear as crystal to eyes that were once blinded to them; and I had to laugh at myself as we walked down the hallway. Madelaine inquired as to the source of my merriment.

"The first night we were here, my Aunt Lydia and Madame Killey shared a bedchamber," I said. "I felt so sorry for my Auntie, for I had a beautiful big bed all to myself; and I believed that there could be no empty chambers left in the house, for why else would my Auntie have to share one with her hostess? I felt guilt at knowing that I could stretch out alone in my bed, while Auntie would have to be content with only half of hers. Now I cannot believe how foolish I was, that I could not have guessed at the reason!" Madelaine laughed also, and so we made our way to the feather bed that I knew would no longer be mine alone.

Madelaine closed the bedchamber door softly behind us; and we were alone once more. This time she very slowly undressed me, and I simply stood, enjoying the touch of her fingers upon my skin. As much as I had enjoyed our first encounter in her private apartments, this was much nicer again; for there was no hesitation on her part, no questions on mine; both of us were aware of what was happening, and both of us wanted it as badly as the other, and instead of being confused and asking what she was doing to me, I needed only to stand and thrill in her attention to me, and long to touch her in return and perhaps show her even a portion of the pleasure which was so unselfishly being offered to me.

This time Madelaine allowed me to undress her, which again was a very new experience for me. Like you, Alicia, I have very seldom dressed or undressed myself; I was always assisted by Nursie, or by a maid. So I must admit that I fumbled a great deal as I performed my appointed task, and even I was not fully aware of the number of buttons and laces that had to be unfastened before a garment could be removed! I suppose it is just another indication of how we press upon others to look after us; and I am therefore not surprised that so few women have ever learned the pleasures they are capable of providing for themselves, when so few of us can even take off our own garments without the help of another.

But even in my fumbling, I enjoyed my experience much more than I could have imagined. Madelaine has the smooth, milky-white skin that so many Frenchwomen enjoy; you cannot imagine it without seeing it, Alicia, for it is so unlike ours, almost creamy in its consistency, and all but translucent for it is so very feminine. She had smoothed upon it some type of exotic lotion, which had a delicious flowery scent that could only be detected occasionally, for it was very soft and understated; and I hovered about her, trying to breathe it in. I soon found myself placing tiny kisses upon the skin as I uncovered it, and she smiled and made a purring sound in her throat, to signal her approval of my touch upon her. You may one day know how good it feels to know that you are pleasing someone else in this manner.

Very shortly she was entirely unclothed as well, and once again I was able to admire the beauty of her body. I was comparing it to mine, for the naked female form is one that I have never had the opportunity to study; and Madelaine understood this, and inquired as to what I knew of women. I had to admit that my knowledge was woefully inadequate compared to hers.

She bade me lie upon the bed, which I did; she then went to the dresser, and returned with a small hand-held looking glass. She placed two pillows under my head, so that I might see, and then she gently pushed my legs apart, so that the dark spot between my legs was exposed to her; and then she placed the looking glass in such a way that it reflected this area, and could be easily and fully viewed by me.

Indeed, Alicia, this was a wonder to me, for I had never seen such a thing, not even with Madelaine, for on our first night she had concentrated on my body alone; and as this part of me was always hidden from view, and I had never thought to train a looking glass upon it as she had, it was a mystery to me even as I carried it about with me. At first it appeared very confusing, and very unusual; dark, with a lot of hair upon it, and I did not know exactly what to make of it. But together we examined it, Madelaine and myself, both with the mirror and later, with Mad-elaine showing me the same parts upon her own body.

She called the dark spot a "cunny," and said that it was only one of the many names that might be used to indicate it; but this was her favorite, for it sounded soft and cuddly. She showed me that it was covered by fleshy lips on either side, from which sprouted my hair, and that these lips could be pulled apart with the fingers; and when she did so, I felt the same stirrings at her touch that she had created in me the day before, and that I had produced for myself that evening.

There was a fleshy bulb at the top, and when Madelaine touched it, my whole body was warmed from within, and I knew right away that this had been the seat of the pleasure that I had known. Her fingers then slipped further down, and she showed me that there was a tunnel—a tunnel into my very body, if you can imagine that, Alicia—and she twisted her finger all about its rim, and when she brought it away, she showed me how her fingertip was wet. She told me that my body was producing this sweet juice, and that it was an indication of the need for pleasure which she assured me I was soon to receive. Then she showed me how she might insert her finger into this tunnel, and I felt an inner warmth as she did so; and to my surprise, I could feel her digit within me, moving about me. It was an unusual sensation, but most appreciated; and then Madelaine bade me give her my hand, and she had me insert my own finger into this tunnel. Alicia, it was as if I were touching wet velvet, and the walls of this tunnel pressed heartily upon my finger even as I inserted it; and Madelaine told me that in the future we would give this special tunnel its own pleasure; but I kept my finger inside of it for a long time, for I could not believe how velvety soft it was, and I was amazed that such a place had existed in my body for as many years as I had been alive and yet I had been completely ignorant of its presence. I did not understand why we were kept so untutored, and told Madelaine so; and she replied that most women knew all about keeping a household, and the latest fashions, and how to sew and paint and read, but knew absolutely naught about the body they would be within all of their lives; and I was saddened for them, but happy to know that such ignorance was no longer to be my lot.

Thus we moved farther down, and Madelaine

showed me how I might stir myself by gently moving my fingers along my fleshy lips, and then she caressed my bottom, and how lovely did her hands move upon me. Then she took the looking glass from my hands, and said that it was time I learned more of the ways of love that she was only too happy to teach me.

She reached down, and I did not understand why she did so; but then I realized that she was laying sweet kisses upon those love-swollen cunny-lips, and how wonderful it felt! I told her that I had never imagined such a thing, but she said that it was very common, and that once I had felt its exquisite stirrings I would long for more. Then she continued to kiss me, and my flesh cried out for more; whereupon she stuck out her tongue, and proceeded to lick at me.

You might find this shocking, Alicia, and indeed I did at first, for it seemed such an unusual thing for her to do. But my shock lasted only a moment, for it seemed that nothing had never been done to me before to create such a feeling inside of me. I could feel that my tunnel was filled with the juices of wanting that she had showed me upon her finger, and far from being repulsed by it, Madelaine was positively thrilled, for she licked it up and pronounced it delicious, and proceeded to lick all around my lips and on the inside of my thighs, and I could only moan with desire for her. Then she went to that fleshy bulb, the one I spoke to you of before; and when her tongue touched that sweet knob, it was as if something inside of me broke loose, and I gasped and moaned as she lapped at me faster and faster. Before I knew it, Alicia, my hands were in her untethered hair, and I was pressing her face into me, harder, harder, for I simply could not get enough of her tongue upon my cunny, and I did not ever want her to stop!

It was as if my whole body was in a whirlwind, with these emotions coursing through my blood as she moved upon me with her hot tongue, and then I was drawn into the middle of the storm, and I forgot everything as a wave rushed through me and took me with it, and left me weak and tingling in its wake. Madelaine smiled, and told me that I had "spent"; and it was indeed an accurate word, for I was completely drawn, and my limbs felt heavy with love and desire, and the antics she had played upon me with her fingers were nothing compared to the blissful feelings I had from the tip of her small pink tongue.

I caught my breath, and Madelaine held me; and then I told her something that made her very happy, for indeed I desired to confer upon her the pleasure which she had brought upon me. She asked if I were sure; but how else was I to respond, except in the affirmative? I had never wanted anything so badly as to taste her as she had tasted me.

She stretched out upon the bed, then, and I moved as she had, to position myself between her legs. Her cunny was a slightly lighter shade than mine, and the hair was soft and long, and I spent a great deal of time just looking at it, and running my fingers over the lips and touching the soft button that had been the seat of my own pleasure. Then my desire overcame me, and I bent down and touched my tongue greedily to her swollen sex.

The taste is difficult to describe, Alicia, for mere ink cannot do it justice. Imagine, then, that a thousand bees visited a thousand flowers, and each took a drop of precious nectar from the petals, and transformed it into a honey that tasted of the flowers but was sweeter still. That was the juice which trickled from her tunnel, and I loved it so much that I had to place my fingers in the puddle, and smear it all over her sex, so that I might taste it in every crevice that my tongue had reason to explore.

Alicia, you know as well as I do that in almost every instance of our lives, we have to be taught—taught to use a knife and fork, taught to read, taught to behave properly in polite company. But no teaching was necessary for me on this occasion. It was as if an animal instinct had taken me over, and I was swept along helplessly as a shell pressed by the tide. I knew from Madelaine's tongue upon me the spots that would feel the best, and I made my way toward these, listening to her groans of passion and feeling her soft hands upon my neck. I licked at her cunny as she had licked at mine, and my tongue explored all of her flesh and then made its way to that sweet knob at the top; and when I had given all of myself over to it, Madelaine reacted in the same manner which I had, and groaned and thrashed about on the bed, and cried out in her sweet rush of relief, and she spent herself as I had; and I arose, my lips shiny and sweet with her heavy perfumed nectar, and my whole body glad of what I had done for this extraordinary friend.

We stayed together on the bed for some time, wrapped in each other's arms. I had many questions regarding what had happened, and Madelaine was more than happy to answer them for me; and I asked if this was all that we could share and she laughed and said no, that this was only the beginning. Oh, Alicia, I feel as if I am still in school, and have just been taught my A-B-Cs, but have looked over and seen volumes of Shakespeare and Chaucer waiting upon the shelf and have realized that one day I will comprehend them no matter how long it takes. Except that in this case, there will be no dreary drills, no endless pages, and the occasional crack of the headmistress's ruler when a task is not completed to her satisfaction; for I have a teacher who is both kind and loving, and lessons that can never be taught or learned improperly, but enjoyed no matter how the class progresses!

We did not spend all day in the bedchamber for, as Madelaine told me, there is more to this lifestyle than the sharing of physical pleasure; there is warm companionship, and friendship, and a thousand little things all joined together in love and harmony to make this path of life a most joyous and incredible one. And so we dressed, and took the carriage, and saw more of this amazing city, although I now saw it through eyes opened fully; and when we returned, Aunt Lydia and Madame Killey were waiting for us, and in my joy I could only hold my Auntie while tears coursed down my cheeks, for my heart was so filled I thought it might burst upon me even as she hugged me, and called me her own.

Your loving friend,
Elaine

Dearest Alicia,

This letter brings with it a pair of conflicting emotions, both of them extremely strong; one is sorrow, the other great joy, and of course I will explain both of them in due course.

The sorrow came about when Auntie gently informed me that our time in Paris was about to come to a close, for another leg of our journey was about to begin.

I had known from the very beginning that Paris was to be just our first stop, and at that time, I knew that I would explore the city carefully, and then pack my trunks eagerly and prepare for our next expedition. But that, of course, was before I had met Madelaine.

I must admit that I sobbed in her arms, for the thought of leaving her behind was so repugnant to me. But in her calm French way, she wiped away my tears and hugged me to her, and assured me that such a parting would not be a good-bye, but simply a pause in our relationship. She was so composed and mature that I felt ashamed at my childish outburst, and I dried my eyes with my handkerchief and tried to smile.

"Do you not realize," she said, "that your Auntie plans to return to Paris and make it your final stop before your trip back to London?"

Alicia, in my sorrow, this fact had completely slipped my mind. Indeed, our plans were to come back to Madame Killey's before we crossed the English Channel again, and it would be my opportunity to hold my Madelaine again.

"You must remember that I have never had the opportunity to leave my homeland," Madelaine said, and I felt a twinge as I realized she was actually jealous of my adventures. "When you return, you will be able to tell me all about these magnificent countries which I have never seen, and which you will visit shortly."

"Then for your sake, I will go gladly," I told her. "I am still not happy to leave you behind, but I will describe the sights for you, and send letters to you, and purchase souvenirs which I think will delight you."

She stayed the night with me, in Madame

Killey's house, and all of us retired early for the evening. Aunt Lydia said it was because we would rise at dawn to commence our travels, but all of us smiled as she said so, because we knew that there was far more to her comment than merely the hour of her awakening. Madelaine and I proved this a short time later in my room, when we started with simple kisses and hugs, and ended up in a hot, passionate embrace with Madelaine applying her fingers to my hungry cunny while I licked at hers until both of us spent with a fury that surprised us.

It was all too soon that the maid knocked upon the door, and reluctantly we rose and dressed for an early breakfast. Then, while the sun was still fresh in the sky, I hugged Madame Killey, and kissed my Madelaine good-bye, and got into the coach with my Auntie Lydia. I tried so hard, Alicia, but the tears still came, and I was quick to notice that Madelaine's eyes were wet as well and that she occasionally touched at them with her handkerchief. The night before, I had asked her if she had introduced many of Madame Killey's friends to the joys of womanly love; and she replied in the affirmative, but quickly assured me that I had been her very favorite. Alicia, that is the sort of thing that is easily said amongst people who wish to curry favor with others; but in the case of Madelaine, I truly believe that she was sincere when she said so, and no matter how many women I shall meet or how many friends I have, I will always be grateful that it was she who introduced me into this brave new world.

The coach left us at the station, to wait for the train that will take us to Switzerland. Auntie told me that we shall stay in the city of Bern for a while (did I mention, dear Alicia, that it is the capital of the country we journey to?) and then we shall visit Italy, and Spain, and finally go back to Paris before returning to London. How exciting, and how amazing that a young woman such as myself will have such an opportunity for such adventures.

While we were waiting, I took the opportunity to examine my surroundings closely; and in the course of doing so, I met a young Frenchwoman of my age, who spoke my language, and who struck up a conversation with me while we waited. She said her name was Courtney, and that she was traveling with a friend of her Mother's for a chaperone, and that she would ride the train to Bern as we would; but in that Swiss city, she would change trains and from there travel to Austria, to stay with her aunt and uncle while she attended school there. It was her first visit outside of her homeland as well, and with our age and our travels in common, we had a grand time speaking with each other. Although I had expected the time to drag along, it fairly flew as we chatted, and before I knew it, the sharp French commands were called out by the stationmaster, and with a great clattering and whistle and exhaust of steam, the train was waiting for us to board.

To my disappointment, Courtney and her chaperone were located in a separate coach; but Auntie assured me that once the journey began, we would be free to move about the train and if seats were available, we might have the opportunity to sit together. As our trip would last over the night, when viewing from the windows would be impossible, I looked forward to the diversion.

The countryside was extremely beautiful, and I spent much of the day just watching the scenery as it raced by my window; and to my surprise, the day did go by quickly, and when darkness fell, my eyes grew heavy and the thought of retiring to my berth seemed a favorable one. Alicia, do I sound like the same young woman who attended a party that ended at dawn? I laughed to think of it, even as Auntie and I made our way to the sleeping-car.

The conductor looked at our tickets, and led the way down the long aisle to show us to our berths. But it was cause for embarrassment, for there had been a mix-up at the station with our tickets, and while each berth held two beds, one atop the other, our tickets indicated that my bed was in one berth, and Auntie's in another!

The conductor's face was very red, and he apologized and assured us that the matter would be rectified very quickly, with both Auntie and myself sharing the same berth. But just at that moment, the owners of the corresponding tickets appeared in the sleeping-car, and who should it be but Courtney and her chaperone!

My new friend and I had quite a surprise at this turn of events, even as the poor conductor grew even more flustered. But my Auntie, who was very merry in the face of this adversity, looked at the chaperone and said, "Do you think it would bother you to remain with your ticket as it is?"

"I do not understand," the woman said. "Well," Aunt Lydia replied, "as you know, your ward and my niece became fast friends while waiting at the station; and now their tickets indicate that they are to share their sleeping-quarters. I will gladly exchange my ticket with yours, if you wish to remain with your charge; but I should think that sharing a berth would be more like a party for these new friends; we will be only in the next berth, so they would be well represented by their elders; and as for me, I am a quiet sleeper, and hear nothing once I am asleep, and to retire in one bed while you retire in the other would be no hardship for me."

The woman thought about this for a moment, and then said, "Well, I cannot see any harm in it; and madam, if it bothers you not to take the upper berth, then I shall be happy to take the lower."

"I have no quarrel with that," Aunt Lydia replied; and the woman turned to Courtney, and admonished her to behave and not to keep me up all night chattering, although it was obvious to both my Auntie and Courtney's companion that the likelihood of such an occurrence was not only expected but unavoidable. Perhaps, Alicia, this older lady was recalling her youth, and similar experiences, and wishing her young ward well.

In due time I was in my sleeping-clothes, and I got into the lower berth. It was a comfortable bed, naturally smaller than that which I was accustomed to, but the wall behind me and the curtains in front made it a very cozy nest, and the bed linens were fresh and very warm; and this delightful private alcove, combined with the steady rocking of the train, was a most enjoyable experience.

Courtney, also in her nightclothes, came inside the curtains and climbed the small ladder to the bed over me. We could, with great difficulty, hear Aunt Lydia bidding Courtney's chaperone good night in the berth beside ours, and we realized that it would be very difficult for them to hear us; and so we naturally continued the conversations we had entered into earlier during the day.

Courtney asked several questions of me, many of them personal, and I thought it might be something that French girls learn at school, for I had been asked virtually the same questions by everyone I had met on my trip: where are you from, what are your interests, have you any sisters or brothers, are you engaged, and (when I answer in the negative), have you ever had a beau? Once again I replied in the negative; for although I considered her as such, it might have not been in the best light to name Madelaine to such an exalted position as that of my "beau."

There was a bit of a pause, and then Courtney said, "Elaine, I am not comfortable here."

I was surprised, for I was as cozy as a kitten curled on a pillow, and I said, "My bed is quite soft, Courtney; is yours different from mine?"

"It is not the mattress, Elaine," she replied. "I do not like the height of the bed. I am afraid that I shall fall out throughout the night."

"I shall trade with you, then," I offered.

"Oh, but I am cold as well," she said. "It would be best if I had a companion. Elaine, may I share your berth?"

Alicia, I am sure you may know my answer; and in moments, Courtney had descended the ladder, and I pushed aside the bed linen and bade her enter. It was very crowded in the small bed, but I was overjoyed at having my new friend beside me; to have her warm body close to me, and smell the delicious subtle perfume she wore.

She snuggled in with me, and remarked on the coziness of our position; and because she was experiencing difficulty obtaining a comfortable place to lay her arm, she requested permission to place it around me. I accepted; and she placed her hand close to my bosom; and we spent a few moments discussing various items of interest; and Alicia, I thought it was at first my imagination that her fingers were straying across my body, but very shortly I had no doubt that her hand was caressing me!

I must have started with surprise, for she drew her fingers back; but then she whispered in my ear, "Does it bother you that I touch you?"

Indeed it did not; and very quietly, I told her that her hand upon this private area was welcome, and in an even lower tone, I let her know that because of my dear friend Madelaine, I now considered myself to be of the lesbian persuasion. At this point she kissed my cheek, and said, "I was beginning to think that I would never meet another on this trip!"

Yes, Alicia, it is true; my new friend enjoyed the same pleasures I did. Aware of my preference, she kissed me deeply, and I returned the caresses of her tongue with my own; and shortly we were moaning softly as our hands found each other's breasts under our light sleeping-clothes. She had a way of pinching my nipples gently and twisting them softly that sent the now-familiar chills throughout my entire body, and I begged her to continue in this manner, until I could feel my cunny juices flowing and thoroughly wetting the spot between my legs that I had so learned to please.

It was difficult, due to the intimate nature of the small bed, but Courtney managed to pull my nightclothes down to expose my bosom, and she positioned herself so that her sweet mouth was over me; and then she licked and sucked at me until my nipples were hard, and stood out straight from my body; and my only regret was that she could not spend her attention upon both of them at the same time, for as one was pleasured, the other was left wanting.

She pulled up her skirt and I did not have to be prompted in my duty. My fingers found her sweet tunnel immediately, and it was as wet as my own; and my hand was soon soaked with this delicious nectar, and my fingers slipped over her flesh easily.

It was quickly obvious that mutual pleasure was to be ours, for Courtney pulled up my own night-dress, and placed her hand in that area which was throbbing with my sweet hot desire. "You are so wet," she murmured to me, and I told her that her own body was producing copious amounts of this wine itself, and she smiled and kissed me again.

She called my sex a "mound," and as she rubbed it, she entered into a steady conversation, whispered into my ear; and while I cannot reproduce all of it here, she said things such as, "Your pretty little mound just loves the feel of my fingers, for it is so wet, so juicy; I love to have my hand inside of it, to rub your sex and make you feel so hot; please, dear Elaine, rub my mound harder, put your fingers inside of me; right there, oh yes, rub me there, for it feels so good; etc., etc." The effect upon me was to heighten my own excitement, and I loved to listen to her even as her fingers danced their waltz over my hot, wet flesh.

Her speech also had the effect of spurring me on to increase my own work upon her cunny, and she told me that she liked to be treated with firmness, even a bit of roughness; and I pressed my fingers hard against her swollen sex, and probed with my thumb on the little button that is the seat of our pleasure; and she responded by gasping and writhing about in our small bed. And Alicia, you may find this shocking, but her excitement transferred itself to me, and I desired firmness and roughness alike; and it seemed that she could not rub hard enough on me, but that I wanted more, and harder.

I was sure that the whole train must know what we were doing, for we were now gasping, and moving about on the bed, and our hands were moving as quickly and as firmly as they possibly could. My body was as tight as I could ever imagine, and I begged my friend for release; and so she selected my fleshy button, and pressed upon it and pushed it from side to side; and I spent with a force that erupted throughout my entire being. Courtney kept her hand upon my cunny, which now throbbed with a draining satisfaction, and I rubbed at her until she also released her tension, and gushed over my hand as she reached her climax.

It took a long time before we were able to calm down, and stop gasping; but even then, my cunny was tender and satisfied, and my friend gently laid her hand over it and cupped it tenderly, and created within me a feeling of complete gratification.

Courtney did not return to her bed, but we made room for each other, and lay cuddled in each other's arms as we told each other how happy we were to have met. She was extremely surprised that my Auntie Lydia had taken me on this journey with the obvious intention of introducing me to this life-style; and I pondered aloud if my Auntie and my friend's chaperone were enjoying the same type of arrangement that we had shared.

"Oh, heavens no!" Courtney exclaimed, and then laughed at the idea of her mother's friend enjoying such forbidden pleasures. "Madame S—— would sooner believe in flying horses than in women giving each other satisfaction, I am sure. She is one of those poor unenlightened souls who believes that sex is only for procreation and never for delight. I will feel sorry for her, and for all like her, all my life."

"Then my Auntie will simply sleep this evening," I said.

Courtney laughed, with some mischief. "I doubt that very much," she said. "Madame S—— has one major accomplishment in her life, and it is that she can snore louder than anyone I have ever heard!"

We both giggled like schoolgirls, and snuggled into each other's arms; and with the warmth of the blankets, and my friend's arms around me, and the gentle constant rocking of the train, I felt as comforted as a small child, and slept as if I were oblivious to the world. The next morning, refreshed and relaxed, both Courtney and I chatted constantly throughout breakfast; Madame S—— was bright-eyed, if quiet; but poor Aunt Lydia's eyes were half-closed with sleep, and her manner was irritable as she sipped at her coffee. Later through the morning I asked how she had slept; and she gave a sideways glance at Madame S——, unseen by the source of her displeasure, and said that there had been considerable noise upon the train, so it had been difficult for her to sleep. Madame S—— very innocently said that she had heard no such noises, and had slept very well; and although I am sure that at any other time, Auntie would have been pleased for me had I told her about Courtney and myself, under the circumstances I felt it best to hold my tongue, and instead tell my secret to this letter instead.

Your dearest friend,
Elaine

Dearest Alicia,

It is still difficult for me to believe that I, a young woman who had seldom left the street she was born in prior to this trip, am now writing to you from the second country she has visited so far. Yes, I am currently in the land of the Swiss, and what a beautiful place it is.

Our locomotive arrived at the train station, and while all four of us descended from the train together, Courtney and her chaperone remained behind, while Auntie and I watched our trunks being loaded into the carriage that was waiting for us. I hugged my new friend close to me, and kissed her good-bye as friends do when parting, although I desired to kiss her deeply with all the passion within me, and I knew that she felt the same. Her chaperone Madame S—— smiled at us, thinking us simply girlfriends who were sorry to leave each other; while Aunt Lydia looked at me with one raised eyebrow, and a questioning look which I understood at once. Still I gave her no indication, for I knew the wrath of a woman who had not slept the night, and to gloat with the fact that I had enjoyed a special love while Auntie watched the ceiling and listened to the dulcet tones of her companion—I am sure it would have been too much for her to take! Courtney and I exchanged our addresses and promised to write each other, and then my new friend and I parted.

The carriage waiting for us had been sent by Fraulein Kant. Alicia, it seems that my Auntie has friends all over the world, and all of them rather successful, for the vehicle that waited for us was a very fine one, decorated liberally with polished brass and lanterns, with a hot-blooded team in shiny harness to draw it. The coachman and foot-man wore expensive uniforms, and they bowed low to us and held the carriage doors for us as we ascended. Then, with a final wave to my friend Courtney, I was off for yet another experience in a new city.

Auntie had visited Switzerland many, many times, and as we rode through the streets from the train station, she told me several interesting things about the city I was now visiting. The city of Bern has been the capital of Switzerland for only forty years, although it is almost seven hundred years old, as Auntie informed me. It is a beautiful city, its buildings made of light colored stone, and they line the roads with hardly a space between them; and each of them has many windows to catch the sunlight, all with shutters brightly painted, and window-boxes which were filled with all manner of tiny, brightly colored blooms.

This country is more like an amalgamation of the countries surrounding it, and as we rode through the busy streets I must have heard a half-dozen tongues spoken; but the primary one is German, with French and English heard after it. It is a very sharp, guttural language, not like the lilting French which I had grown accustomed to; but nevertheless interesting to the ears, and I longed to learn it.

I asked her the nature of the lady we will be staying with; and Auntie replied that Fraulein Kant was a good friend of hers, whom she had met while Fraulein Kant was visiting a mutual friend in London. By the gentle way in which Auntie described her friend, I knew immediately, even without being told, the circumstances under which they had become friends. Alicia, experience is a most amazing thing; not only does it increase one's perception to that which is in front of one, but it also allows one to understand that which is only implied.

You must also understand that another of the benefits of this journey was that I had Auntie's full attention; and I had come to know her more in the last week than I had during the nineteen years of my life. She likewise had come to know me; and I soon discovered that we now shared an unspoken language, shared unmade gestures, and a secret that we could both have and comprehend without it even being mentioned by either of us. So when I asked Auntie whether Fraulein Kant had young friends close to my age, there was no need to be explicit or even to lift an eyebrow in her direction; for Auntie knew precisely what I was truly trying to inquire of her.

"Fraulein Kant is in the same situation I now happily find myself in," Aunt Lydia said. "Many years ago, her brother and his wife were killed in a horrible fire, and their daughter Helga was left without a family. Fraulein Kant took her niece in and raised her as her own, and Helga still lives with her."

"How old is she?" I inquired.

"Twenty-one," Auntie smiled, and my heart leaped. Alicia, could it be true that I would find another friend to satisfy me the way Madelaine and Courtney had? I looked at Auntie, but she was carefully examining the scenery from our carriage, and I kept my peace, but secretly prayed that this would not be a holiday for Auntie alone!

Alicia, our final destination turned out to be a

street known as the Junkerngasse—the names are so strange to my English tongue—which Auntie told me was the most prestigious avenue in the entire city. And we are to be guests here! Dear friend, I knew I would see so much on this trip, but I did not for a moment imagine that I would be treated as finely as royalty while I did so.

It certainly seemed as if kings and queens lived upon this street, judging by the hugeness and the grandeur of the homes there. Finally our carriage turned at the entrance to one, which seemed to me to be the largest upon the street, and stopped for us at the door.

I have always heard that the German people are a very cold and reserved race, but Fraulein Kant immediately proved me wrong as soon as she appeared. With a squeal of delight, she grasped my Auntie to her bosom and hugged her hard, murmuring in her own language and pressing kisses upon my Auntie, which were returned with as much enthusiasm. I could only stand by silently watching them. Then it was my turn to be introduced, and Fraulein Kant was just as demonstrative with me, hugging me to her and kissing both my cheeks in the French manner.

I had my opportunity to meet Fraulein Kant's niece at dinner, which was held in the huge dining room, and I felt a little overwhelmed with only four of us at the enormous mahogany table, waited on by what seemed like an army of servants—all of them female—who filled our glasses, adjusted our napkins, and brought to us anything we desired. Shall I ever become accustomed again to my ordinary life back in London?

I expect that I had my own picture of what Helga would look like; and judging by her name, I had envisioned a plump, ruddy-cheeked, rough-hewn peasant girl with her blonde hair in braids. How wrong had I been, Alicia! Only the blonde portion of my vision was correct, but that blonde hair was loose, in a carefree, windswept style that was so foreign to my eyes (being so used to all women with their hair coiffured so painstakingly, and held with many pins and much yarn) and at the same time, inviting to the point that I longed to reach out to touch it. It was so blonde as to be almost white.

She was tall and willowy, yet shapely, and her body was accentuated by the light clothes which she wore; a dress with a jacket, yet the skirt hung gently, without the discomfort of petticoats beneath. When I was introduced, she shook my hand with enthusiasm, and her smile was repeated in her deliciously blue eyes. "I am sure we will be good friends," she said, her English accented with her German heritage; and I could only reply that I was sure it would be so.

Indeed, Alicia, as I ate my dinner I could not help but steal glances at her, for she had captivated me. Have I told you that I have continued to wear my underthings as Madelaine taught me—that is, not at all? Yes, for as shocking as it is to imagine, I wore my skirts and my petticoats and nothing more; my cunny was as naked under my clothing as if I were newborn, and it rubbed against my skirts in such an enticing manner when I squirmed in my chair. Alicia, I declare, I shall never wear underdrawers again, as long as I live; and if you should only try it once, you shall vow this as well.

But I digress. The reason for squirming in my chair was, certainly, my newfound friend. She spoke little, and I did the same; for Aunt Lydia and Fraulein Kant held most of the discussion at dinner, not having seen each other for more than a year. This time, having a knowledge that I did not have when I arrived at my last hostess's home, their affection for each other was as obvious as if it were written on their foreheads, and I smiled to myself and wished my Auntie well for the glorious evening I knew she would share.

My cunny was hot and throbbing when I stood up, and I suppose I was almost overcome with jealousy when it was finally time to retire; for Aunt Lydia and Fraulein Kant were to share a bedchamber (of course I was not told as much, but I certainly knew nevertheless), but the servant led me to a room of my own, while Helga wished me good night and walked down the long hall to a chamber of her own.

I undressed and got into my nightdress; and this enormous bed was surely the most comfortable yet, for I snuggled into it right away. But the place between my legs was begging for a touch, and before I knew it, my hand had strayed down to it, and was softly caressing the dark hair, and pulling apart the fleshy lips that protected the object of my desire.

My tunnel was so wet that my fingers were soaked immediately, and this juice helped me to slip my hand inside and explore the velvet walls so secretly hidden inside of me. Within moments I was gasping for breath, my heart beating hard in my chest, as the warmth swelled up through my body from that spot. Now I wanted two fingers inside, then three; I wanted to feel full. I could not help but thrust my hand in and out, while my other hand rubbed the hot button between my cunny-lips, and my hips moved with a life of their own. I could imagine Helga there, wanted her there, wanted to push her against me and have her tongue into me and have her fingers deep inside my tunnel, thrusting hard into me. I whispered her name, begged her to lick my cunny, begged her to push into me. "Lick me! Lick my hole, lick my slit!" I demanded of my invisible companion; "Help me to spend, to reach my desire!"

I felt as if my whole hand must be inside of me, and my button was hot and hard. When I finally exploded in a stream of release, I cried out with my passion, and my body trembled and leaped with emotion. Alicia, it was amazing.

As I lay there, my fingers strayed to my mouth, and I sucked at them—the taste of a woman is a delicious nectar. I wondered how Helga's sweet cunny would taste, and I longed to be near it, to smell it, to taste it, to make it spend.

I could only dream that Helga was laying in her bed thinking the same thoughts of me, Alicia; for now that I have tasted of this love, I seem to want it all of the time, and I want every woman I believe will taste of this love also. Think of me often, Alicia, for as you may know, I think constantly of you.

Your dearest friend,
Elaine

Valentina Cilescu
THE ROSEBUD SUTRA

While the maiden is lying on her bed, the mistress should loosen the girdle and the knot of her dress, and when the maiden begins to dispute with her, she should overwhelm her with kisses. Having gained this point, the mistress should loosen the knot of her undergarments, and turning up her lower garment should massage the joints of her naked thighs.

—The Rosebud Sutra

Miss Catherstone's face was like thunder, her thin, bony fingers twisting and untwisting the knot of her lace-edged handkerchief.

"This cannot be," she gasped, but her face was white with the shock of realization. "You have betrayed me!"

Dorothea Strong, still weak from loss of blood, lay stretched out on the couch, her normally smooth dark hair ruffled about her tanned face.

"I...am sorry," she said quietly.

"Sorry!" snapped Miss Catherstone. "That seems scarcely adequate in the circumstances. The understanding between us was that you would enjoy the girl's company for the afternoon, and if you were satisfied with her, you would pay me the sum of two hundred pounds to engage her services as your...travelling companion.

"I entrusted the girl to your care. She is a valuable asset, and yet you saw fit to lead her into danger! And having done so, you then chose to abandon her to her fate...."

Dorothea raised herself up on one elbow. A white bandage, stained with red, was wound around the flesh wound in her upper arm.

"Miss Catherstone, I had no idea... There was nothing I could do..."

"You foolish, stubborn woman. You knew very well that the hills are full of outlaws and brigands, and yet you led an innocent girl into their very arms. They have stolen her away from me. Do you know what they will be doing to her now? Sullying her virginal purity with their filthy hands..."

"I...I will try to find her. As soon as I can, I will ride into the mountains to look for her and bring her back. I swear it."

"Yes, Dr. Strong. You will. Or you will never be

received at the academy again. Never, do you hear?"

Without waiting for a reply, Miss Catherstone turned and stalked out of the room, leaving Dorothea to tormented thoughts of what she had done, of what might have been.

Out on the landing, Mary Bates listened with mounting anger. She had not trusted Dorothea Strong the first time she saw her, and she certainly did not trust her now, with all her promises and her apologies. Mary thought tearfully of her lover Amelia, and of the terrible things that might be happening to her—all because of some convenient financial arrangement between Dorothea Strong and Miss Catherstone.

As soon as Dorothea had raised the alarm, a search party from the Jainapur garrison had ridden out in search of Amelia, but that had been three days ago, and there was still no news of Amelia. Still nothing to say if she was alive or dead. Mary looked through the doorway at Dorothea Strong and felt a surge of bitter rage. In that moment she made her decision.

If Dorothea did not go to look for Amelia, she would.

Amelia had lost all track of time. For two days—or was it three?—she had been led higher and higher into the mountains towards the distant, snow-capped peaks. Her wrists bound and tethered by a long hemp rope, she stumbled behind the lead horse, her yellow gown torn and muddied by the red dust that kept getting into her eyes and lungs.

They travelled mostly by night, when the air was so cold that it made Amelia shiver uncontrollably. In the daytime, they rested in the shade of the rocks, but still the sun beat down on her half-naked body with a vengeful intensity. She was far from home, far from friends. She even missed the stern face of Miss Catherstone, chiding her for some minor transgression.

Here, with these tall, hard-faced tribeswomen, the prospect of one of Miss Catherstone's beatings held no fears for Amelia. She feared that in her captivity her treatment would be far more severe than anything she had ever suffered at the academy. And she dared not show her fear, for each sign of weakness was punished with a blow across the shoulders from a flexible leather thong. Even protected by the material of her dress and camisole, her flesh stung from the blows.

On the morning of the fourth day, as dawn turned the sky blush pink over the high Himalayan peaks, she saw the encampment: an untidy jumble of tents and horses, sheltering around a series of caves hollowed out of the bare rock.

At first the camp seemed deserted, save for a few scrawny goats and chickens and a piebald pony tethered beside the stream. But as they approached, figures emerged from the tents: young women clad in coarse woolen tunics, their dark hair falling loose and glossy about their shoulders. They ran forward to greet their lovers, who leapt down from the saddle and gathered them into their arms, embracing them with hunger.

Tears sprang to Amelia's eyes as more curious fingers explored her body, running over the silky skin of her arms and throat, loosening the tangles in her golden hair and spreading it out in a shimmering curtain that fell below her waist. She listened to the women chattering amongst themselves, understanding their dialect because it was so similar to the speech of the ayah who had cared for her as a child.

"Look at her skin—it's soft and juicy as a mango. Would it taste as sweet if I tried to bite it...?"

A hand insinuated itself between the buttons of Amelia's torn camisole and fingers pinched her breast, making her squeal in protest. She wriggled and tried to pull away, but other hands were exploring her more intimately still—girlish fingers pulling up her skirts, discovering the bare secret of her sex through the split crotch of her linen drawers.

"She is bare and wet!"

"She is ready for sex. Let us enjoy her now. Please, Mistress, we have been so long without fresh slaves..."

Nails raked the skin of her breast and she gasped with the exhilaration of sudden discomfort, astonishingly pleasurable through the sense-dulling mist of her exhaustion and fear. Another hand, stronger than the first, pried the fingers away, and she saw that the chief of the raiding party had intervened.

"No—you must not mark her. She is not for us. She is for Khara."

Little murmurs of disappointment filled the air.

"But why? We have waited so long. Our breasts ache for love, our cunts are so empty…"

The outlaw chief spoke again, her sonorous voice full of authority.

"She is a virgin."

The murmurs were instantly silenced, and the women drew away, as though in awe. Amelia stood stock-still, afraid to move or speak, terrified that if she did anything that offended the tribeswomen she would instantly be killed.

"She is a virgin, and therefore must be given as a gift to Khara. Come, slave."

A jerk on the rope that bound her hands together forced Amelia to move forward, half walking, half dragged across the stony ground which cut cruelly into her bare feet. She was being led toward one of the tents, by far the most magnificent, which stood in the center of the camp. It was made of dozens of multi-coloured blankets and tapestries, slung Bedouin-style over ropes and sticks which formed a large, boxy framework with an overhanging canopy.

Beneath the canopy sat a naked woman in an attitude of meditation, with her legs in the lotus position and a wickedly sharp dagger lying on the ground before her. Her outspread thighs displayed the shameless secret of her sex: the plump love-lips, that seemed to pout in a kiss of welcome; the glistening pink heart running with secret dew.

Despite her fear, Amelia looked at the girl with interest. She seemed very young, yet utterly self-possessed. Her neck was stretched into a slender column by dozens of solid gold rings, her arms and ankles encircled by many jeweled bracelets, her nose pierced by a jeweled chain which ran to a headdress of gold and rubies. Her eyes closed and her hands outstretched, she seemed oblivious to the world around her, but as they approached she spoke, her voice as unearthly and distant as an automaton's.

"Who approaches?"

"Makhani and a slave girl."

"What do you desire?"

"To make humble supplication to our queen."

"You may pass."

The outlaw chief Makhani jerked on the rope again and Amelia stumbled forward into the interior of the tent, blinking as her eyes gradually grew accustomed to the half-light.

There, on a bed of silken cushions, sat a beautiful woman dressed in the garb of a man, her full-breasted yet slender form attired in the rich, close-fitting finery of a maharajah. Her slim hips were encased in tight silver breeches which hugged the curves of her small, taut asscheeks. Her large breasts strained for release from the blue silk tunic, their size emphasized by the broad cummerbund wrapped tightly about her tiny waist.

Instead of the turban, she wore a plain gold toque on her long black hair, which was drawn back into a tight plait braided with multi-coloured silks. On either side of her stood naked girls, their firm young breasts slick with sweat as they cooled their queen with long-handled fans fashioned from gilded wood and peacock feathers.

"What gift have you brought to amuse me this time, Makhani?" Her voice was sweeter than Amelia had expected, yet it held a note of steel.

Makhani knelt before her queen and pulled on the rope so violently that Amelia was forced to follow suit, tumbling to her knees on the carpeted floor of the tent.

"I have brought you a new slave, your Highness," replied Makhani. "We captured her in the hills near the town of Jainapur."

"She is a fine enough English bitch," observed Khara coolly. "But I have many fine bitches to relieve my boredom."

"She is a virgin, your Highness. Tight as a child, hot as a tigress. I wager she will give you pleasure."

"A virgin! How quaint. And the girl must be all

of eighteen, nineteen years old! How jealously the English guard the useless trinket of their virginity."

Khara got to her feet and Amelia noticed that she was wearing brocade slippers with curled toes. She looked like a picture from the Arabian Nights book Amelia had been given for her tenth birthday.

"You have verified her virginity?"

"Not personally, your Highness. The girl tells me that she is a virgin and from her fear I judge that she speaks the truth."

Khara laughed.

"These English fillies are full of willfulness and deception. I shall examine the girl myself."

"No!" Amelia tried to scramble to her feet but Makhani caught her, winding the rope from her wrists around her throat, so tightly that she could scarcely breathe.

"Silence, slave!"

"I am not your slave," gasped Amelia. "I am…"

"Slave!" Makhani struck her with the side of her hand and she fell to the ground, fat teardrops trickling down her cheeks, all her spirit spent. "Do you dare defy your queen?"

"She is indeed a willful and spirited filly," observed Khara, with a degree of satisfaction. "Breaking that spirit might perhaps prove an agreeable diversion."

"Shall I prepare her for your examination?" Makhani looked up adoringly into her queen's face. It had been many moons since she had last been honoured to share Khara's bed, longer still since Khara had allowed her the joy of tonguing her beautiful hard clitoris. She burned with longing, praying that her gift would find favour in Khara's eyes.

"Strip her and make her lie down on the bed," Khara instructed her. "And light more lamps. I want to see every inch of this proud little filly's body. She must be taught that she can hide nothing from our eyes."

Amelia struggled in Makhani's arms, finding resources of strength she had thought long since lost on her grueling journey. She bit and spat like a she-cat as Makhani wrestled to remove her clothes. Khara watched and laughed, evidently delighted by this battle of wills.

"Restrain her." Khara clapped her hands and the two naked fan-bearers glided to her side. "I hunger to see the girl naked."

With three pairs of hands holding her, Amelia gave up her struggle. It was futile. Everything was hopeless. She had been carried off into a life of slavery and not a soul in the world knew where she was—not even Dorothea Strong, who had led her to this terrible fate.

Makhani unfastened Amelia's belt and drew it off, running the plaited silk with satisfaction over the palm of her hand. It would make a fine instrument of discipline to redden this filly's white skin and teach her the meaning of obedience. Then she turned her attention to the dress—the yellow muslin soiled and torn now from the long days' journeying through the mountains. The single button holding the waistband yielded easily and the remnants of the dress fell in a sighing whisper to the ground.

The petticoats proved a more difficult problem. Stiff with starch, their drawstrings were tightly knotted and impossible to untie. Not in the least daunted, Makhani took the knife from her belt and slit the crisp cotton from waist to hem, tearing it away to expose the knee-length bloomers beneath.

Amelia could scarcely believe that this was happening to her. It was all like some dreadful, surreal dream. And the worst of it was that something deep inside her—something shameful that no one should ever admit to—was pleased to be a slave, happy to become the victim of these women's lust. Even Makhani's ungentle touch awoke sensations of pleasure in her yearning flesh, so long deprived of the means of its own satisfaction.

"Such inexplicable garments these English girls wear," commented Khara, circling Amelia so that she could observe her from different angles. "They primp and preen themselves with dresses and jewels, but underneath they are wearing these...these abominations." She plucked at the coarse linen of

Amelia's camisole. "It is almost as though they are ashamed of their bodies, afraid of the pleasure that they can give."

"It is rumoured that the English take no pleasure from the sports of the flesh, your Highness," replied Makhani. "They are cold-blooded, sexless as eunuchs."

Khara tweaked the fabric of Amelia's drawers and the vent bulged open, exposing the golden curls at her crotch.

"Is that so? And yet, for all their pretended modesty, they expose themselves with such vulgarity," mused Khara, running the tip of her silver ferrule down over Amelia's belly and pushing it up against the soft wet flesh of her bare sex. Amelia moaned and instinctively pushed down against the cold silver-tipped cane; when Khara slid it out from between her thighs, it was wet with her juices. She breathed in Amelia's scent and licked a drop of juice from the silver tip. "Terrible garments. Remove them."

Makhani obeyed, first unbuttoning the camisole and sliding it off over Amelia's shoulders, then slitting the drawstring of her bloomers and pulling them down over her rounded hips.

"Step out of them," snapped Makhani. When Amelia hesitated for just one moment, she felt the cold hardness of Khara's ferrule slicing down onto her exposed buttocks. "Now."

Completely naked now, she shivered, suddenly

cold in the chilly mountain air. Khara stood behind her, her strong hands toying with the matted veil of her golden hair.

"A charming enough gift," she conceded, "though a little travelworn. Make her lie down on the bed. I wish to examine her more closely."

Amelia made no attempt to resist as hands seized her by the arms and made her lie down on the wide, soft-cushioned couch which served as Khara's bed. Indeed, after so many long days and nights in the mountains, she yearned for the softness of a bed, for the gentleness of sleep.

But sleep could not have been further from Khara's mind as she stood over her helpless victim. She began by examining Amelia minutely from head to toe, stroking and pinching her skin, forcing open her mouth to examine the regularity and whiteness of her teeth.

"Hmm. She has a good form, though it is not yet fully developed. Her breasts are a little small for my taste, but the nipples erect quite adorably to the touch." She pinched and squeezed them with such skillful cruelty that Amelia felt a trickle of juice well up from the deepest heart of her, emerging from her swollen love-lips to stain the ruby red bed covering beneath her. Even this indignity did not escape Khara's attention.

"Ah, I see the slave has a certain aptitude. I can smell her hunger. That is good." Khara returned to her examination. "The umbilicus is deeply sunken, and that also is an auspicious sign. How pretty it would be if pierced for a ruby or an emerald..."

She pressed the tip of her long-nailed finger into Amelia's navel, and the English girl gave a yelp of surprised pleasure. She had never imagined that such a touch could be so discomfiting and yet so sensual. To her profound shame, she felt her clitoris swell with blood between her pouting love-lips, its engorged stalk the certain betrayer of her carnal lust.

Khara's hands moved slowly over the surface of Amelia's taut belly, tracing the slight downward curve from navel to groin, then the plump swell of her mount of Venus, garnished with a tangle of bright gold curls.

"Her maidenhair is of a pleasing silkiness; the sex-lips are full and plump, and the inner lips protrude slightly...that is a sure sign of a well-developed sexual sense. Ah..." She pulled apart Amelia's outer cunny-lips and peered inside. "I see that the fruit of her sex is juicy and a fine, deep pink. And see, Makhani—her love-bud is round and glossy as a fine freshwater pearl."

Her fingers were cool, the nails long and sharp as knife blades, and Amelia held her breath in fear and excitement as Khara ran the very tip of her index finger along the deep, wet groove of her sex. It was the sweetest torment, and Amelia let out a long sigh of pleasure as the hood of her clitoris slipped over the hard, round head. Syrupy sex juice was welling up inside her, oozing and dripping from between her gaping cunt-lips at each new and skillful caress.

"Good. Very good." Khara's voice became a low purr of satisfaction as she scooped up a little of the sex fluid and smeared it over the head of Amelia's clitty. "The English filly has a natural instinct for the ways of pleasure." She rubbed a little harder, and Amelia gave a cry of despair. Her body was no longer her own, each nerve ending crying out for the bliss she had felt that morning—it seemed so long ago now—when Mary Bates had teased her to her first orgasm. "So much so that I begin to doubt her purity."

Amelia sobbed her distress and her shameful longing as Khara's finger left her clitoris and traced a slow, lingering path toward the entrance to her vagina.

"No...please, don't touch me there." Her cunt muscles clenched instinctively as Khara's fingertip pressed a little way in to her sex. "You'll hurt me..."

Khara laughed.

"There are worse things than the pain of love, slave," she replied, good-humoredly. "In time you will come to understand that pain is an inextricable part of that love."

The index finger of her other hand rubbed hard on Amelia's clitoris, and the girl writhed in a torment of guilty lust, her hips bucking as though trying to take this new lover deep inside her. She could not break free; Makhani and the two naked girls were holding her down, pinning her shoulders to the bed so that she could only look up at the gently moving canopy of blankets that formed the roof of the tent. She could no longer see Khara, but only feel her as her cunt grew wetter and more welcoming and her crisis approached.

As Amelia's cunt muscles relaxed, Khara slid her finger smoothly into the wet tunnel of her sex, so tight that even her slender finger seemed to stretch its walls. With a wicked delight, she jabbed her sharp fingernail a little further in, and was rewarded with a sharp cry of pain.

"Please...please! That hurts!"

"Well, well." With as much brutality as it had entered, Khara's finger slid out of Amelia's cunt. Khara licked it clean with a reflective enjoyment.

"She is a virgin, your Highness?"

"She is indeed a virgin, Makhani. Tight as a bird. So, so deliciously tight, and with a hymen as thick and as tough as glove leather."

"You intend to keep her and deflower her yourself, your Highness?" Makhani amused herself by taking Amelia's nipples between finger and thumb and pinching them long and hard.

"It is a tempting thought, Makhani, but no. I have other plans for this delicious English slut." Khara looked down at the bed, where Amelia's body was still writhing in the spasms of frustrated lust, her thighs spread wide and the pink oyster of her sex running with honey-sweet juice. "I shall sell her to the merchant, Indhira. With her golden hair and her beautifully tight cunt, she will fetch an excellent price."

"Indhira, your Highness? But she takes only those who are fit for training. She will take no virgins…"

"Very true, my dear Makhani." Khara's eyes gleamed as brightly as the gold toque on her glossy hair. "And so she must be relieved of her troublesome virginity, and initiated into the first stages of her training. When the merchandise is presented to Indhira, we must be able to show her that the filly has an aptitude for the sensual arts.

"Tonight, Makhani, when we have celebrated your return with food and wine, you and five of your sisters shall deflower the girl. I shall observe. I am sure that it will make an excellent and stimulating spectacle."

The moon rose slowly over the mountains, its fat white disc gazing down blankly from a sky of blackest velvet, sprinkled with stars. It was a beautiful night, filled with moonlight and the scent of flowers, but Amelia scarcely noticed its beauty. The sweet, thick wine she had been given to drink had made her brain muddled, and yet she felt curiously alert, as though all power of rational thought had been taken away from her, leaving only the hypersensitivity of touch, of taste, of smell.

Her whole body felt alive to the wealth of sensations around it. As she moved across the stony ground, her white silk robe brushed lightly over the buds of her breasts, already erect, already filled with the need to be sucked, licked, stroked, bitten. It felt as though a million eager tongues were running over her flesh, a million soft and skillful fingers stroking her wherever the silken fabric flowed and touched.

She heard Khara's voice, but it seemed a long way away.

"Bring her into the circle. Into the very center, where I can see her."

She felt hands closing again about her arms, and she moved forward obediently, forced to trust the hands because she could see nothing but a host of dancing, dreamlike images, images of things that she had never even imagined before and could scarcely believe were real.

There were naked women with painted breasts, and others moving about them in a slow and sinuous dance, their bodies heavy with jewelled chains that hung from pierced nipples and cunt-lips. Coloured and scented smoke rose from incense burners placed all around the margin of the wide circle, and between them burned flickering fires in copper braziers, orange and yellow flames rising up from the white-hot coals.

For a moment, Amelia quite forgot where she was, losing all sense of time and space as her eyes fought to focus on the chimerical dancing pictures—figures that moved so close she thought she could touch them, but when she reached out they were gone.

A nagging ache of memory kept drifting back in waves, like waves of sadness—yearningly real for a few moments, and then gone. She was Amelia Courtnay, a proud English girl who had been stolen away by brigands—savage, ruthless women who intended to sate their lust on her defenseless body. She must find some way to resist...

But it was futile. The thought lingered only a mo-ment, and then it was gone, so far away that she could scarcely glimpse it any more, just one more dancing figure in the circle of leaping flames.

"She has been prepared?"

"As you instructed, your Highness. Her body hair has been shaved and she has been massaged with sweet oils."

"Then the ceremony may begin."

Khara clapped her hands, and at once a sweet, strange music filled the air. Amelia did not recognize the instruments, but the woody, rippling sound of pipes mingled with the clamor of strings, bowed and plucked. In the darkness beyond the circle of fire, a woman began to sing as the drummer's supple hands set the beat.

The rhythm was elemental and compelling, the woman's voice low and sensual, rising from time to time to a passionate crescendo that echoed the need in Amelia's aching body. The massage which the two naked girls had given her had left her warm and hungry, her breasts tingling and the tight amber rose of her asshole twitching and stinging where the scented oil had been rubbed into it.

She felt strangely naked beneath the white silk robe; almost childlike now that the hair of her cunt and axillae had been shaved away, leaving her helpless and pure. The shame had faded away as the sweet wine had done its work, the mulled spices kindling a low heat in her belly whilst the alcohol annihilated all her inhibitions. As the music swooped and soared around her, she let her instincts lead her into the dance.

Slowly she began to move, her body swaying in time to the chant, her feet shifting on the bare earth as the drumbeat called her to her destiny.

"Take off your robe, Amelia. Show your nakedness to me."

Automatically, with no pause for thought, Amelia took hold of the white silk robe and pulled it over her head. The night air was chill in the mountains, but she did not notice it. A furnace of desire was burning inside her, far brighter and far hotter than the leaping flames of the fires around her. She wanted to be naked; wanted to exorcise the terrible need within her.

"Now touch yourself, Amelia. I want to see how you give yourself pleasure."

Khara's voice seemed like another theme in the symphony of sound around her, and it seemed the most natural thing in the world to obey it. Yet how could she tell her mistress that she did not know how to give herself pleasure, that until Mary had kissed her and caressed her, her lewdest touch had been to stroke her nipples gently, in the dark seclusion of the dormitory?

"Put your hands on your breasts and touch yourself, Amelia."

She let her hands wander to the small, firm mounds of her breasts. It felt as though she was touching them for the first time, discovering them as a lover would. She had become her own lover, her fingers innocent yet knowing as they roamed over the bare flesh. Beneath her palms, the pink cones of her nipples were puckered and fiercely erect, so hard that it seemed impossible that they could be part of the same, soft flesh that made up the body of her breasts. They seemed alien in their hardness—not soft like flesh, but tough like rubber or wood, love-buttons that could be touched to turn on her desire.

Inspiration guided her fingers and she moved the palms of her hands in a sweeping, circular motion over her breasts, so that the nipples ground gently against them. The effect was electric, sending lingering aftershocks of pleasure right through her body from breast to cunt, from her nipples to the exposed pink triangle of her pubis.

"Very good, Amelia. But I want to see more. I want to see what else you can do."

Amelia drew her fingers up so that they were like pincers and fastened them on the twin buds of her nipples. At first she touched them only gently, her supersensitive body hardly able to bear even such a light caress; but as her flesh grew more accustomed to the touch, her hunger burned more fiercely and her body grew greedy for more piquant sensations.

She pinched and rolled the breast flesh with an almost brutal intensity, discovering with a child's delight how wonderful it could be to take herself to the narrow margin between pleasure and pain. The slight discomfort of the stinging, burning sensation seemed to intensify her sensual hunger, and as she pinched a little harder she felt an answering wetness grow between her thighs.

In her innocence, she had never caressed herself between her legs, never stroked herself to orgasm. Only Mary had ever taken her there—poor, sweet Mary, so many miles away in another world, or so it seemed now. Instinctively she pressed her thighs together more tightly and was rewarded with a burst of the most exquisite sensation. She rubbed her thighs together, and discovered that this stimulated the sensual hot spot between her cunt-lips to a burning frenzy of pleasure. If she kept on doing it, would she reach the same peak of ecstasy that she had enjoyed on that one ecstatic morning in Jainapur?

"You feel pleasure, Amelia; that is good." Khara's syrupy voice penetrated Amelia's brain and, like a child rewarded for good behavior, she felt the pleasing warmth of satisfaction. "But I want to see more. I want to see you touch yourself, Amelia. Open up your legs and touch yourself for me."

Amelia slid her feet a little farther apart on the soft earth and felt instantly bereft. All the wonderful warmth in her clitty seemed to ebb away, leaving only the terrible yearning for release. She felt so ignorant, so angry to have been kept so long in innocence. What must she do to please her new mistress—and to assuage the unbearable longing within her belly?

Keeping the fingers of her left hand on her nipple, she slipped her right hand over her smooth, shaven pubis and down between her thighs. She was amazed at the hot wetness she felt when she touched herself there, between the twin lobes of her plump pussy-lips. They seemed so swollen, so fat with juice that she scarcely recognized the feel of them.

What was this, this long, hard stalk that pushed against her hand and sent electric shocks through her body whenever she touched it? Could it really be the pert little clitty she had sometimes touched when she was washing herself? She had never known it could be so huge and hard. She pressed on it and the touch was almost painful in its intensity. It was too dry, too sensitive, its little pink hood forced right back so that the whole shaft of her clitoris was exposed.

She must be gentle, answer the cravings of her body with the lightest, the softest of caresses. She pushed her finger into the tight, wet tunnel of her sex and loaded it with the clear, slippery pre-come, then smeared it over the head of her clitty as Khara had done. The sensation was blissful, and somewhere, very far away, she heard her own voice moaning softly in harmony with the music.

"She is a born slut," observed Khara, drinking from a silver goblet as she watched Amelia stroking her own clitty. The girl seemed in a world of her own, lost to reality as she focused on the intensity of her need, her quest for the ultimate pleasure that still eluded her clumsy fingers. "Innocent of course, but then that is to be desired in one who is to be trained as a slave. She will learn quickly, and since she knows nothing, there are no bad habits for her new mistress to break."

Amelia trembled at the new, unknown pleasure of her fingers on her clitty, learning by touch the pathway to purest delight. Even now she could feel the sensations building inside her, the mounting excitement as the heat spread from her breasts and clitty to fill her whole body. It was as though her entire being was caught in time, waiting, breathless, for the moment of release. A few more strokes, a few more sweet caresses on her pleasure-bud and she would be there. She could feel the ecstasy almost upon her, feel the muscles of belly and ass and cunt beginning to tense in the seconds before the spasm overtook her.

She screamed out her pleasure as her cunt blossomed into orgasm, releasing a flood of fragrant nectar which dripped like honey from her nether-lips, anointing the barren earth on which she stood. All control had left her, all consciousness save the consciousness of overwhelming pleasure.

It was too much, the pleasure too powerful for her to bear; Amelia sank to the ground in a swoon, her body white and quivering in the dancing firelight.

"Excellent, excellent." Khara clapped her hands in delight. "I had not expected her to be such an apt pupil. I feel sure that her defloration will make an entertaining spectacle." She parted the folds of her robe to reveal her bare, shaven cunt, the left lobe of her outer sex-lips pierced by a silver ring set with emeralds. "Bring me the instrument of her initiation."

A serving girl, naked except for a filmy veil which obscured the lower half of her face, approached and knelt before the queen, holding out a cushion of dark blue velvet. On it lay a dildo of yellowed ivory, about seven inches long and its surface carved with lascivious scenes from the Hindu holy books: women kissing and stroking each other's breasts, massaging each other with sweet oils, masturbating with long, smooth sticks that distended their vulvas.

Khara picked up the dildo and kissed it—once on the shaft, once on the tip.

"It is yet fragrant with the spendings of our last slave," she observed with a nostalgic pleasure. It had been most agreeable, initiating the last girl. Although only a simple peasant from a village in the hills, she had proved both apt and willing. But her cunt had been a little large, and Khara felt sure that Amelia Courtnay would prove a still more interesting pupil.

She slid the dildo over her belly and placed its head at the entrance to her shaven vulva. Then, with a single thrust, she forced it inside her cunt, so deep that its entire length vanished between her love-lips, and she gave a sigh of satisfaction. As the outlaws' queen, she had many lovers—as many pretty virgins and knowing sluts as any woman could wish for—but none had the power to pleasure her as beautifully as she pleasured herself.

The dildo slid, glistening, out of her cunt and in the next second disappeared inside her once more, forced in by a second powerful thrust.

"You may masturbate me, Makhani," said Khara, her eyes closed as she slid the dildo into her cunt and held it there with tightly clenched cunt muscles. "Place your lips upon my rosebud and bring me swiftly to orgasm."

Makhani knelt before her queen and opened her lips, putting out the tip of her tongue and wriggling it into the deep pink furrow between Khara's thighs. She lapped like a she-cat, teasing and tormenting the little pink stalk with her lips and teeth whilst her tongue flicked repeatedly across its head. Khara sat with eyes closed, her face betraying no trace of her excitement, but her breathing quickening as her cunt walls gripped the carved dildo, sucking it into her as though it alone could give her the release she craved.

She came with the merest sigh of contentment, the walls of her cunt rippling with wave after wave of pleasure, and the dildo slid slowly out of her onto the ground, its carved surface wet with her sex juice.

"Take it, Makhani. The honour shall first be yours this night." Khara smiled as she handed the dildo to Makhani, laying it across her hands as though it were some precious, sacred object. "The girl is prepared. I wish to see you enjoy her."

Amelia, waking from her swoon, felt strong arms holding her down, pulling apart her thighs, making her draw up her knees so that her sex was shamelessly displayed between her outspread legs, a coral pink sea-shell at the base of her creamy belly.

"Hold her still," commanded Makhani. Amelia tried to focus on the woman's face, but it blurred and merged into dream images in her head, images of painted dancing girls, whirling and laughing, their hands touching and caressing each other's bodies as the music bubbled and swirled to a climax.

Her body ached. She longed for a release from this torment of frustration, this burning, itching ache that racked her whole body and made her clitoris throb to the pulse of her insatiable desire. Hands touched her, some holding her down, others stroking and pinching her breasts and belly, producing little starbursts of pain that served only to intensify her longing.

"Please, please, please...," she heard herself gasp. What was she pleading for? She no longer knew—only that she wanted the touching to go on, to become deeper, stronger, more extreme.

The pointed tip of the dildo nudged between her love-lips, seeking out the white-hot heart of her desire. At the first touch, Amelia arched her back and let out a shuddering gasp, the surrogate dick of carved ivory teasing and stretching the tight entrance to her hole.

"No!" The first twinge of pain brought with it some distant remembrance of fear. This could not be. There was not room, she was too small...

"Your Highness, she is very tight," observed one of the serving girls. "The initiation may pain her."

"In all pleasure there should be an element of pain," replied Khara with a shrug of serene indifference. "In time, the pain will heighten her pleasure. Proceed."

Makhani pushed the dildo into Amelia's wet haven, but she moaned and twisted, trying to escape its inexorable advance. Her cunt was so tight that it felt as though she would split in two.

"Harder," commanded Khara, a note of excitement entering her voice. "Do not let her fight you. Push it deep inside her."

As the tip of the dildo met the unyielding membrane of Amelia's hymen, she gave a little sob of discomfort. But she no longer struggled. There was a terrible inevitability about the pain, the fear. And her whole body throbbed with the desire she was ashamed to admit, the desire that she could no longer conceal, for the juices were running freely from her cunt, anointing both the dildo and Makhani's relentless hand.

"Now!" Khara's voice summoned up the moment of her immolation, and—pressing on Amelia's love-bud with a skillful finger—Makhani gave the dildo a violent thrust. Amelia's back arched and she gave a shuddering cry as the dildo tore through her hymen, possessing her, releasing her at last from the prison of her virginity into womanhood in a shattering, breathtaking orgasm.

As one of the serving girls lapped at the scarlet pool of Amelia's virgin blood, soothing her hurts with the soft wet tip of her tongue, Khara sat back and smiled to Makhani.

"Such an apt pupil," she sighed. "She is sure to fetch an excellent price—now that she has been relieved of her virginity—for no virgin may ever enter the Temple of the Rosebud Sutra.

The Masquerade Erotic Newsletter

◆ ◆ ◆ ◆ ◆ ◆ ◆ ◆ ◆ ◆ ◆ ◆ ◆ ◆ ◆ ◆ ◆ ◆

FICTION, ESSAYS, REVIEWS, PHOTOGRAPHY, INTERVIEWS, EXPOSÉS, AND MUCH MORE!

"One of my favorite sex zines featuring some of the best articles on erotica, fetishes, sex clubs and the politics of porn."   —*Factsheet Five*

"I recommend a subscription to *The Masquerade Erotic Newsletter*.... They feature short articles on "the scene"...an occasional fiction piece, and reviews of other erotic literature. Recent issues have featured intelligent prose by the likes of Trish Thomas, David Aaron Clark, Pat Califia, Laura Antoniou, Lily Burana, John Preston, and others.... it's good stuff."   —*Black Sheets*

"A classy, bi-monthly magazine..."   —*Betty Paginated*

"It's always a treat to see a copy of *The Masquerade Erotic Newsletter*, for it brings a sophisticated and unexpected point of view to bear on the world of erotica, and does this with intelligence, tolerance, and compassion." —Martin Shepard, co-publisher, The Permanent Press

"Publishes great articles, interviews and pix which in many cases are truly erotic and which deal non-judgementally with the full array of human sexuality, a far cry from much of the material which passes itself off under that title.... *Masquerade Erotic Newsletter* is fucking great."   —*Eddie, the Magazine*

"We always enjoy receiving your *Masquerade Newsletter* and seeing the variety of subjects covered...."   —*body art*

"*Masquerade Erotic Newsletter* is probably the best newsletter I have ever seen."   —*Secret International*

"The latest issue is absolutely lovely. Marvelous images...."
                                                    —*The Boudoir Noir*

"I must say that the *Newsletter* is fabulous...."

                                                    —Tuppy Owens,
                                    Publisher, Author, Sex Therapist

"Fascinating articles on all aspects of sex..."   —*Desire*

◆ ◆ ◆ ◆ ◆ ◆ ◆ ◆ ◆ ◆ ◆ ◆ ◆ ◆ ◆ ◆ ◆ ◆

The Masquerade
Erotic Newsletter

*"Here's a very provocative, very professional
[newsletter]...made up of intelligent erotic
writing... Stimulating, yet not sleazy photos
add to the picture and also help make this zine
a high quality publication."* —Gray Areas

From **Masquerade Books**, the World's Leading Publisher of
Erotica, comes *The Masquerade Erotic Newsletter*—the best
source for provocative, cutting-edge fiction, sizzling pictorials, scin-
tillating and illuminating exposes of the sex industry, and probing
reviews of the latest books and videos.

Featured writers and articles have included:

Lars Eighner • *Why I Write Gay Erotica*
Pat Califia • *Among Us, Against Us*
Felice Picano • *An Interview with Samuel R. Delany*
Samuel R. Delany • *The Mad Man* (excerpt)
Maxim Jakubowski • *Essex House: The Rise and Fall of
Speculative Erotica*
Red Jordan Arobateau • *Reflections of a Lesbian Trick*
Aaron Travis • *Lust*
Nancy Ava Miller, M. Ed. • *Beyond Personal*
Tuppy Owens • *Female Erotica in Great Britain*
Trish Thomas • *From Dyke to Dude*
Barbara Nitke • *Resurrection*
and many more....

The newsletter has also featured stunning photo essays by such
masters of fetish photography as **Robert Chouraqui**, **Eric
Kroll**, **Richard Kern**, and **Trevor Watson**.

A one-year subscription (6 issues) to the *Newsletter* costs $30.00.
Use the accompanying coupon to subscribe now—for an uninter-
rupted string of the most provocative of pleasures (as well as a special gift, offered to subscribers only!).

ROSEBUD BOOKS

THE ROSEBUD READER

Rosebud Books—the hottest-selling line of lesbian erotica available—here collects the very best of the best. Rosebud has contributed greatly to the burgeoning genre of lesbian erotica—to the point that authors like Lindsay Welsh, Aarona Griffin and Valentina Cilescu are among the hottest and most closely watched names in lesbian and gay publishing. Here are the finest moments from Rosebud's contemporary classics. $5.95/319-8

ALISON TYLER

THE BLUE ROSE

The tale of a modern sorority—fashioned after a Victorian girls' school. Ignited to the heights of passion by erotic tales of the Victorian age, a group of lusty young women are encouraged to act out their forbidden fantasies—all under the tutelage of Mistresses Emily and Justine, two avid practitioners of hard-core discipline! $5.95/335-X

ELIZABETH OLIVER

PAGAN DREAMS

Cassidy and Samantha plan a vacation at a secluded bed-and-breakfast, hoping for a little personal time alone. Their hostess, however, has different plans. The lovers are plunged into a world of dungeons and pagan rites, as the merciless Anastasia steals Samantha for her own. B&B—B&D-style! $5.95/295-7

SUSAN ANDERS

PINK CHAMPAGNE

Tasty, torrid tales of butch/femme couplings—from a writer more than capable of describing the special fire ignited when opposites collide. Tough as nails or soft as silk, these women seek out their antitheses, intent on working out the details of their own personal theory of difference. $5.95/282-5

LAVENDER ROSE

Anonymous

A classic collection of lesbian literature: From the writings of Sappho, Queen of the island Lesbos, to the turn-of-the-century *Black Book of Lesbianism*; from *Tips to Maidens* to *Crimson Hairs*, a recent lesbian saga—here are the great but little-known lesbian writings and revelations. $4.95/208-6

EDITED BY LAURA ANTONIOU

LEATHERWOMEN II

A follow-up volume to the popular and controversial *Leatherwomen*. Laura Antoniou turns an editor's discerning eye to the writing of women on the edge—resulting in a collection sure to ignite libidinal flames. Leave taboos behind—because these Leatherwomen know no limits.... $4.95/229-9

LEATHERWOMEN

These fantasies, from the pens of new or emerging authors, break every rule imposed on women's fantasies. The hottest stories from some of today's newest and most outrageous writers make this an unforgettable exploration of the female libido. $4.95/3095-4

LESLIE CAMERON

THE WHISPER OF FANS

"Just looking into her eyes, she felt that she knew a lot about this woman. She could see strength, boldness, a fresh sense of aliveness that rocked her to the core. In turn she felt open, revealed under the woman's gaze—all her secrets already told. No need of shame or artifice...." $5.95/259-0

ROSEBUD BOOKS

AARONA GRIFFIN
PASSAGE AND OTHER STORIES
An S/M romance. Lovely Nina is frightened by her lesbian passions until she finds herself infatuated with a woman she spots at a local café. One night Nina follows her and finds herself enmeshed in an endless maze leading to a mysterious world where women test the edges of sexuality and power. $4.95/3057-1

VALENTINA CILESCU
THE ROSEBUD SUTRA
"Women are hardly ever known in their true light, though they may love others, or become indifferent towards them, may give them delight, or abandon them, or may extract from them all the wealth that they possess." So says *The Rosebud Sutra*—a volume promising women's inner secrets. One woman learns to use these secrets in a quest for pleasure with a succession of lady loves.... $4.95/242-6

THE HAVEN
The shocking story of a dangerous woman on the run—and the innocents she takes with her on a trip to Hell. J craves domination, and her perverse appetites lead her to the Haven: the isolated sanctuary Ros and Annie call home. Soon J forces her way into the couple's world, bringing unspeakable lust and cruelty into their lives. The Dominatrix Who Came to Dinner! $4.95/165-9

MISTRESS MINE
Sophia Cranleigh sits in prison, accused of authoring the "obscene" *Mistress Mine*. For Sophia has led no ordinary life, but has slaved and suffered—deliciously—under the hand of the notorious Mistress Malin. How long had she languished under the dominance of this incredible beauty? $4.95/109-8

LINDSAY WELSH
PROVINCETOWN SUMMER
This completely original collection is devoted exclusively to white-hot desire between women. From the casual encounters of women on the prowl to the enduring erotic bonds between old lovers, the women of *Provincetown Summer* will set your senses on fire! A nationally best-selling title.$5.95/362-7

NECESSARY EVIL
What's a girl to do? When her Mistress proves too systematic, too by-the-book, one lovely submissive takes the ultimate chance—choosing and creating a Mistress who'll fulfill her heart's desire. Little did she know how difficult it would be—and, in the end, rewarding,.... $5.95/277-9

A VICTORIAN ROMANCE
Lust-letters from the road. A young Englishwoman realizes her dream—a trip abroad under the guidance of her eccentric maiden aunt. Soon the young but blossoming Elaine comes to discover her own sexual talents, as a hot-blooded Parisian named Madelaine takes her Sapphic education in hand. $5.95/365-1

A CIRCLE OF FRIENDS
The author of the nationally best-selling *Provincetown Summer* returns with the story of a remarkable group of women. Slowly, the women pair off to explore all the possibilities of lesbian passion, until finally it seems that there is nothing—and no one—they have not dabbled in. $4.95/250-7

PRIVATE LESSONS
A high voltage tale of life at The Whitfield Academy for Young Women—where cruel headmistress Devon Whitfield presides over the in-depth education of only the most talented and delicious of maidens. Elizabeth Dunn arrives at the Academy, where it becomes clear that she has much to learn—to the delight of Devon Whitfield and her randy staff of Mistresses! $4.95/116-0

ROSEBUD BOOKS

BAD HABITS

What does one do with a poorly trained slave? Break her of her bad habits, of course! The story of te ultimate finishing school, *Bad Habits* was an immediate favorite with women nationwide. "Talk about passing the wet test!... If you like hot, lesbian erotica, run—don't walk...and pick up a copy of *Bad Habits*."—*Lambda Book Report* $4.95/3068-7

ANNABELLE BARKER

MOROCCO

A luscious young woman stands to inherit a fortune—if she can only withstand the ministrations of her cruel guardian until her twentieth birthday. With two months left, Lila makes a bold bid for freedom, only to find that liberty has its own excruciating and delicious price.... $4.95/148-9

A.L. REINE

DISTANT LOVE & OTHER STORIES

A book of seductive tales. In the title story, Leah Michaels and her lover Ranelle have had four years of blissful, smoldering passion together. One night, when Ranelle is out of town, Leah records an audio "Valentine," a cassette filled with erotic reminiscences.... $4.95/3056-3

RHINOCEROS BOOKS

EDITED BY AMARANTHA KNIGHT

FLESH FANTASTIC

Humans have long toyed with the idea of "playing God": creating life from nothingness, bringing Life to the inanimate. Now Amarantha Knight, author of the "Darker Passions" series of erotic horror novels, collects stories exploring not only the allure of Creation, but the lust that follows.... $6.95/352-X

GARY BOWEN

DIARY OF A VAMPIRE

"Gifted with a darkly sensual vision and a fresh voice, [Bowen] is a writer to watch out for."   **—Cecilia Tan**
The chilling, arousing, and ultimately moving memoirs of an undead—but all too human—soul. Bowen's Rafael, a red-blooded male with an insatiable hunger for same, is the perfect antidote to the effete malcontents haunting bookstores today. *Diary of a Vampire* marks the emergence of a bold and brilliant vision, firmly rooted in past *and* present. $6.95/331-7

RENE MAIZEROY

FLESHLY ATTRACTIONS

Lucien Hardanges was the son of the wantonly beautiful actress, Marie-Rose Hardanges. When she decides to let a "friend" introduce her son to the pleasures of love, Marie-Rose could not have foretold the erotic excesses that would lead to her own ruin and that of her cherished son. $6.95/299-X

EDITED BY LAURA ANTONIOU

NO OTHER TRIBUTE

A collection of stories sure to challenge Political Correctness in a way few have before, with tales of women kept in bondage to their lovers by their deepest passions. Love pushes these women beyond acceptable limits, rendering them helpless to deny the men and women they adore. Laura Antoniou brings together the most provocative women's writing in this companion volume to *By Her Subdued*. $6.95/294-9

RHINOCEROS BOOKS

THE MARKETPLACE

"Merchandise does not come easily to the Marketplace.... They haunt the clubs and the organizations.... Some of them are so ripe that they intimidate the poseurs, the weekend sadists and the furtive dilettantes who are so endemic to that world. And they never stop asking where we may be found...." $6.95/3096-2

THE CATALYST

After viewing a controversial, explicitly kinky film full of images of bondage and submission, several audience members find themselves deeply moved by the erotic suggestions they've seen on the screen. "Sara Adamson"'s sensational debut volume! $5.95/328-7

DAVID AARON CLARK

SISTER RADIANCE

From the author of the acclaimed *The Wet Forever*, comes a chronicle of obsession, rife with Clark's trademark vivisections of contemporary desires, sacred and profane. The vicissitudes of lust and romance are examined against a backdrop of urban decay and shallow fashionability in this testament to the allure—and inevitability—of the forbidden. $6.95/215-9

THE WET FOREVER

The story of Janus and Madchen, a small-time hood and a beautiful sex worker, *The Wet Forever* examines themes of loyalty, sacrifice, redemption and obsession amidst Manhattan's sex parlors and underground S/M clubs. Its combination of sex and suspense led Terence Sellers to proclaim it "evocative and poetic." $6.95/117-9

ALICE JOANOU

BLACK TONGUE

"Joanou has created a series of sumptuous, brooding, dark visions of sexual obsession and is undoubtedly a name to look out for in the future."
—*Redeemer*

Another seductive book of dreams from the author of the acclaimed *Tourniquet*. Exploring lust at its most florid and unsparing, *Black Tongue* is a trove of baroque fantasies—each redolent of the forbidden. Joanou creates some of erotica's most mesmerizing and unforgettable characters. $6.95/258-2

TOURNIQUET

A heady collection of stories and effusions from the pen of one our most dazzling young writers. Strange tales abound, from the story of the mysterious and cruel Cybele, to an encounter with the sadistic entertainment of a bizarre after-hours cafe. A sumptuous feast for all the senses.. $6.95/3060-1

CANNIBAL FLOWER

"She is waiting in her darkened bedroom, as she has waited throughout history, to seduce the men who are foolish enough to be blinded by her irresistible charms....She is the goddess of sexuality, and *Cannibal Flower* is her haunting siren song."—Michael Perkins $4.95/72-6

MICHAEL PERKINS

EVIL COMPANIONS

Set in New York City during the tumultuous waning years of the Sixties, *Evil Companions* has been hailed as "a frightening classic." A young couple explores the nether reaches of the erotic unconscious in a shocking confrontation with the extremes of passion. With a new introduction by science fiction legend Samuel R. Delany. $6.95/3067-9

RHINOCEROS BOOKS

AN ANTHOLOGY OF CLASSIC ANONYMOUS EROTIC WRITING

Michael Perkins, acclaimed authority on erotic literature, has collected the very best passages from the world's erotic writing—especially for *Rhinoceros* readers. "Anonymous" is one of the most infamous bylines in publishing history—and these steamy excerpts show why! $6.95/140-3

THE SECRET RECORD: Modern Erotic Literature

Michael Perkins, a renowned author and critic of sexually explicit fiction, surveys the field with authority and unique insight. Updated and revised to include the latest trends, tastes, and developments in this misunderstood and maligned genre. An important volume for every erotic reader and fan of high quality adult fiction. $6.95/3039-3

HELEN HENLEY

ENTER WITH TRUMPETS

Helen Henley was told that woman just don't write about sex—much less the taboos she was so interested in exploring. So Henley did it alone, flying in the face of "tradition" by producing *Enter With Trumpets*, a touching tale of arousal and devotion in one couple's kinky relationship. $6.95/197-7

PHILIP JOSE FARMER

FLESH

Space Commander Stagg explored the galaxies for 800 years, and could only hope that he would be welcomed home by an adoring—or at least *appreciative*—public. Upon his return, the hero Stagg is made the centerpiece of an incredible public ritual—one that will repeatedly take him to the heights of ecstasy, and inexorably drag him toward the depths of hell. One of Farmer's most successful voyages into the sexual future, *Flesh* is both highly erotic and sharply satirical. $6.95/303-1

A FEAST UNKNOWN

"Sprawling, brawling, shocking, suspenseful, hilarious..."
—Theodore Sturgeon

Farmer's supreme anti-hero returns. *A Feast Unknown* begins in 1968, with Lord Grandrith's stunning statement: "I was conceived and born in 1888." Slowly, Lord Grandrith—armed with the belief that he is the son of Jack the Ripper—tells the story of his remarkable and unbridled life. Beginning with his discovery of the secret of immortality, Grandrith's tale proves him no raving lunatic—but something far more bizarre.... $6.95/276-0

THE IMAGE OF THE BEAST

Herald Childe has seen Hell, glimpsed its horror in an act of sexual mutilation. Childe must now find and destroy an inhuman predator through the streets of a polluted and decadent Los Angeles of the future. One clue after another leads Childe to an inescapable realization about the nature of sex and evil.... $6.95/166-7

SAMUEL R. DELANY

EQUINOX

The *Scorpion* has sailed the seas in a quest for every possible pleasure. Her crew is a collection of the young, the twisted, the insatiable. A drifter comes into their midst, and is taken on a fantastic journey to the darkest, most dangerous sexual extremes—until he is finally a victim to their boundless appetites. Delany's classic *The Tides of Lust*, now issued under the author's original title, returns from exile to establish him as one of the pioneers of modern erotic literature. $6.95/157-8

RHINOCEROS BOOKS

ANDREI CODRESCU

THE REPENTANCE OF LORRAINE

"One of our most prodigiously talented and magical writers."

—NYT Book Review

An aspiring writer, a professor's wife, a secretary, gold anklets, Maoists, Roman harlots—and more—swirl through this spicy tale of a harried quest for a mythic artifact. Written when the author was a young man, this lusty yarn was inspired by the heady—and hot—days and nights of the Sixties. Includes a special Introduction by the author, painting a vivid portrait of *Lorraine*'s creation. $6.95/329-5

DAVID MELTZER

ORF

He is the ultimate musician-hero—the idol of thousands, the fevered dream of many more. And like many musicians before him, he is misunderstood, misused—and totally out of control. Every last drop of feeling is squeezed from a modern-day troubadour and his lady love. $6.95/110-1

LEOPOLD VON SACHER-MASOCH

VENUS IN FURS

This classic 19th century novel is the first uncompromising exploration of the dominant/submissive relationship in literature. The alliance of Severin and Wanda epitomizes Sacher-Masoch's dark obsession with a cruel, controlling goddess and the urges that drive the man held in her thrall. The letters exchanged between Sacher-Masoch and Emilie Mataja—an aspiring writer he sought as the avatar of his forbidden desires—are also included in this special volume. $6.95/3089-X

SOPHIE GALLEYMORE BIRD

MANEATER

Through a bizarre act of creation, a man attains the "perfect" lover—by all appearances a beautiful, sensuous woman but in reality something far darker. Once brought to life she will accept no mate, seeking instead the prey that will sate her hunger for vengeance. A biting take on the war of the sexes, this debut goes for the jugular of the "perfect woman" myth. $6.95/103-9

TUPPY OWENS

SENSATIONS

A piece of porn history. Tuppy Owens tells the unexpurgated story of the making of *Sensations*—the first big-budget sex flick. Originally commissioned to appear in book form after the release of the film in 1975, *Sensations* is finally released under Masquerade's stylish Rhinoceros imprint. $6.95/3081-4

DANIEL VIAN

ILLUSIONS

Two disturbing tales of danger and desire in Berlin on the eve of WWII. From private homes to lurid cafés to decaying streets, passion is explored, exposed, and placed in stark contrast to the brutal violence of the time. A singularly arousing volume. $6.95/3074-1

PERSUASIONS

"The stockings are drawn tight by the suspender belt, tight enough to be stretched to the limit just above the middle part of her thighs..." A double novel, including the classics *Adagio* and *Gabriela and the General*, this volume traces desire around the globe. International lust! $6.95/183-7

RHINOCEROS BOOKS

LIESEL KULIG
LOVE IN WARTIME
An uncompromising look at the politics, perils and pleasures of sexual power. Madeleine knew that the handsome SS officer was a dangerous man. But she was just a cabaret singer in Nazi-occupied Paris, trying to survive in a perilous time. When Josef fell in love with her, he discovered that a beautiful and amoral woman can sometimes be wildly dangerous. $6.95/3044-X

MASQUERADE BOOKS

THE GEEK   *Tiny Alice*
"An adventure novel told by a sex-bent male mini-pygmy. This is an accomplishment of which anybody may be proud."
                                                        —Philip José Farmer
A notorious cult classic. *The Geek* is told from the point of view of, well, a chicken who reports on the various perversities he witnesses as part of a traveling carnival. When a gang of renegade lesbians kidnaps Chicken and his geek, all hell breaks loose. A strange tale, filled with outrageous erotic oddities, that finally returns to print after years of infamy. $5.95/341-4

SEX ON THE NET   *Charisse van der Lyn*
Electrifying erotica from one of the Internet's hottest and most widely read authors. Encounters of all kinds—straight, lesbian, dominant/submissive and all sorts of extreme passions—are explored in thrilling detail. Discover what's turning on hackers from coast to coast! $5.95/399-6

BEAUTY OF THE BEAST   *Carole Remy*
A shocking tell-all, written from the point-of-view of a prize-winning reporter. And what reporting she does! All the secrets of an uninhibited life are revealed, and each lusty tableau is painted in glowing colors. Join in on her scandalous adventures—and reap the rewards of her extensive background in Erotic Affairs! $5.95/332-5

NAUGHTY MESSAGE   *Stanley Carten*
Wesley Arthur, a withdrawn computer engineer, discovers a lascivious message on his answering machine. Aroused beyond his wildest dreams by the unmentionable acts described, Wesley becomes obsessed with tracking down the woman behind the seductive voice. His search takes him through strip clubs and no-tell motels—and finally to his randy reward.... $5.95/333-3

The Marquis de Sade's JULIETTE   *David Aaron Clark*
The Marquis de Sade's infamous Juliette returns—and at the hand of David Aaron Clark, she emerges as the most powerful, perverse and destructive nightstalker modern New York will ever know. Under this domina's tutelage, two women come to know torture's bizarre attractions, as they grapple with the price of Juliette's promise of immortality.
Praise for Dave Clark:
"David Aaron Clark has delved into one of the most sensationalistically taboo aspects of eros, sadomasochism, and produced a novel of unmistakable literary imagination and artistic value."   —Carlo McCormick, *Paper*
                                                        $5.95/240-X

THE PARLOR   *N.T. Morley*
Lovely Kathryn gives in to the ultimate temptation. The mysterious John and Sarah ask her to be their slave—an idea that turns Kathryn on so much that she can't refuse! But who are these two mysterious strangers? Little by little, Kathryn comes to know the inner secrets of her stunning keepers. Soon, all is revealed—to the delight of everyone involved! $5.95/291-4

MASQUERADE BOOKS

NADIA *Anonymous*

"Nadia married General the Count Gregorio Stenoff—a gentleman of noble pedigree it is true, but one of the most reckless dissipated rascals in Russia..." Follow the delicious but neglected Nadia as she works to wring every drop of pleasure out of life—despite an unhappy marriage. A classic title providing a peek into the secret sexual lives of another time and place. **$5.95/267-1**

THE STORY OF A VICTORIAN MAID *Nigel McParr*

What were the Victorians really like? Chances are, no one believes they were as stuffy as their Queen, but who would have imagined such unbridled libertines! One maid is followed from exploit to smutty exploit! **$5.95/241-8**

CARRIE'S STORY *Molly Weatherfield*

"I had been Jonathan's slave for about a year when he told me he wanted to sell me at an auction. I wasn't in any condition to respond when he told me this..." Desire and depravity run rampant in this story of uncompromising mastery and irrevocable submission. **$5.95/228-0**

CHARLY'S GAME *Bren Flemming*

Charly's a no-nonsense private detective facing the fight of her life. A rich woman's gullible daughter has run off with one of the toughest leather dykes in town—and Charly's hired to lure the girl back. One by one, wise and wicked women ensnare one another in their lusty nets! **$4.95/221-3**

ANDREA AT THE CENTER *J.P. Kansas*

Kidnapped! Lithe and lovely young Andrea is, without warning, whisked away to a distant retreat. Gradually, she is introduced to the ways of the Center, and soon becomes quite friendly with its other inhabitants—all of whom are learning to abandon all restraint in their pursuit of the deepest sexual satisfaction. **$5.95/324-4**

ASK ISADORA *Isadora Alman*

An essential volume, collecting six years' worth of Isadora Alman's syndicated columns on sex and relationships. Alman's been called a "hip Dr. Ruth," and a "sexy Dear Abby," based upon the wit and pertinence of her advice. Today's world is more perplexing than ever—and Isadora Alman is just the expert to help untangle the most personal of knots. **$4.95/61-0**

THE SLAVES OF SHOANNA *Mercedes Kelly*

Shoanna, the cruel and magnificent, takes four maidens under her wing—and teaches them the ins and outs of pleasure and discipline. Trained in every imaginable perversion, from simple fleshly joys to advanced techniques, these students go to the head of the class! **$4.95/164-0**

LOVE & SURRENDER *Marlene Darcy*

"Madeline saw Harry looking at her legs and she blushed as she remembered what he wanted to do.... She casually pulled the skirt of her dress back to uncover her knees and the lower part of her thighs. What did he want now? Did he want more? She tugged at her skirt again, pulled it back far enough so almost all of her thighs were exposed...." **$4.95/3082-2**

THE COMPLETE *PLAYGIRL* FANTASIES *Editors of* **Playgirl**

The best women's fantasies are collected here, fresh from the pages of *Playgirl*. These knockouts from the infamous "Reader's Fantasy Forum" prove, once again, that truth can indeed be hotter, wilder, and *better* than fiction. **$4.95/3075-X**

STASI SLUT *Anthony Bobarzynski*

Need we say more? Adina lives in East Germany, far from the sexually liberated, uninhibited debauchery of the West. She meets a group of ruthless and corrupt STASI agents who use her as a pawn in their political chess game as well as for their own perverse gratification— until she uses her talents and attractions in a final bid for total freedom! **$4.95/3050-4**

MASQUERADE BOOKS

BLUE TANGO
Hilary Manning

Ripe and tempting Julie is haunted by the sounds of extraordinary passion beyond her bedroom wall. Alone, she fantasizes about taking part in the amorous dramas of her hosts, Claire and Edward. When she finds a way to watch the nightly debauch, her curiosity turns to full-blown lust! $4.95/3037-7

LOUISE BELHAVEL

FRAGRANT ABUSES

The saga of Clara and Iris continues as the now-experienced girls enjoy themselves with a new circle of worldly friends whose imaginations match their own. Perversity follows the lusty ladies around the globe! $4.95/88-2

DEPRAVED ANGELS

The final installment in the incredible adventures of Clara and Iris. Together with their friends, lovers, and worldly acquaintances, Clara and Iris explore the frontiers of depravity at home and abroad. $4.95/92-0

TITIAN BERESFORD

THE WICKED HAND

With a special Introduction by *Leg Show*'s Dian Hanson. A collection of fanciful fetishistic tales featuring the absolute subjugation of men by lovely, domineering women. From Japan and Germany to the American heartland—these stories uncover the other side of the "weaker sex." $5.95/343-0

CINDERELLA

Beresford triumphs again with this intoxicating tale, filled with castle dungeons and tightly corseted ladies-in-waiting, naughty viscounts and impossibly cruel masturbatrices—nearly every conceivable method of erotic torture is explored and described in lush, vivid detail. $4.95/305-8

JUDITH BOSTON

Young Edward would have been lucky to get the stodgy old companion he thought his parents had hired for him. Instead, an exquisite woman arrives at his door, and Edward finds his compulsively lewd behavior never goes unpunished by the unflinchingly severe Judith Boston! $4.95/273-6

NINA FOXTON

An aristocrat finds herself bored by amusements for "ladies of good breeding." Instead of taking tea with proper gentlemen, Nina invents a contraption to "milk" them of their most private essences. No man ever says "No" to Nina! $4.95/145-4

A TITIAN BERESFORD READER

Beresford's fanciful settings and outrageous fetishism have established his reputation as modern erotica's most imaginative and spirited writer. Wild dominatrixes, perverse masochists, and mesmerizing detail are the hallmarks of the Beresford tale—and encountered here in abundance. $4.95/114-4

CHINA BLUE

KUNG FU NUNS

"When I could stand the pleasure no longer, she lifted me out of the chair and sat me down on top of the table. She then lifted her skirt. The sight of her perfect legs clad in white stockings and a petite garter belt further mesmerized me. I lean particularly towards white garter belts." China Blue returns! $4.95/3031-8

HARRIET DAIMLER

DARLING • INNOCENCE

In *Darling*, a virgin is raped by a mugger. Driven by her urge for revenge, she searches New York in a furious sexual hunt that leads to rape and murder. In *Innocence*, a young invalid determines to experience sex through her voluptuous nurse. Two critically acclaimed novels in one volume! $4.95/3047-4

MASQUERADE BOOKS

AKBAR DEL PIOMBO

SKIRTS
Randy Mr. Edward Champdick enters high society—and a whole lot more—in his quest for ultimate satisfaction. For it seems that once Mr. Champdick rises to the occasion, nothing can bring him down. Rampant ravishment follows this libertine wherever he goes! $4.95/115-2

DUKE COSIMO
A kinky romp played out against the boudoirs, bathrooms and ballrooms of the European nobility, who seem to do nothing all day except each other. The lifestyles of the rich and licentious are revealed in all their glory. Lust-styles of the rich and infamous! $4.95/3052-0

A CRUMBLING FAÇADE
The return of that incorrigible rogue, Henry Pike, who continues his pursuit of sex, fair or otherwise, in the most elegant homes of the most debauched aristocrats. No one can resist the irrepressible Pike! $4.95/3043-1

PAULA
"How bad do you want me?" she asked, her voice husky, breathy. I shrank back, for my desire for her was swelling to unspeakable proportions. "Turn around," she said, and I obeyed....This canny seductress tests the mettle of every man who comes under her spell—and every man does! $4.95/3036-9

ROBERT DESMOND

PROFESSIONAL CHARMER
A gigolo lives a parasitical life of luxury by providing his sexual services to the rich and bored. Traveling in the most exclusive circles, this gun-for-hire will gratify the lewdest and most vulgar sexual cravings! This dedicated pro leaves no one unsatisfied. $4.95/3003-2

THE SWEETEST FRUIT
Connie is determined to seduce and destroy Father Chadcroft. She corrupts the unsuspecting priest into forsaking all that he holds sacred, destroys his parish, and slyly manipulates him with her smoldering looks and hypnotic aura. $4.95/95-5

MICHAEL DRAX

SILK AND STEEL
"He stood tall and strong in the shadows of her room... Akemi knew what he was there for. He let his robe fall to the floor. She could offer no resistance as the shadowy figure knelt before her, gazing down upon her. Why would she resist? This was what she wanted all along...." $4.95/3032-6

OBSESSIONS
Victoria is determined to become a model by sexually ensnaring the powerful people who control the fashion industry: Paige, who finds herself compelled to watch Victoria's conquests; and Pietro and Alex, who take turns and then join in for a sizzling threesome. $4.95/3012-1

LIZBETH DUSSEAU

TRINKETS
"Her bottom danced on the air, pert and fully round. It would take punishment well, he thought." A luscious woman submits to an artist's every whim—becoming the sexual trinket he had always desired. $5.95/246-9

THE APPLICANT
"*Adventuresome young woman who enjoys being submissive sought by married couple in early forties. Expect no limits.*" Hilary answers an ad, hoping to find someone who can meet her needs. Beautiful Liza turns out to be a flawless mistress; with her husband Oliver, she trains Hilary to be submissive. $4.95/306-6

MASQUERADE BOOKS

SPANISH HOLIDAY

She didn't know what to make of Sam Jacobs. He was undoubtedly the most remarkable man she'd ever met.... Lauren didn't mean to fall in love with the enigmatic Sam, but a once-in-a-lifetime European vacation gives her all the evidence she needs that this hot man might be the one for her.... A tale of romance and insatiable desires, this is one holiday that may never end! $4.95/185-3

CAROLINE'S CONTRACT

After a life of repression, Caroline goes out on a limb. On the advice of a friend, she meets with the alluring Max Burton—a man more than willing to indulge her fantasies of domination and discipline. Caroline soon learns to love his ministrations—and agrees to a very *special* arrangement.... $4.95/122-5

MEMBER OF THE CLUB

"I wondered what would excite me.... And deep down inside, I had the most submissive thoughts: I imagined myself … under the grip of men I hardly knew. If there were a club to join, it could take my deepest dreams and make them real. My only question was how far I'd really go?" A woman finally goes all the way in a quest to satisfy her hungers, joining a club where she *really* pays her dues—with any one of the many men who desire her! $4.95/3079-2

SARA H. FRENCH

MASTER OF TIMBERLAND

"Welcome to Timberland Resort," he began. "We are delighted that you have come to serve us. And…be assured that we will require service of you in the strictest sense. Our discipline is the most demanding in the world. You will be trained here by the best. And now your new Masters will make their choices." A tale of sexual slavery at the ultimate paradise resort. $5.95/327-9

RETURN TO TIMBERLAND

It's time for a trip back to Timberland, the world's most frenzied sexual resort! Prepare for a vacation filled with delicious decadence, as each and every visitor is serviced by unimaginably talented submissives. These nubile maidens are determined to make this the raunchiest camp-out ever! $5.95/257-4

SARAH JACKSON

SANCTUARY

Tales from the Middle Ages. *Sanctuary* explores both the unspeakable debauchery of court life and the unimaginable privations of monastic solitude, leading the voracious and the virtuous on a collision course that brings history to throbbing life. $5.95/318-X

HELOISE

A panoply of sensual tales harkening back to the golden age of Victorian erotica. Desire is examined in all its intricacy, as fantasies are explored and urges explode. Innocence meets experience time and again. $4.95/3073-3

JOYCELYN JOYCE

PRIVATE LIVES

The illicit affairs and lecherous habits of the illustrious make for a sizzling tale of French erotic life. A wealthy widow has a craving for a young busboy; he's sleeping with a rich businessman's wife; her husband is minding his sex business elsewhere! $4.95/309-0

CANDY LIPS

The world of publishing serves as the backdrop for one woman's pursuit of sexual satisfaction. From a fiery femme fatale to a voracious Valentino, she takes her pleasure where she can find it. Luckily for her, it's most often found between the legs of the most licentious lovers! $4.95/182-9

MASQUERADE BOOKS

KIM'S PASSION

The life of a beautiful English seductress. Kim leaves India for London, where she quickly takes upon herself the task of bedding every woman in sight! One by one, the lovely Kim's conquests accumulate, until she finds herself in the arms of gentry and commoners alike. $4.95/162-4

CAROUSEL

A young American woman leaves her husband when she discovers he is having an affair with their maid. She then becomes the sexual plaything of various Parisian voluptuaries. Wild sex, low morals, and ultimate decadence in the flamboyant years before the European collapse. $4.95/3051-2

SABINE

There is no one who can refuse her once she casts her spell; no lover can do anything less than give up his whole life for her. Great men and empires fall at her feet; but she is haughty, distracted, impervious. It is the eve of WW II, and Sabine must find a new lover equal to her talents. $4.95/3046-6

THE WILD HEART

A luxury hotel is the setting for this artful web of sex, desire, and love. A newlywed sees sex as a duty, while her hungry husband tries to awaken her to its tender joys. A Parisian entertains wealthy guests for the love of money. Each episode provides a new variation in this lusty Grand Hotel! $4.95/3007-5

JADE EAST

Laura, passive and passionate, follows her husband Emilio to Hong Kong. He gives her to Wu Li, a connoisseur of sexual perversions, who passes her on to Madeleine, a flamboyant lesbian. Madeleine's friends make Laura the centerpiece in Hong Kong's infamous underground orgies. Slowly, Laura descends into the depths of depravity, eventually becoming one of lecherous Emilio's slaves—for sale! $4.95/60-2

RAWHIDE LUST

Diana Beaumont, the young wife of a U.S. Marshal, is kidnapped as an act of vengeance against her husband. Jack Beaumont sets out on a long journey to get his wife back, but finally catches up with her trail only to learn that she's been sold into white slavery in Mexico. $4.95/55-6

THE JAZZ AGE

The time: the Roaring Twenties. A young attorney becomes suspicious of his mistress while his wife has an fling with a lesbian lover. *The Jazz Age* is a romp of erotic realism from the heyday of the speakeasy. $4.95/48-3

AMARANTHA KNIGHT

THE DARKER PASSIONS:
THE FALL OF THE HOUSE OF USHER

The Master and Mistress of the house of Usher indulge in every form of decadence, and are intent on initiating their guests into the many pleasures to be found in utter submission. But something is not quite right in the House of Usher, and the foundation of its dynasty begins to crack.... $5.95/313-9

THE DARKER PASSIONS: *FRANKENSTEIN*

What if you could create a living, breathing human? What shocking acts could it be taught to perform, to desire, to love? Find out what pleasures await those who play God.... $5.95/248-5

THE DARKER PASSIONS: *DR. JEKYLL AND MR. HYDE*

It is an old story, one of incredible, frightening transformations achieved through mysterious experiments. Now, Amarantha Knight explores the steamy possibilities of a tale where no one is quite who—or what—they seem. Victorian bedrooms explode with hidden demons. $4.95/227-2

MASQUERADE BOOKS

THE DARKER PASSIONS: *DRACULA*

"Well-written and imaginative, Amarantha Knight gives fresh impetus to this myth, taking us through the sexual and sadistic scenes with details that keep us reading.... This author shows superb control. A classic in itself has been added to the shelves."   —*Divinity* $5.95/326-0

ALIZARIN LAKE

THE EROTIC ADVENTURES OF HARRY TEMPLE

Harry Temple's memoirs chronicle his amorous adventures from his initiation at the hands of insatiable sirens, through his stay at a house of hot repute, to his encounters with a chastity-belted nympho—and many other exuberant and over-stimulated partners. $4.95/127-6

EROTOMANIA

The bible of female sexual perversion! It's all here, everything you ever wanted to know about kinky women past and present. From simple nymphomania to the most outrageous fetishism, all secrets are revealed in this look into the forbidden rooms of feminine desire. $4.95/128-4

AN ALIZARIN LAKE READER

A selection of wicked musings from the pen of Masquerade's perennially popular author. It's all here: *Business as Usual, The Erotic Adventures of Harry Temple, Festival of Venus,* the mysterious *Instruments of the Passion,* the devilish *Miss High Heels*—and more. $4.95/106-3

MISS HIGH HEELS

It was a delightful punishment few men dared to dream of. Who could have predicted how far it would go? Forced by his sisters to dress and behave like a proper lady, Dennis finds he enjoys life as Denise much more! Crossdressed fetishism run amuck! $4.95/3066-0

THE INSTRUMENTS OF THE PASSION

All that remains is the diary of a young initiate, detailing the twisted rituals of a mysterious cult institution known only as "Rossiter." Behind sinister walls, a beautiful young woman performs an unending drama of pain and humiliation. Will she ever have her fill of utter degradation? $4.95/3010-5

FESTIVAL OF VENUS

Brigeen Mooney fled her home in the west of Ireland to avoid being forced into a nunnery. But the refuge she found in the city turned out to be dedicated to a very different religion. The women she met there belonged to the Old Religion, devoted to the ways of sex and sacrifices. $4.95/37-8

PAUL LITTLE

THE PRISONER

Judge Black has built a secret room below a penitentiary, where he sentences the prisoners to hours of exhibition and torment while his friends watch. Judge Black's House of Corrections is equipped with one purpose in mind: to administer his own brand of rough justice! $5.95/330-9

TUTORED IN LUST

This tale of the initiation and instruction of a carnal college co-ed and her fellow students unlocks the sex secrets of the classroom. Books take a back seat to secret societies and their bizarre ceremonies in this story of students with an unquenchable thirst for knowledge! $4.95/78-5

DANGEROUS LESSONS

A compendium of corporeal punishment from the twisted mind of bestselling Paul Little. Incredibly arousing morsels abound: *Tears of the Inquisition, Lust of the Cossacks, Poor Darlings, Captive Maidens, Slave Island,* even the scandalous *The Metamorphosis of Lisette Joyaux.* $4.95/32-7

MASQUERADE BOOKS

NAUGHTIER AT NIGHT

"He wanted to seize her. Her buttocks under the tight suede material were absolutely succulent—carved and molded. What on earth had he done to deserve a morsel of a girl like this?" $4.95/3030-X

RACHEL PEREZ

ODD WOMEN

These women are lots of things: sexy, smart, innocent, tough—some even say odd. But who cares, when their combined ass-ettes are so sweet! There's not a moral in sight as an assortment of Sapphic sirens proves once and for all that comely ladies come best in pairs. $4.95/123-3

AFFINITIES

"Kelsy had a liking for cool upper-class blondes, the long-legged girls from Lake Forest and Winnetka who came into the city to cruise the lesbian bars on Halsted, looking for breathless ecstasies...." A scorching tale of lesbian libidos unleashed, from an uncommonly vivid writer. $4.95/113-6

CHARLOTTE ROSE

A DANGEROUS DAY

A new volume from the best-selling author who brought you the sensational *Women at Work* and *The Doctor Is In*. And if you thought the high-powered entanglements of her previous books were risky, wait until Rose takes you on a journey through the thrills of one dangerous day! $5.95/293-0

THE DOCTOR IS IN

"Finally, a book of erotic writing by a woman who isn't afraid to get down—and with deliciously lavish details that open out floodgates of lust and desire. Read it alone ... or with somebody you really like!"
—Candida Royalle

From the author of the acclaimed *Women at Work* comes a delectable trio of fantasies inspired by one of life's most intimate relationships. Charlotte Rose once again writes about women's forbidden desires, this time from the patient's point of view. $4.95/195-0

WOMEN AT WORK

Hot, uninhibited stories devoted to the working woman! From a lonesome cowgirl to a supercharged public relations exec, these women know how to let off steam after a tough day on the job. Includes "A Cowgirl's Passion," ranked #1 on Dr. Ruth's list of favorite erotic stories for women! $4.95/3088-1

SYDNEY ST. JAMES

RIVE GAUCHE

Decadence and debauchery among the doomed artists in the Latin Quarter, Paris circa 1920. Expatriate bohemians couple with abandon—before eventually abandoning their ambitions amidst the intoxicating temptations waiting to be indulged in every bedroom. $5.95/317-1

THE HIGHWAYWOMAN

A young filmmaker making a documentary about the life of the notorious English highwaywoman, Bess Ambrose, becomes obsessed with her mysterious subject. It seems that Bess touched more than hearts—and plundered the treasures of every man and maiden she met on the way. $4.95/174-8

GARDEN OF DELIGHT

A vivid account of sexual awakening that follows an innocent but insatiably curious young woman's journey from the furtive, forbidden joys of dormitory life to the unabashed carnality of the wild world. Pretty Pauline blossoms with each new experiment in the sensual arts. $4.95/3058-X

MASQUERADE BOOKS

ALEXANDER TROCCHI

THONGS

"...In Spain, life is cheap, from that glittering tragedy in the bullring to the quick thrust of the stiletto in a narrow street in a Barcelona slum. No, this death would not have called for further comment had it not been for one striking fact. The naked woman had met her end in a way he had never seen before—a way that had enormous sexual significance. My God, she had been..." $4.95/217-5

HELEN AND DESIRE

Helen Seferis' flight from the oppressive village of her birth became a sexual tour of a harsh world. From brothels in Sydney to harems in Algiers, Helen chronicles her adventures fully in her diary. Each encounter is examined in the scorching and uncensored diary of the sensual Helen! $4.95/3093-8

THE CARNAL DAYS OF HELEN SEFERIS

Private Investigator Anthony Harvest is assigned to save Helen Seferis, a beautiful Australian who has been abducted. Following clues in Helen's explicit diary of adventures, he Helen, the ultimate sexual prize. $4.95/3086-5

WHITE THIGHS

A fantasy of obsession from a modern erotic master. This is the story of Saul and his sexual fixation on the beautiful, tormented Anna. Their scorching passion leads to murder and madness every time they submit to their lusty needs. Saul must possess Anna again and again. $4.95/3009-1

SCHOOL FOR SIN

When Peggy leaves her country home behind for the bright lights of Dublin, her sensuous nature leads to her seduction by a stranger. He recruits her into a training school where no one knows what awaits them at graduation, but each student is sure to be well schooled in sex! $4.95/ 89-0

MY LIFE AND LOVES (THE 'LOST' VOLUME)

What happens when you try to fake a sequel to the most scandalous autobiography of the 20th century? If the "forgers" are two of the most important figures in modern erotica, you get a masterpiece, and THIS IS IT! One of the most thrilling forgeries in literature. $4.95/52-1

MARCUS VAN HELLER

TERROR

Another shocking exploration of lust by the author of the ever-popular *Adam & Eve*. Set in Paris during the Algerian War, *Terror* explores the place of sexual passion in a world drunk on violence. $5.95/247-7

KIDNAP

Private Investigator Harding is called in to investigate a mysterious kidnapping case involving the rich and powerful. Along the way he has the pleasure of "interrogating" an exotic dancer named Jeanne and a beautiful English reporter, as he finds himself enmeshed in the crime underworld. $4.95/90-4

LUSCIDIA WALLACE

KATY'S AWAKENING

Katy thinks she's been rescued after a terrible car wreck. Little does she suspect that she's been ensnared by a ring of swingers whose tastes run to domination and unimaginably depraved sex parties. With no means of escape, Katy becomes the newest initiate into this sick private club—much to her pleasure! $4.95/308-2

FOR SALE BY OWNER

Susie was overwhelmed by the lavishness of the yacht, the glamour of the guests. But she didn't know the plans they had for her. Sexual torture, training and sale into slavery! $4.95/3064-4

MASQUERADE BOOKS

THE ICE MAIDEN

Edward Canton has ruthlessly seized everything he wants in life, with one exception: Rebecca Esterbrook. Frustrated by his inability to seduce her with money, he kidnaps her and whisks her away to his remote island compound, where she emerges as a writhing, red-hot love slave! $4.95/3001-6

DON WINSLOW

THE MANY PLEASURES OF IRONWOOD

Seven lovely young women are employed by The Ironwoood Sportsmen's club for the entertainment of gentlemen. A small and exclusive club with seven carefully selected sexual connoisseurs, Ironwood is dedicated to the relentless pursuit of sensual pleasure. $5.95/310-4

CLAIRE'S GIRLS

You knew when she walked by that she was something special. She was one of Claire's girls, a woman carefully dressed and groomed to fill a role, to capture a look, to fit an image crafted by the sophisticated proprietress of an exclusive escort agency. High-class whores blow the roof off! $4.95/108-X

GLORIA'S INDISCRETION

"He looked up at her. Gloria stood passively, her hands loosely at her sides, her eyes still closed, a dreamy expression on her face ... She sensed his hungry eyes on her, could almost feel his burning gaze on her body...." $4.95/3094-6

THE MASQUERADE READERS

THE COMPLETE EROTIC READER

The very best in erotic writing together in a wicked collection sure to stimulate even the most jaded and "sophisticated" palates. $4.95/3063-6

THE VELVET TONGUE

An orgy of oral gratification! *The Velvet Tongue* celebrates the most mouthwatering, lip-smacking, tongue-twisting action. A feast of fellatio and *soixanteneuf* awaits readers of excellent taste at this steamy suck-fest. $4.95/3029-6

A MASQUERADE READER

Strict lessons are learned at the hand of *The English Governess*. Scandalous confessions are found in *The Diary of an Angel*, and the story of a woman whose desires drove her to the ultimate sacrifice in *Thongs* completes the collection. $4.95/84-X

THE CLASSIC COLLECTION

SCHOOL DAYS IN PARIS

The rapturous chronicles of a well-spent youth! Few Universities provide the profound and pleasurable lessons one learns in after-hours study—particularly if one is young and available, and lucky enough to have Paris as a playground. A stimulating look at the pursuits of young adulthood. $5.95/325-2

MAN WITH A MAID

The adventures of Jack and Alice have delighted readers for eight decades! A classic of its genre, *Man with a Maid* tells an outrageous tale of desire, revenge, and submission. Over 200,000 copies in print! $4.95/307-4

MAN WITH A MAID II

Jack's back! With the assistance of the perverse Alice, he embarks again on a trip through every erotic extreme. Jack leaves no one unsatisfied—least of all, himself, and Alice is always certain to outdo herself in her capacity to corrupt and control. An incendiary sequel! $4.95/3071-7

MAN WITH A MAID: The Conclusion

The final chapter in the epic saga of lust that has thrilled readers for decades. The adulterous woman who is corrected with enthusiasm and the maid who receives grueling guidance are just two who benefit from these lessons! $4.95/3013-X

MASQUERADE BOOKS

CONFESSIONS OF A CONCUBINE II: HAREM SLAVE

The concubinage continues, as the true pleasures and privileges of the harem are revealed. For the first time, readers are invited behind the veils that hide uninhibited, unimaginable pleasures from the world.... $4.95/226-4

CONFESSIONS OF A CONCUBINE

What *really* happens behind the plush walls of the harem? An inexperienced woman, captured and sentenced to service the royal pleasure, tells all in an outrageously unrestrained memoir. No affairs of state could match the passions of a young woman learning to relish a life of ceaseless sexual servitude. $4.95/154-3

INITIATION RITES

Every naughty detail of a young woman's breaking in! Under the thorough tutelage of the perverse Miss Clara Birchem, Julia learns her wicked lessons well. During the course of her amorous studies, the resourceful young lady is joined by an assortment of lewd characters. $4.95/120-9

TABLEAUX VIVANTS

Fifteen breathtaking tales of erotic passion. Upstanding ladies and gents soon adopt more comfortable positions, as wicked thoughts explode into sinfully scrumptious acts. Carnal extremes and explorations abound in this tribute to the spirit of Eros—the lustiest common denominator! $4.95/121-7

LADY F.

An uncensored tale of Victorian passions. Master Kidrodstock suffers deliciously at the hands of the stunningly cruel and sensuous Lady Flayskin—the only woman capable of taming his wayward impulses. $4.95/102-0

SACRED PASSIONS

Young Augustus comes into the heavenly sanctuary seeking protection from the enemies of his debt-ridden father. Within these walls he learns lessons he could never have imagined and soon concludes that the joys of the body far surpass those of the spirit. $4.95/21-1

CLASSIC EROTIC BIOGRAPHIES

JENNIFER III

The further adventures of erotica's most daring heroine. Jennifer, the quintessential beautiful blonde, has a photographer's eye for detail—particularly details of the masculine variety! A raging nymphomaniac! $5.95/292-2

JENNIFER AGAIN

One of contemporary erotica's hottest characters returns, in a sequel sure to blow you away. Once again, the insatiable Jennifer seizes the day—and extracts from it every last drop of sensual pleasure! $4.95/220-5

JENNIFER

From the bedroom of an internationally famous—and notoriously insatiable—dancer to an uninhibited ashram, *Jennifer* traces the exploits of one thoroughly modern woman. $4.95/107-1

ROSEMARY LANE *J.D. Hall*

The ups, downs, ins and outs of Rosemary Lane. Raised as the ward of Lord and Lady D'Arcy, after coming of age she discovers that her guardians' generosity is boundless—as they contribute to her carnal education! $4.95/3078-4

THE ROMANCES OF BLANCHE LA MARE

When Blanche loses her husband, it becomes clear she'll need a job. She sets her sights on the stage—and soon encounters a cast of lecherous characters intent on making her path to sucksess as hot and hard as possible! $4.95/101-2

KATE PERCIVAL

Kate, the "Belle of Delaware," divulges the secrets of her scandalous life, from her earliest sexual experiments to the deviations she learns to love. Nothing is secret, and no holes barred in this titilating tell-all. $4.95/3072-5

MASQUERADE BOOKS

THE AMERICAN COLLECTION

LUST *Palmiro Vicarion*
A wealthy and powerful man of leisure recounts his rise up the corporate ladder and his corresponding descent into debauchery. A tale of a classic scoundrel with an uncurbed appetite for sexual power! $4.95/82-3

WAYWARD *Peter Jason*
A mysterious countess hires a tour bus for an unusual vacation. Traveling through Europe's most notorious cities, she picks up friends, lovers, and acquaintances from every walk of life in pursuit of pleasure. $4.95/3004-0

LOVE'S ILLUSION
Elizabeth Renard yearned for the body of Dan Harrington. Then she discovers Harrington's secret weakness: a need to be humiliated and punished. She makes him her slave, and together they commence a journey into depravity that leaves nothing to the imagination—*nothing!* $4.95/100-4

THE RELUCTANT CAPTIVE
Kidnapped by ruthless outlaws who kill her husband and burn their prosperous ranch, Sarah's journey takes her from the bordellos of the Wild West to the bedrooms of Boston, where she's bought by a stranger from her past. A rough, rough ride through the Old West. $4.95/3022-9

A RICHARD KASAK BOOK

EDITED BY RANDY TUROFF
LESBIAN WORDS: State of the Art
Lesbian Words collects one of the widest assortments of lesbian nonfiction writing in one revealing volume. Dorothy Allison, Jewelle Gomez, Judy Grahn, Eileen Myles, Robin Podolsky and many others are represented by some of their best work, looking at not only the current fashionability the media has brought to the lesbian "image," but important considerations of the lesbian past via historical inquiry and personal recollections. A fascinating, provocative volume, *Lesbian Words* is a virtual primer to contemporary trends in lesbian thought. $10.95/340-6

MICHAEL ROWE
WRITING BELOW THE BELT: Conversations with Erotic Authors
Award-winning journalist Michael Rowe interviewed the best and brightest erotic writers—both those well-known for their work in the field and those just starting out—and presents the collected wisdom in *Writing Below the Belt*. Rowe speaks frankly with cult favorites such as Pat Califia, crossover success stories like John Preston, and up-and-comers Michael Lowenthal and Will Leber. $19.95/363-5

EURYDICE
f/32
"Its wonderful to see a woman...celebrating her body and her sexuality by creating a fabulous and funny tale." —Kathy Acker
f/32 has been called "the most controversial and dangerous novel ever written by a woman." With the story of Ela (whose name is a pseudonym for orgasm), Eurydice won the National Fiction competition sponsored by Fiction Collective Two and Illinois State University. A funny, disturbing quest for unity, *f/32* prompted Frederic Tuten to proclaim "almost any page ... redeems us from the anemic writing and banalities we have endured in the past decade of bloodless fiction." $10.95/350-3

A RICHARD KASAK BOOK

LOOKING FOR MR. PRESTON

Edited by Laura Antoniou, *Looking for Mr. Preston* includes work by Lars Eighner, Pat Califia, Michael Bronski, Felice Picano, Joan Nestle, Larry Townsend, Michael Lowenthal, and others who contributed interviews, essays and personal reminiscences of John Preston—a man whose career spanned the industry from the early pages of the *Advocate* to various national bestseller lists. Preston was the author of over twenty books, including *Franny, the Queen of Provincetown*, and *Mr. Benson*. He also edited the noted *Flesh and the Word* erotic anthologies, *Personal Dispatches: Writers Confront AIDS*, and *Hometowns*,. More importantly, Preston became a personal inspiration, friend and mentor to many of today's gay and lesbian authors and editors. Ten percent of the proceeds from sale of the book will go to the AIDS Project of Southern Maine, for which Preston had served as President of the Board. **$23.95/288-4**

MICHAEL LOWENTHAL, EDITOR

THE BEST OF THE BADBOYS

A collection of the best of Masquerade Books' phenomenally popular Badboy line of gay erotic writing. Badboy 's sizable roster includes many names that are legendary in gay circles. The very best of the leading Badboys is collected here, in this testament to the artistry that has catapulted these "outlaw" authors to bestselling status. John Preston, Aaron Travis, Larry Townsend, John Rowberry, Clay Caldwell and Lars Eighner are here represented by their most provocative writing. Michael Lowenthal both edited this remarkable collection and provides the Introduction. **$12.95/233-7**

GUILLERMO BOSCH

RAIN

An adult fairy tale, *Rain* takes place in a time when the mysteries of Eros are played out against a background of uncommon deprivation. The tale begins on the 1,537th day of drought—when one man comes to know the true depths of thirst. In a quest to sate his hunger for some knowledge of the wide world, he is taken through a series of extraordinary, unearthly encounters that promise to change not only his life, but the course of civilization around him. **$12.95/232-9**

LUCY TAYLOR

UNNATURAL ACTS

"A topnotch collection..." —*Science Fiction Chronicle*

A remarkable debut volume from a provocative writer. *Unnatural Acts* plunges deep into the dark side of the psyche, far past all pleasantries and prohibitions, and brings to life a disturbing vision of erotic horror. Unrelenting angels and hungry gods play with souls and bodies in Taylor's murky cosmos: where heaven and hell are merely differences of perspective; where redemption and damnation lie behind the same shocking acts. **$12.95/181-0**

SAMUEL R. DELANY

THE MOTION OF LIGHT IN WATER

"A very moving, intensely fascinating literary biography from an extraordinary writer. Thoroughly admirable candor and luminous stylistic precision; the artist as a young man and a memorable picture of an age."
—William Gibson

The first unexpurgated American edition of award-winning author Samuel R. Delany's riveting autobiography covers the early years of one of science fiction's most important voices. Delany paints a vivid and compelling picture of New York's East Village in the early '60s—a time of unprecedented social transformation. Startling and revealing, *The Motion of Light in Water* traces the roots of one of America's most innovative writers. **$12.95/133-0**

A RICHARD KASAK BOOK

SKIN TWO

THE BEST OF *SKIN TWO* Edited by Tim Woodward

For over a decade, *Skin Two* has served the international fetish community as a groundbreaking journal from the crossroads of sexuality, fashion, and art. *Skin Two* specializes in provocative, challenging essays by the finest writers working in the "radical sex" scene. Collected here are the articles and interviews that established the magazine's reputation. Including interviews with cult figures Tim Burton, Clive Barker and Jean Paul Gaultier. $12.95/130-6

CARO SOLES

MELTDOWN!
An Anthology of Erotic Science Fiction and Dark Fantasy for Gay Men

Editor Caro Soles has put together one of the most explosive collections of gay erotic writing ever published. *Meltdown!* contains the very best examples of this increasingly popular sub-genre: stories meant to shock and delight, to send a shiver down the spine and start a fire down below. An extraordinary volume, *Meltdown!* presents both new voices and provocative pieces by world-famous writers Edmund White and Samuel R. Delany. $12.95/203-5

BIZARRE SEX

BIZARRE SEX AND OTHER CRIMES OF PASSION
Edited by Stan Tal

Stan Tal, editor of *Bizarre Sex*, Canada's boldest fiction publication, has culled the very best stories that have crossed his desk—and now unleashes them on the reading public in *Bizarre Sex and Other Crimes of Passion*. Over twenty small masterpieces of erotic shock make this one of the year's most unexpectedly alluring anthologies. Including such masters of erotic horror and fantasy as Edward Lee, Lucy Taylor and Nancy Kilpatrick, *Bizarre Sex and Other Crimes of Passion*, is a treasure-trove of arousing chills. $12.95/213-2

PAT CALIFIA

SENSUOUS MAGIC
A new classic, destined to grace the shelves of anyone interested in contemporary sexuality.

Sensuous Magic is clear, succinct and engaging even for the reader for whom S/M isn't the sexual behavior of choice.... Califia's prose is soothing, informative and non-judgmental—she both instructs her reader and explores the territory for them.... When she is writing about the dynamics of sex and the technical aspects of it, Califia is the Dr. Ruth of the alternative sexuality set.... —Lambda Book Report

Don't take a dangerous trip into the unknown—buy this book and know where you're going!—SKIN TWO $12.95/131-4

GAUNTLET

THE BEST OF *GAUNTLET* Edited by Barry Hoffman
No material, no opinion is taboo enough to violate Gauntlet's *purpose of 'exploring the limits of free expression'—airing all views in the name of the First Amendment.*
—Associated Press

Gauntlet has, with its semi-annual issues, taken on such explosive topics as race, pornography, political correctness, and media manipulation—always publishing the widest possible range of opinions. Only in *Gauntlet* might one expect to encounter Phyllis Schlafley *and* Annie Sprinkle, Stephen King *and* Madonna—often within pages of one another. The most provocative articles have been gathered by editor-in-chief Barry Hoffman, to make *The Best of Gauntlet* a riveting exploration of American society's limits. $12.95/202-7

A RICHARD KASAK BOOK

THE EROTIC COMEDIES

A collection of stories from America's premier erotic philosopher. Marco Vassi was a dedicated iconoclast, and *The Erotic Comedies* marked a high point in his literary career. Scathing and humorous, these stories reflect Vassi's belief in the power and primacy of Eros in American life, as well as his commitment to the elimination of personal repression through carnal indulgence. $12.95/136-5

THE SALINE SOLUTION

During the Sexual Revolution, Marco Vassi established himself as an intrepid explorer of an uncharted sexual landscape. During this time he also distinguished himself as a novelist, producing *The Saline Solution* to great acclaim. With the story of one couple's brief affair and the events that lead them to desperately reassess their lives, Vassi examines the dangers of intimacy in an age of freedom. $12.95/180-2

CHEA VILLANUEVA

JESSIE'S SONG

"It conjures up the strobe-light confusion and excitement of urban dyke life, moving fast and all over the place, from NYC to Tucson to Miami to the Philippines; and from true love to wild orgies to swearing eternal celibacy and back. Told in letters, mainly about the wandering heart (and tongue) of writer and free spirit Pearly Does; written mainly by Mae-Mae Might, a sharp, down-to-earth but innocent-hearted Black Femme. Read about these dykes and you'll love them."   —Rebecca Ripley

A rich collection of lesbian writing from this uncompromising author. Based largely upon her own experience, Villanueva's work is remarkable for its frankness, and delightful in its iconoclasm. Widely published in the alternative press, Villanueva is a writer to watch. Toeing no line, *Jessie's Song* is certain to redefine all notions of "mainstream" lesbian writing, and provide a reading experience quite unlike any other this year. $9.95/235-3

SHAR REDNOUR, EDITOR

VIRGIN TERRITORY

An anthology of writing about the most important moments of life. Tales of first-time sensual experiences, from the pens of some of America's most uninhibited literary women. No taboo is unbroken as these women tell the whole truth and nothing but, about their lives as sexual women in modern times.

Included in this daring volume are such cult favorites as Susie Bright, Shannon Bell, Bayla Travis, Carol Queen, Lisa Palac and others. They leave no act undescribed, and prove once and for all that "beginner's luck" is the very best kind to have! $12.95/238-8

BADBOY BOOKS

THE JOY SPOT *Phil Andros*

"Andros gives to the gay mind what Tom of Finland gives the gay eye—this is archetypal stuff. There's none better."   —*John F. Karr,* **Manifest Reader**
A classic from one of the founding fathers of gay porn. *The Joy Spot* looks at some of Andros' favorite types—cops, servicemen, truck drivers—and the sleaze they love. Nothing's too rough, and these men are always ready. So get ready to give it up—or have it taken by force! $5.95/301-5

THE ROPE ABOVE, THE BED BELOW *Jason Fury*

The irresistible Jason Fury returns! Once again, our built, blond hero finds himself in the oddest—and most compromising—positions imaginable. And his combination of heat and heart has made him one of gay erotica's most distinctive voices. $4.95/269-8

BADBOY BOOKS

SUBMISSION HOLDS *Key Lincoln*
A bright talent unleashes his first collection of gay erotica. From tough to ten-
der, the men between these covers stop at nothing to get what they want.
These sweat-soaked tales show just how bad boys can get.... $4.95/266-3

SKIN DEEP *Bob Vickery*
Skin Deep contains so many varied beauties no one will go away unsatisfied. From
Daddy's Boys to horny go-go studs, no tantalizing morsel of manflesh is over-
looked—or left unexplored! Beauty may be only skin deep, but a handful of beautiful skin is a tempting proposition. $4.95/265-5

ANIMAL HANDLERS *Jay Shaffer*
Another volume from a master of scorching fiction. In Shaffer's world, each
and every man finally succumbs to the animal urges deep inside. And if
there's any creature that promises a wild time, it's a beast who's been caged
for far too long.... $4.95/264-7

RAHM *Tom Bacchus*
A volume spanning the many ages of hardcore queer lust—from Creation to
the modern day. The overheated imagination of Tom Bacchus brings to life
an extraordinary assortment of characters, from the Father of Us All to the
cowpoke next door, the early gay literati to rude, queercore mosh rats. No
one is better than Bacchus at staking out sexual territory with a swagger and a
sly grin. $5.95/315-5

REVOLT OF THE NAKED *D. V. Sadero*
In a distant galaxy, there are two classes of humans: Freemen and Nakeds.
Freemen are full citizens in this system, which allows for the buying and sell-
ing of Nakeds at whim. Nakeds live only to serve their Masters, and obey
every sexual order with haste and devotion. Until the day of
revolution—when an army of sex toys rises in anger.... By the author of *In the
Alley.* $4.95/261-2

WHiPs *Victor Terry*
Connoisseurs of gay writing have known Victor Terry's work for some time.
With *WHiPs,* Terry joins Badboy's roster at last. Cruising for a hot man?
You'd better be, because one way or another, these WHiPs—officers of the
Wyoming Highway Patrol—are gonna pull you over for a little impromptu
interrogation.... $4.95/254-X

PRISONERS OF TORQUEMADA *Torsten Barring*
The infamously unsparing Torsten Barring (*The Switch, Peter Thornwell,
Shadowman*) weighs in with another volume sure to push you over the edge. How
cruel *is* the "therapy" practiced at Casa Torquemada? Rest assured that Barring is
just the writer to evoke such steamy malevolence. $4.95/252-3

SORRY I ASKED *Dave Kinnick*
Up close and very personal! Unexpurgated interviews with gay porn's rank
and file. Haven't you wondered what it's like to be in porn pictures? Kinnick,
video reviewer for *Advocate Men*, gets personal with the guys behind (and
under) the "stars," and reveals the dirt and details of the porn business.
   $4.95/3090-3

THE SEXPERT *Edited by Pat Califia*
For many years now, the sophisticated gay man has known that he can turn to
one authority for answers to virtually any question on the subject of man-to-
man intimacy and sexual performance. Straight from the pages of *Advocate
Men* comes The Sexpert! From penis size to toy care, bar behavior to AIDS
awareness, The Sexpert responds to real concerns with uncanny wisdom and
a razor wit. $4.95/3034-2

BADBOY BOOKS

DEREK ADAMS

MY DOUBLE LIFE

Every man leads a double life, dividing his hours between the mundanities of the day and the outrageous pursuits of the night. In this, his second collection of stories, the author of *Boy Toy* and creator of sexy P.I. Miles Diamond shines a little light on what men do when no one's looking. Derek Adams proves, once again, that he's the ultimate chronicler of our wicked ways. $5.95/314-7

BOY TOY

Poor Brendan Callan—sent to the Brentwood Academy against his will, he soon finds himself the guinea pig of a crazed geneticist. Brendan becomes irresistibly alluring—a talent designed for endless pleasure, but coveted by others with the most unsavory motives.... $4.95/260-4

CLAY CALDWELL

SERVICE, STUD

From the author of the sexy sci-fi epic *All-Stud*, comes another look at the gay future. The setting is the Los Angeles of a distant future. Here the all-male populace is divided between the served and the servants—an arrangement guaranteeing the erotic satisfaction of all involved. Until, of course, one pugnacious young stud challenges authority, and the sexual rules it so rigidly enforces.... $5.95/336-8

STUD SHORTS

"If anything, Caldwell's charm is more powerful, his nostalgia more poignant, the horniness he captures more sweetly, achingly acute than ever."
—Aaron Travis

A new collection of this legendary writer's latest sex-fiction. With his customary candor, Caldwell tells all about cops, cadets, truckers, farmboys (and many more) in these dirty jewels. $5.95/320-1

QUEERS LIKE US

A very special delivery from one of gay erotica's premier talents. For years the name Clay Caldwell has been synonymous with the hottest, most finely crafted gay tales available. *Queers Like Us* is one of his best: the story of a randy mailman's trek through a landscape of willing, available studs. $4.95/262-0

CLAY CALDWELL/LARS EIGHNER

QSFx2

A volume of the wickedest, wildest, other-worldliest yarns from two master storytellers. Caldwell and Eighner take a trip to the furthest reaches of the sexual imagination, sending back stories proving that as much as things change, one thing will always remain the same.... $5.95/278-7

LARS EIGHNER

WHISPERED IN THE DARK

Hailed by critics, Lars Eighner continues to produce gay fiction whose quality rivals the best in the genre. *Whispered in the Dark* demonstrates Eighner's unique combination of strengths: poetic descriptive power, an unfailing ear for dialogue, and a finely tuned feeling for the nuances of male passion.
$5.95/286-8

AMERICAN PRELUDE

Praised by the *New York Times*, Eighner is widely recognized as one of our best, most exciting gay writers. What the *Times* won't admit, however, is that he is also one of gay erotica's true masters. Scalding heat blends with wry emotion in this red-blooded bedside volume. $4.95/170-5

ORDERING IS EASY!

MC/VISA orders can be placed by calling our toll-free number

PHONE 800-375-2356 / FAX 212 986-7355

or mail this coupon to:

MASQUERADE BOOKS
DEPT. W74A, 801 2ND AVE., NY, NY 10017

BUY ANY FOUR BOOKS AND CHOOSE ONE ADDITIONAL BOOK, OF EQUAL OR LESSER VALUE, AS YOUR FREE GIFT.

QTY.	TITLE	NO.	PRICE
			FREE
			FREE

W74A

SUBTOTAL	
POSTAGE and HANDLING	

We Never Sell, Give or Trade Any Customer's Name.

TOTAL

In the U.S., please add $1.50 for the first book and 75¢ for each additional book; in Canada, add $2.00 for the first book and $1.25 for each additional book. Foreign countries: add $4.00 for the first book and $2.00 for each additional book. No C.O.D. orders. Please make all checks payable to Masquerade Books. Payable in U.S. currency only. New York state residents add 8¼% sales tax. Please allow 4-6 weeks delivery.

NAME _____

ADDRESS _____

CITY _____ STATE _____ ZIP _____

TEL ( ) _____

PAYMENT: ☐ CHECK   ☐ MONEY ORDER   ☐ VISA   ☐ MC

CARD NO. _____ EXP. DATE _____